# MISSISSIPPI KING

## AN AZALEA NOVEL

## CELIA AARON

Cover art by Deranged Doctor Designs

Cover image by Scott Hoover

Content Editing by J. Brooks

Copy Editing by Spell Bound

# CONTENTS

he man with the light blue eyes watched as I spun the dial to the safe hidden in my credenza. My fingers shook—and not just from age this time. I entered the combination and pulled at the thick steel handle. It stayed put. I must have fumbled the combination.

"No games, old man." His voice sliced through me like a razor, and I couldn't still the staccato beat of my heart.

"I'm sorry. I'll get it this time." My shaky words barely rose above a whisper. Concentrating harder than I ever had in my life, I spun the dial and held my breath. My fingers worked back and forth until I knew I'd entered the correct combination.

I pulled the handle and sighed with relief as the metal gave way, a familiar scrape from the mechanism cutting through the quiet office.

"About fucking time." The man with the light eyes had stepped closer, his voice right over my shoulder.

Sweat beaded along my upper lip, and I could smell

the acrid perspiration seeping into my dress shirt beneath my suit jacket.

With another hefty pull, the dark gray metal door swung all the way open, and my breath caught in my throat.

Empty.

I fell back into my chair, one of the wheels squeaking along the wood floor.

"What the fuck is this?" The man with the light eyes didn't raise his voice. He didn't have to.

"I-I don't know." I turned to stare up at him, but my gaze didn't make it past the gun barrel pointed at me.

"Where's the money?" His eyebrows drew together though his hand remained steady, the gun never wavering.

I shook my head as bile rose in my throat. "I don't know."

"Cut the shit."

"I really don't know." I gawked at the empty safe, the blank metal walls. "Someone must have broken in and taken it."

He rushed forward and slammed the butt of the gun against my forehead. My vision blacked, then sputtered back in skittering sparks as I cowered away from him. Tears welled, and I swallowed my cry for help. It wouldn't do any good in my empty law office in the dead of night.

Blood trickled down my cheek, dropping onto my shoulder as I slumped in my chair. "I don't know what happened to it. A thief must have—"

"Where's the fucking money?" His calm tone was like

the smooth surface of deep, cold water. Almost soothing. Definitely lethal.

"I don't know." My tears mixed with the blood, the desperate cocktail sliding down my wrinkled face as if I were melting away. And I was. When the man with the light eyes had called asking for the money, I knew this was the end for me, that I was a dead man.

He pulled a phone from his pocket. Keeping his gun trained on me, he made a call. "It's not here... Yeah... He claims he doesn't know."

I held my shaking hands up, throwing myself on whatever mercy he had. "I don't—"

"Shh." He shook his head slowly, his crystal eyes sending a shiver through me.

I quieted as he pressed the phone to his ear again.

"What do you want me to do?" He stood unnervingly still, getting instructions from his boss as I sat and waited for the life or death judgment.

"Got it." Pocketing his phone, he took a step back. "Are you going to tell me where the money is?"

"I don't know!" I slammed my hand on my desk to add a little drama to the lie. "Someone took it!"

He tsked and slid his finger off the trigger guard and onto the slim piece of metal behind it. The smallest bit of pressure would send the hammer hurtling forward, igniting the gunpowder, and expelling the bullet that would end my life. *Pressure.* How fitting.

I clenched my eyes shut and forced myself to sit up straight. This was justice. Not the shit I pretended to deal in at my law firm, but the real thing. I'd had this coming long before the man with the light eyes had stepped into my office.

He gave me a perfunctory nod. His finger twitched in a nearly imperceptible movement.

The gun roared, and then my world fell silent.

2

## BENTON

"*M*r. King." Margaret greeted me as I walked into the office. Her iron-gray curls and cloying perfume had been a constant at the front desk of King & Morris for as long as I could remember.

"Morning, Margaret." I strode past her, the familiar creaks in the one-hundred-and-fifty-year-old floor another reminder of how neither the office nor the people in it ever seemed to change. To me, the stasis was comforting, like a child's well-loved blanket.

The double doors to my father's office were closed, but a light shone through the crack. He was an early riser, so it was no surprise he was already hard at work.

I glanced at the long line of portraits as I made my way down the hall, each one an image of a King or a Morris lawyer, their hair and clothing styles changing with the decades. Each one gave me a gruff stare, silently telling me to get to work, do a good job, and keep the family names unblemished. I wouldn't let them down.

My secretary's desk was empty as I strode past. I mentally

5

made a black mark against Jenny for it. Other than death, there was never any good excuse for missing work. I'd been out of law school for ten years, never missed a day at the firm.

"Hey, tight ass, was wondering when you'd show up." Porter sat in my office chair, his dusty boots propped on my spotless desk. "Can't believe I beat you here."

"Put your feet down and get out of my office." I smoothed my tie, even though there was no chance at it having a wrinkle. Not on my watch.

The morning sun streamed through the wide wood shutters along the side of my office, and a slight twitch pulled at the corner of my eye as my valuable time ticked away.

"Don't be a dick." Porter swung his feet down but snagged the hat off his head and dropped it on my keyboard. I could almost feel the grime from it transferring to the keys.

"What do you want?" I unbuttoned my dark suit coat and crossed my arms over my chest.

"First, I'd like it if you got the stick out of your ass." He grinned, his easy charm lost on me. "Go ahead and move that to the top of your to-do list. Second, we need to talk about Dad's birthday party."

I ignored his initial request and moved on to the birthday party. "What about it?"

The clacking sound in the hallway told me Jenny had finally arrived.

"Sorry I'm late, Mr. King. A logging truck spilled all over the—" She walked into the room and stopped, her gaze stilling on my brother. "Well if it isn't Sheriff King."

Porter flicked his badge and winked at her. "Yes, ma'am, here to maintain law and order. It's my job around these here parts."

She giggled like a schoolgirl, a rose hue rising into her spray-tanned cheeks.

I didn't have time for this. "Porter, this isn't even your jurisdiction. We're inside the Azalea city limits."

Porter cocked his head to the side, his eyes squinting as he tried, and failed, to do the math. "So that means…"

"That means you have to defer to the city police department. You're the *county* sheriff. This is the *city*."

His grin resurfaced. "I know that, man. I'm just yanking your chain."

I wasn't so sure. "You're wasting my time. I have work to do."

Porter plucked my fountain pen from my desk and twirled it in his fingers. "We need to talk about Dad's birthday."

"Can I get you boys some coffee, drinks, anything?" Jenny practically purred the words.

Porter gave her an up and down perusal. One I'd seen too many times to count. This wouldn't end well.

"Yeah, I'd like to take a drink of y—"

"No thank you, Jenny." I turned to her, her gaze roving back and forth between us. "We have family business to discuss. Please close the door on your way out." I punctuated the word "out" with a stern glare. At least she followed my instructions—but only after swaying her hips so hard I thought she might knock something out of joint.

Once the door clicked shut, Porter whistled. "You hit that yet?"

"No, of course not. We have a strict no-fraternization policy, and she's only twenty-three." *And I'm simply not interested in vapid women who gossip more than they work.*

"Oh, come on. She's not too young for you, and definitely not for me. You're what?" He tapped his fingers on his chin. "Thirty-two now? Why do you act like it's seventy-two? You're worse than Dad. At least he flirts with Widow Brewer every chance he gets. Not to mention what he gets up to with ol' Letty. Let's see. The last girl you dated was, hmm."

I hadn't seriously dated anyone in a while. Dating was a distraction, and all the women in Azalea who gravitated toward me were focused on getting their Mrs. Degree with a specialty in King. No, thanks. "I have things to do. Unlike some people who lucked up on a position that was way out of their skill range, I actually have to work for a living."

He smirked. "I totally have the skill set to be sheriff."

"You worked as a process server for a couple years, and now, thanks to this foolish county, you're a glorified process server with a badge." I walked the rest of the way to the desk, snatched his hat from it, and handed it to him. "If you want to discuss Dad's party, we should wait until Charlotte is back in town."

"Yeah, but I had this great idea. You know how he was the king of Mardi Gras over in New Orleans when he was, I don't know, twenty or something?"

I shook my head. "I think that story was made up."

He shrugged, the black radio attached to his shoulder

wobbling a little. "Whatever. How about we throw him a Mardi Gras party? Let him be the king of ceremonies again. He'd love it! Maybe we could even find a date for you. Some gal who likes stuffy types. A librarian or something."

"Out." I tossed his hat onto the visitor's chair and walked around to him. He stood and ran a hand through his dark blond hair. "I thought we were really having a moment there. You were going to open up to me about why you've always had a corn cob wedged between your cheeks, then we were going to discuss party planning, curl our hair, maybe stay up late and talk about what boys we liked." He stepped out of the way as I swiped the grit off my desk.

A brown smudge marred the edge of my planner. No way that was coming out.

"If that's all you have to discuss—"

A knock sounded on the door, and Jenny's voice rang out. "Mr. King?"

"Yes?" Porter and I answered in unison.

I shook my head. "You're *Sheriff* King now, remember?"

He plopped his hat on his head. "Right you are, big brother." He opened the door for Jenny whose cheeks somehow seemed even pinker, her lips too red.

"I'm sorry to interrupt, but Mr. Kitston is here to see your father, but he isn't answering his phone. Would you mind checking on him? I'd go myself, but..."

"He scares you, huh?" Porter's voice was conspiratorial. "Afraid he'll chase you around the office like an episode of Mad Men?"

9

She laughed and placed her hand on his forearm. "You're so funny."

I stifled my irritation and walked toward the front of the office as Porter and Jenny trailed behind me, their tone hushed. I knocked on Dad's door. No answer.

"Dad, Mr. Kitston is here about his will." My voice seemed to stop at the wood, but surely he would have heard me. I glanced over at Porter as a cold sensation rushed up my spine. "Maybe he's not here?"

He shrugged and turned his attention back to Jenny. "Now, about that coffee, sweetheart."

I gripped the right door handle. "Dad? I'm coming in."

Pushing the door open, I found Dad sitting at his desk. Everything seemed exactly the same as I remembered it.

Except the smell. And the blood everywhere. And Jenny's piercing scream.

## 3

ARABELLA

*J* stuffed half a donut into my mouth and logged onto my computer. The office was just waking up from the overnight shift. Azalea, Mississippi had its fair share of inebriates and ne'er-do-wells, two of which were hanging out in the drunk tank; otherwise, the days were slow and the nights slower.

"You save me one?" Logan dropped into his chair across from me and yawned.

"Nope," I spoke through the donut and worked on biting all of it into a more manageable shape in my mouth.

He rubbed his eyes. His dark hair was desperately in need of a comb, and I suspected he hadn't changed clothes in days.

"You tie one on this weekend?" I swallowed and wondered for a second if it would all go down. Maybe I'd be in the Azalea Gazette: "Azalea Detective's Death by Donut."

"I hit Crawley's Saturday night, yeah." He rubbed his jaw, and I noticed the small bruise appearing there.

Pointing, I asked, "Who was it this time?"

"This?" He gingerly touched the bruise. "This was when Brenda saw me talking to Vorayna."

"Brenda did that?" I whistled. "I didn't think she had it in her." I tapped random keys, trying to wake my dinosaur of a computer.

"She'd been drinking tequila."

"Ah-ha." I sipped my coffee and considered getting him a cup.

Then he grinned. "Don't worry. I got them to play nice. Real nice. All three of us."

My coffee consideration poured down the drain, and I returned to banging on my keys and mouse.

"You go out this weekend?"

"Yeah." I met his dark brown eyes. "You know me. Just a party a minute."

"So that's a no." He squinted.

"No. Vivienne caught a cold at daycare, and she snotted and was generally miserable from about Friday at five till this morning at about seven."

"Lucky you."

I tipped my coffee cup to him. "You know it."

"What are we working on today, fearless leader?"

I wrinkled my nose. Logan had a few years on me. I was thirty-one to his thirty-four, but we'd both started working for the Azalea Police Department the same year. We'd worked the city beat—both of us in a car during the sweltering summers—for a few years until some of the older guard retired, leaving two detective spots open within six months of each other. I got promoted first—mainly because of the rumors that Logan had slept with one of the retiring detective's daughters on the old man's desk.

I cycled through our handful of cases in my mind. "You're still on that okra theft case, right?"

He groaned. "That's not a thing."

"Millie Lagner says it's a thing, so it's a thing."

"No one is sneaking into her garden at night and taking her okra. They're also not stockpiling alien goods in her garage. It's not happening. None of it. And it's definitely not worth the time of the great City of Azalea's second-best detective."

My computer finally flickered to life, and I entered my password, then began the five-minute wait for it to wake the rest of the way up.

"It doesn't matter what you think. It's our job to investigate any and all crimes in the city limits."

"This is just stupid." He rubbed his face, the scratchy sound of his stubble reminding me of the last time I had seen Dale. He'd been haggard, in need of a shave, and strung out like a clothesline.

"It's not like you have anything better to do." My computer finally began to function, and I logged into the case filing system.

"Fine." He stood. "If I'm not back in an hour, call in the SWAT team."

"We don't have a SWAT team."

"The National Guard, then." He clipped his badge to the waistband of his jeans.

"If you don't get your ass out of here, I'll call the chief.

How about that?" I cut my eyes at him as he glowered at me.

"You always were a tattletale." He walked to my desk, his heavy boots thunking on the tile floor.

"You always were a crybaby." I tried and failed to stifle my smile. Our insult routine was familiar and comfortable, like a favorite pair of jeans.

He shrugged, a grin tugging at his lips. "Okra is itchy as all hell. You'd cry too."

I hated okra and anything to do with gardening, so I couldn't argue too much with his point. Luckily, I didn't have to, because the phone rang.

I swiped up the receiver before he could. "Yeah?"

"Benton King is on the phone. He says his father's been shot and killed at the law firm." Helen, our dispatcher, spoke with an uncharacteristically shaky voice. "The chief isn't in his office right now. I called his cell phone, but he didn't answer that either."

"He must be busy with Lina."

"That's what I thought, too. But someone needs to get out there, and I wasn't sure if I should send Trevor since he's—"

"Too green," I finished for her.

"Right."

"I'm out." Logan strode away from me, almost to the door.

"Hang on," I called. He turned and gave me a curious look as I spoke into the receiver.

"Tell Benton King that Logan and I are on our way."

"Yes, ma'am."

I hung up and stood, then grabbed my service weapon

from my side drawer and looped the lanyard with my badge around my neck.

Logan's eyebrows rose. "Something must be really wrong."

"Randall King has been killed." I tried to keep my tone nonchalant despite the surge of adrenaline firing through my veins. We hadn't had a murder investigation in over a year. I should have been proud of our stats, glad that we lived in a community without a measurable homicide rate. And I was, but I couldn't deny my excitement at the thought of a new case, especially one involving the larger-than-life Randall King.

Logan whistled. "You've got to be shitting me. Does Garvey know?"

"No. Helen hasn't been able to get him on the phone."

"Lina?"

I closed the desk drawer and grabbed my keys. "Probably."

Logan held the door for me as we hustled out to my unmarked car. He hesitated at the passenger door. "Look, I don't want to hold up the investigation or anything, but I have an okra theft case that is very important. Millie Lagner is going to get mighty upset if we don't take her complaints serious—"

"Get in the car, smart ass."

THE FAMILIAR GRAY brick building of King and Morris, ferns hanging along the front porch and flowers pouring from planters along the walk, looked particularly pale in the morning light. I parked next to the sheriff's SUV in the small lot to the side of the building.

"What's the dipshit sheriff doing here?" Logan was opening his door as I threw it into park.

"He's a King. I assume his brother must've called him in when they found the body." I gave up the crisp air conditioning of the car and strode into the muggy late summer air. Fresh cut grass and the scent of distant honeysuckle tickled my nose as we strode up the front stairs.

Logan pushed through the ancient wood door, and we stepped into the reception area, the wooden boards creaking beneath us.

An older woman with iron-gray hair sat at the front desk. "Where's Garvey?"

"He's busy on another matter." I took the lead and approached the desk, noting the two business card holders displayed with the names Randall and Benton King in bold print. "I'm Detective Matthews and this is Detective Dearborn."

She gave me a withering stare, her no-nonsense demeanor verging on hostile. "It's a sad state of affairs when the chief of police is too busy to have any care for poor Mr. King."

I took her name from the small placard on the edge of her desk. "Margaret, I can assure you that Chief Garvey will be here as soon as he can." If I hadn't been looking right at her, I would've missed the slight tremble in her chin and the watering of her eyes. Despite the stone façade, she was shaken. I softened my tone. "I'm going to need you to close the office. Lock the front door, and keep people out of here so that we can establish a secure perimeter."

"Mr. King would never allow us to close the office." Her eyes watered even more. "He-he prided himself on working hard every day."

"I understand, but we need to—"

"Where's Garvey?" A taller man, mid 30s with light brown hair and dark blue eyes strode into the reception area from the hallway behind the desk.

"He sent these detectives." Margaret wrinkled her nose.

"I'm Detective Matthews and this is Detective Dearborn. You are?"

"Benton King." He looked down his nose at both of us. His dark gray suit was pressed to perfection, and he gave us a glare reminiscent of his father.

Randall King was the closest thing that Azalea had to a celebrity. His face covered both billboards in town, he always headlined at the Christmas parade, and he'd been a staple of the community for as long as I could remember. Now I supposed he could add "deceased" to his résumé.

"Arabella." Porter King strode out behind his older brother, his usual jovial manner conspicuously absent. He took the phone off the hook and gently patted Margaret's shoulder. "Sweetheart, the firm is closed until further notice."

At his tone, the matron finally crumpled. "All right."

"I expect Arabella and Logan will have some questions for the staff. If you could show everyone into the front conference room, that would be great." Porter pushed his hat back on his head and pinched the bridge of his nose.

I added, "tell the staff not to touch anything. This entire building is a crime scene until I decide differently. Logan, go around back and make sure everything is locked up tight. I don't want anyone walking out of here until I've had a chance to go over everything."

"Got it." He headed out the front door.

"You're in charge?" Benton's scowl deepened as he studied me.

I didn't drop my gaze. "Do you have a problem with that?"

"My father has been murdered, and Chief Garvey sends the B-team to investigate it? I most certainly have a problem with that."

"Benton, take it down a notch." Porter stepped back as Margaret lumbered up from her chair. "Arabella is the lead detective for the city. She's got a lot more experience than I do."

"That's not saying much." Disapproval laced his words.

I took a step toward him and enjoyed it when his eyes widened the slightest bit. "The fact is, it doesn't matter what you think, Mr. King. I'm here to do my job. If you get in my way, I will have you escorted out of the building. And if you have a problem with my methods, I suggest you take it up with Chief Garvey. Otherwise I don't need anything from you except a statement of what happened. Now, show me the body." I stepped around the desk and walked down the back hallway.

The long hallway was lined with paintings of stern men, each of whom had ruled the city during their tenure as a King or a Morris. The sort of men who smoked pipes, sipped brandy or an equally snobby drink, and discussed their tiny kingdom of Azalea.

"Take it easy, Arabella." Porter caught up to my elbow and pointed to a set of closed double doors. "We just lost our father, and Benton is a stuck-up ass even on his best day."

"I can hear you. I'm standing right here." Benton crossed his arms.

I halted. "Both of you need to hang back."

Benton stopped a few paces behind. "Not a problem."

"Who found the body?"

"I did." Benton's gaze never left the doors.

"Has anyone else touched these door handles afterward?"

"No. I opened them and found him." He swallowed hard. "And I'm pretty sure I was the only one who touched them, since I closed the doors soon after."

I pulled a pair of gloves from my inner pocket and worked them on. "Did you go into the room?"

"Not really, no. I could tell..." He clamped his mouth shut, as if finishing the sentence was abhorrent to him.

I moved on, keeping him talking. "Anyone else go in the room?"

"I took a step or two inside, but when I saw that he was—" Porter paused, his eyes watering, before continuing, "gone, I backed out." He cleared his throat.

"All right. We called in a forensics expert from Tupelo, but she won't be here for another couple of hours. I'm going to go in and take a look."

Logan strode toward us from the end of the hallway. "The place is secure."

"Keep it that way." I took a deep breath and gripped the door handles. They opened with a slight creak to reveal a bloody tableau.

A body lay slumped over on the desk. The gray hair on the back of his head was matted with blood and gore. Crimson drops stained the off-white curtains behind the credenza, and the unmistakable smell of death tinged the air. With a gloved finger, I switched on the lights. The rest of the office was untouched, the chairs neatly arranged in front of the desk, and the bookcases on either side stoically looking on.

I glanced back at Benton. He met my gaze, his eyes stark. For all his snobby bluster, I could sense him falling apart on the inside. Maybe his act in the reception area was the only thing that was holding him together. Maybe being haughty and distant was what kept the horror of what happened to his father at bay. Pity filtered through my lens, and I saw him a touch differently. Even so, in a case like this, I couldn't rule out anyone as a suspect just yet. That included Benton and Porter.

"If you'd like to wait with the others in the conference room, that might be best." I said it as mildly as I could.

Benton gave a sharp shake of his head. "I'm fine here. Besides, I want to keep an eye on things and make sure you don't contaminate any evidence."

Logan's dark eyes flashed. "Look, asshole—"

"It's fine." I turned back to the office and stepped inside. No good could come of sparring with Benton King at this point. He was one of two things: a killer or a victim. Given the way he blanched at the sight of the room, I guessed the latter.

Moving farther inward, I took stock of the details—the banker's light with the green shade on the edge of the desk, the liquor decanter with crystal glasses on a neat side table, the worn but well-kept Persian rug beneath my feet. Other than the body and the blood, nothing else seemed amiss.

Continuing around the desk, I cut a wide berth so as not to trample through any of the blood or possible evidence.

A long, low wooden piece of furniture sat nestled under the back windows, one of the cabinets on the side ajar. A metal door hung open, the shiny edge catching the light. "What's in this credenza back here? It looks like maybe a safe? Hard to tell from this angle, and I can't get closer."

"He's had a safe in there for as long as I can remember. But he never kept anything in it except when certain clients used to pay with cash." Porter walked into the room but hovered near the door. "That was a long time ago."

"Porter's correct. We don't use that safe for anything anymore." Benton kept to the doorway and didn't look in my direction. I couldn't blame him. The mess almost turned my stomach, and I didn't even know the man. Not personally.

"No gun here." I knelt and peered at the floor beneath the desk.

"Suicide's out." Logan edged around to the other side of the desk, his back to a bookcase.

"Not necessarily." I glanced at Porter. Would one of the sons have been ashamed of a suicide to the point they'd take the weapon? Or maybe there was more to it. It wouldn't be the first time a suicide was staged to look like a murder so an insurance policy would pay out. My mind hopped from one possibility to the next, never settling on one for too long.

Based on the scene, the most obvious guess at this point was a robbery gone bad. But the fact that the safe hadn't been used as far as either of the King sons knew, was troublesome. On top of that, the front door showed no signs of forced entry, and Logan hadn't mentioned any issues with the back door or any windows, either. We'd need to do a thorough check.

I shuffled farther around the desk and paused when I saw something sticking out of the victim's back. Silver and glinting in the overhead light, a letter opener held a yellow piece of legal paper against Mr. King's bloodied suit coat.

"See anything?" Logan drifted closer.

"Yeah." I put a knee on the edge of the credenza and leaned over to get a better look. "It looks like someone pinned a note to his back."

"Pinned?" Benton's sharp voice cut through the too-thick air.

"Letter opener, I'm afraid."

"Jesus." Benton coughed into his palm.

"What does it say?" Logan couldn't get any nearer, there was too much spatter.

I maneuvered closer, putting both knees on the edge of the credenza and tilting back toward the bloodstained curtains.

In neat blue cursive, the note said, "You're next."

4

BENTON

"*I* already told Detective Matthews." I clasped my hands together on top of the conference table. "I said goodbye to my father Friday night as we left the firm together. I didn't see him again until this morning when I found…"

Detective Dearborn nodded. "Are you sure you can't think of anyone who would've wanted to harm your father?"

I itched to run my fingers through my hair and yank on the strands, a habit I thought I had outgrown. Clearly not. As my irritation grew, so did the need to make the movement. "No one wanted to hurt my father. He dealt mainly with real estate and business disputes, none of which involved him personally. He didn't do criminal law. He never prosecuted anyone. None of this makes sense. This town loved him. I mean, he won the Azalea Dancing With the Stars competition for the past three years running. He knows—*knew*—everyone, and had more friends than he knew what to do with." Talking about him in past tense made my chest hurt.

"And you're sure there was nothing in the safe?" The detective chewed on the end of the King and Morris pen between his fingers as he balanced on the back legs of his chair. I made a mental note that if he left the pen behind, to have Margaret trash it immediately.

"I hadn't seen the inside of that safe in years. And the last time I did see it, it was empty. If my father put something else in there, I wouldn't have known it. But I can tell you that none of the firm funds were stored on the premises. I manage our bank account, and with Margaret's help, keep all of our books in order. There was simply nothing of value in there."

Detective Matthews walked into the conference room with Porter at her elbow.

Though she was dressed casually in jeans and a button-up white shirt, open at the top, she wore her clothes well. The shirt had been ironed, and her simple set of diamond stud earrings added to her femininity. I realized that Porter must've been in shock; otherwise, he would've been hitting on her. Maybe I was in shock too. When I saw my father's body, I just shut off. I was still shut off. It didn't make sense, and I needed time to sort it out and put the puzzle pieces together. But first I had to get the detectives out of my way.

She sank down at the head of the table, completely at ease with taking the lead chair in the room. "We've gone through everyone in the office. No one came in over the weekend. I'm not a forensics analyst, but given the state of the blood and the condition of the body, I would hazard a

guess that he was killed sometime last night." She swept her dark hair behind one shoulder and made a few notes as she spoke.

I'd never met her before, but Porter was somewhat familiar with her. They'd known each other in school. I was older and already at college by the time they'd made it to Azalea High. Porter spoke well of her in the few moments we'd had before our separate interviews. I didn't take his assessment to heart, especially given that he had a tendency to make allowances for women who looked like Arabella Matthews.

She finished scribbling her notes, drummed her pen on the pad, and met my gaze, her green eyes sparkling with an intelligence I didn't trust. "I'm going to need to get a look at all the files Mr. King was working on. I'll also need to visit his home and get a list of known associates from you."

"Files? Absolutely not." I leaned back in my chair. "All files are protected by attorney-client privilege. I can't hand them over to you."

"Ben." Porter gave me a confused stare. "She needs to investigate and find out who killed our father. Of course you'll give her the files."

"I will do no such thing. Those files are confidential. Our clients expect us to safeguard their secrets and to uphold the attorney-client privilege. I don't intend to violate my professional ethics the moment our father is gone. He would never allow this."

Detective Matthews stopped drumming her pen. "Tell me, Mr. King. Now that your father is deceased, you're

the last attorney standing with the King last name at this firm. Isn't that correct?"

My fingers tightened, gripping each other like a life line. "I'm the majority shareholder, yes."

She scribbled some more notes.

"Hey, wait a minute now." Porter snatched his hat off his head. "Ben would never—"

"I'm perfectly capable of defending myself, thank you, Porter." I cut my gaze back to Detective Matthews and gave her the same look my father could give and make anyone feel like a filthy wad of gum stuck to the bottom of a shoe. "You aren't getting the files."

Her partner glanced between us uneasily.

She smiled calmly, almost lazily. It would have been believable if it weren't for the sharpness of her eyes. "If you won't cooperate with this investigation, I'll get a warrant for the files."

"A warrant won't be able to get past attorney-client privilege."

She stood and grabbed her notepad from the table. "I may not be an attorney, but I'm pretty sure I can get a judge to issue a warrant for all of Mr. King's files, particularly if I request an *in camera* review by the court to determine if any of the documents should be withheld based on your claim of privilege."

"Can we do that?" Porter asked her.

She cocked her head to the side. "*Sheriff*, are you asking me if law enforcement can get and enforce a warrant from a judge?"

Porter squinted a bit. "Um, no?"

She shook her head and gave her partner an exasperated glance.

I shrugged. "You do what you have to do, Detective, and I'll do what I have to do." Of course, part of what I had to do was go through each of those files myself to see if I could find any reason for my father's murder. I wasn't going to trust such a crucial part of the investigation to the bumbling B-team from the Azalea City Police Department.

"I'll see you in court." She brushed off my objections like dust from her shoulder. "Now, on the other matters, I'll need a key to your father's house. Do you have one? Unless you'd like me to arrange a warrant for that, too."

I considered my options as she continued making notes. The house was a warrant fight I wouldn't win. A murder victim's home? A judge would grant that warrant request over the phone. Dad had always taught me to choose my battles, and this was one I'd have to let go. I dug around in my pocket and pulled out a key ring. Slipping off the silver one with the square head, I handed it to her. "This will get you in the front door. But I'd like to be present during the search."

She took it and handed it to her partner, then fixed her gaze on me. "If you don't mind, would you tell me where you were last night?"

"Come on." Porter slapped his hat against his leg. "Is this really necessary?"

I shrugged. "It's fine. I had dinner at about 6 o'clock last night. Then I spent the rest of the evening going over a case file and drafting a brief. I went to bed at about 10:30." I held her gaze to make it stick.

Her eyes narrowed a tiny bit, but she turned to Porter. "And you?"

"Seriously, Arabella?"

"Porter, you know as well as I do that I have to cover all the bases here. Just tell me where you were." Her phone beeped and she pulled it from her pocket and read the screen. "Dr. Monroe, the forensic analyst, is almost here."

He snugged his hat on his head. "I had supper at Shady's Diner and then I went over to Vorayna Clearwater's house."

The male detective shifted on his feet and glowered at Porter, but stayed silent.

"You spend the night there?"

Porter chuckled. "Hell no. I was there for two hours tops. Then I went home and played Call of Duty online for an hour before bed."

She nodded. "That's all I need for now. But if I have to verify the hours, would you be willing to submit your gaming console to determine when you were online—" She glanced at me. "And your laptop for evaluation so we can determine the times you were writing your brief?"

I ground my teeth together. "If your investigation proceeds any further into my brother or me, we will lawyer up and fight you every inch of the way. Mainly because you'd be wasting your time instead of doing your job and catching who actually killed our father."

Her direct stare probably made most people sweat. Not me. Though looking at her determined face, her green eyes luminous, was no hardship on my part. "If that's all, I'll show you out." I stood and walked them to

the front door. "Please keep me informed of what you discover."

"I'm sorry Mr. King, but this is an active investigation." She strode out the front door, her partner on her heels. "We'll keep our information close to the vest for as long as necessary to solve this crime. I'm also going to send Brody over to keep an eye on the firm until the evidence has been bagged and the body removed. Given the nature of the note left on the body, I think it would be prudent for us to station a uniform outside your home for the next few days."

I waved the suggestion away. "That won't be necessary. We don't even know who the note was intended for."

She paused, her hand on the Greek column at the head of the stairs. "We don't, but better safe than sorry. There's a killer on the loose."

"I'll just stay over with Benton until this is cleared up," Porter offered. "I don't think anybody's going to roll up on us when they see the Sheriff's car out front."

I didn't particularly want Porter staying at my place, especially considering his love for making a mess and never cleaning up after himself, but it would certainly be preferable to having a police cruiser parked across the street. All my neighbors would be talking as it was.

She stashed her notepad inside her jacket. "You okay with letting him stay, Mr. King?"

I grudgingly gave my answer. "Yes."

"Good. Logan and I are going to head over to your father's house. You're welcome to come and watch the search."

"I will after I speak to the staff."

"Fair enough, but I'm warning you, Mr. King." She put iron in her tone. "Don't get in our way."

"My intention isn't to get in your way, it's to make sure you do your job adequately."

She turned to fully face me. "Let's get one thing straight before we go any further. I'm in charge of this investigation. Not you. If you have a problem with that, I suggest you take it up with Chief Garvey. But if you want your father's killer found, you'll let me do my job. And if I decide that you are willfully interfering in my investigation, I won't hesitate to charge you with obstruction."

Porter held out a hand. "Hey now. We don't need to turn on each other. All of us want to find who did this, me and Benton especially. It was our father, after all." His voice shook before he cleared his throat. "The sheriff's department is at your disposal if you need any assistance."

"Thanks for the offer." She tempered her words, though I could feel irritation simmering beneath her surface. "I realize both of you went through quite a shock, and I'm not trying to be insensitive. But I am going to work this case, and I would prefer to have cooperation— from *both* of you—as we move forward. All right?" She peered up at me.

I chewed my words before spitting them out. "I'm not changing my stance on the attorney-client privilege, but I want to find who did this. I'll help you all I can."

"That's good enough for me. Detective Dearborn and I are going to head to the house." She turned and dropped down the stairs.

"Don't go in until I get there."

Detective Dearborn gave me a half-ass salute and followed Matthews to their car.

A white Camry pulled into the lot, parked, and a woman stepped out. She wore professional attire, and I could have believed she was an attorney coming for business. A young man stepped from the passenger side, his simple khakis and green polo giving the impression of an intern.

"Pauline." Detective Matthews walked down the front steps and greeted the woman. They exchanged words for a few moments before Pauline, her blonde hair restrained in a tight bun at the crown of her head, opened the trunk and directed the man to collect a few items.

"That's the forensic doctor woman from Tupelo and her tech assistant." Porter's stage whisper wafted through the humid air.

The detectives piled into their cruiser as the forensics doctor and her assistant approached.

"Sheriff." The doctor gave a nod of recognition to Porter. "I'm sorry for your loss." Then her tone turned all business. "Show me the way."

Porter walked her into the building, the crime scene tech on her heels, as I watched the detectives pull into the street and head toward the residential area of town.

Porter reappeared. "She's doing her thing, and she said she's already called the coroner to come in behind her. The guy's taking pics and collecting evidence." He put his hands on his belt and stared out at the perfect square of green lawn in front of the firm. We used to play on it when we were kids. Dad would be shut up in his office or meeting with a client, and we'd play tag or toss a football until it was time to go home. I could almost feel the warm sun from those days, but now I stood in the shade.

Porter stirred, kicking the toe of his boot against the railing. "What the hell just happened?"

"I have no idea."

"I can't believe he's gone." His brows drew together as he stared at the flowers along the front walk. "This doesn't seem real."

I had nothing to say. He was right. It didn't feel real. It was as if I could walk into the office and hear my father's voice floating down the hall. But I couldn't. We'd never hear his voice again.

"One question." He stopped his kicking. "Why'd you lie about where you were last night?"

I met his eye. "I could ask you the same thing."

## 5

ARABELLA

"The lawyer one has a stick up his ass, huh?" Logan pulled a can of snuff from his shirt pocket.

"Not in my car." I gave a firm shake of my head. "You know this."

"Come on." He tapped the lid on the Skoal. "Just one little dip."

"Not a chance." I drummed my fingers on the steering wheel as we cut through Azalea's square. The city hadn't changed much over the years, and the square still served as the hub of commerce and government. Large oaks lined the park and fountain at the center, and mom and pop storefronts, some of them older than I was, formed the backbone of Azalea's small-town shopping district.

Many of them had fallen into disrepair over the last decade or so, the paint fading from their signs and business evaporating as big box shopping centers opened on the outskirts of town near the Interstate. Despite the downturn, a few of the businesses had managed to revamp within the last couple of years—the drug store converting to a coffee shop, the old Sears becoming an antique store, and the florist undergoing a flashy renovation. The windows of the brand-new burger joint glinted as we rode past, though I had no idea how it stayed afloat. The food was terrible and the clientele slim.

Logan stuffed the can back into his pocket with a hrmph. "Porter and his brother couldn't be more different."

"I know. I had no idea those two were so night and day."

"Not all different." A sly smirk twisted the corner of his mouth. "They were both eyeing you a little too much."

I arched a brow. "Jealous?"

"Amused." He sighed and settled back into his seat as we passed the older homes along Main Street, their antebellum look heightened by all the columns, balconies, and never-ending azalea bushes along the walks.

"They might look at me differently if I arrest one of them for their father's murder."

"You got a bead on one of them for it?"

"No." In fact, I didn't get a gut feeling about either of them. Nothing bad, anyway. Benton looked down his nose with a haughty arrogance I should have expected from the eldest King, and Porter was the same old jokester I remembered from high school. Neither of them sweated my questions, though I had no doubt they had something to hide. Everyone in a small town like Azalea had more than a few skeletons in the closet, myself included.

My phone buzzed, and I pulled it out. The daycare was

calling.

"Detective Matthews." I answered.

"Hi Arabella. Vivi is running a fever and complaining about her throat being sore. Seems like whatever crud she had over the weekend isn't letting go. I'm afraid we'll have to send her home for the day."

Bad timing. I sighed. "I'll send May Bell to get her, but make sure and help her get Vivienne into the car seat for me, would you?"

"Sure thing. Sorry about this, but we can't keep her with the fever. State regulations—"

"No, it's cool. Not your fault at all. I'll give May Bell a call. She'll be there soon." I hung up and flipped to my mom's number.

"Vivi?" Logan asked.

"Still sick. Has a fever."

"Poor thing." Logan was like an uncle to her, and he gave her more attention and love than her actual father ever had. "Can May Bell handle it?"

"She's going to have to." I called her number. She answered right before it went to voice mail. "Belly?"

"Hey Mom. Can you do me a favor and pick up Vivi from daycare? They called. She's running a fever."

"Sure, of course." She coughed a little.

"Make sure you take your oxygen tank with you."

"This thing is like an albatross around my neck, always trying to drown me." Mixed metaphors were one of my mother's specialties.

She'd lived with us for the past four years, ever since Vivienne was born. Her lung cancer diagnosis came just a year later, but she kept fighting the disease, sending it into remission after a series of treatments that almost claimed her life. Helpful and loving, she was also foul-mouthed and had a penchant for gambling. And did I mention fiercely independent? I could hear her voice, the one that used to be as clear as a piano note, in my mind: "*I never could be just one thing, Belly. You don't have to be, either.*"

"Just put the oxygen tank on your little pull cart and take it, okay? I can't have you gasping for breath while you're behind the wheel with Vivienne in the car."

"Fine." She grumbled, but I knew she'd do whatever was necessary to keep Vivienne safe. Sometimes it seemed like Vivi was just as much her baby as mine. "Enough jawing. Let me go get her."

"Okay. Drive safe." I hung up and got the sneaking suspicion that May Bell would solve Vivi's sore throat with copious amounts of ice cream.

Logan watched as I turned down a lane situated between two long stands of pecan trees. "You know where the Kings live by heart, huh?"

"Everybody knows."

The smooth road unfurled ahead of us like a long black tongue, dappled here and there with patches of sunshine. I knew the way because I'd been out here before. Several times, in fact. When I was younger, poorer, and with a little more time on my hands, I'd drive my old beater down this road and simply sit and stare at the grand King house. It was one of the few truly ante-bellum homes in Azalea, its white columns rising two stories along the front porch and wide windows casting light out into the sultry summer air.

We passed the spot beneath a magnolia where I'd sit in

my car and daydream about living in such a beautiful place. I'd stare for a while, give away my time like it was pennies through my fingers. Then, once I'd been there long enough to feel creepy about it, I would leave and go back to my mom's place on Razor Row—a line of shotgun houses built so close together and so thin that the locals likened them to razors stacked against each other.

The sun was high by the time we rolled up to the side of the house, and my stomach gave a rumble as we exited the car.

Logan didn't seem to notice as he kept his head on a swivel, peering at the carriage house, then the grounds, and finally back to the white mansion. "I'll check out the garage and then the back. Wait for me."

My phone buzzed again. I pulled it out and pressed the button to answer. "Detective Matthews."

"What the hell is going on? Randall King dead?" Chief Garvey's weathered voice crackled like dry logs on a fire.

"Yeah. Pauline is doing the scene now. We're out at Randall's place to have a look. How's Lina?"

"About the same." He coughed. "Hasn't opened her eyes. But they're going to keep trying."

"Sorry Chief." I frowned at Logan, who shook his head, then turned to walk to the garage.

Chief Garvey cleared his throat, the strain evident. "Found anything out yet?"

"No. Both King sons have alibis. We haven't met with their sister yet, but it looks like she was out of town when the killing happened. Got involved in that whole cleanup going on in Browerton where they found those bodies."

"The Blackwood thing? What a mess."

"Yeah. Anyway, King was found slumped over at his desk, one shot through his head. A safe in his desk was open, but empty. And one last thing, there was a note stabbed into his back, post mortem, that said *You're next.*"

"Holy shit. I should have been there."

"No, you needed to be with Lina. It's all right. Logan and I are your detectives. Let us detect."

"I'm going to catch hell from Benton King for not showing up personally. I'll head on over to the law firm now. See if the tech has turned up anything." He cursed under his breath. "In my town, and now of all times."

"We'll get to the bottom of it."

"You better." A hint of the gruff Chief Garvey reappeared. "I've got voicemails from Judge Ingles, half the city council, Mayor Baker, and Letty Cline, just to name a few. Word's spread, and people are already hovering around like flies on shit."

"We're on it."

"One more thing."

"Yeah?" I stepped out of the car.

"Millie Lagner's left me a shit ton of messages about her missing okra."

I shook my head. "Logan will be all over that as soon as we're done with this King business."

"He better. I'm tired of hearing about it. The woman's a nutjob. Logan needs to get his goddamn ass in gear and handle this shit!"

"Yes, sir." I smirked at Logan as he reappeared from the side of the house.

"And be careful." Chief Garvey ended the call.

"What's funny?" Logan cocked his head at me.

"Oh, nothing." I followed him to the front steps. "How's the house look?"

"No signs of forced entry. Everything's clear. Garvey doing okay?" He pulled on a pair of gloves and handed me a set.

"About as well as could be expected. Lina still hasn't opened her eyes yet." I headed up the steps and grabbed the key from my pocket. "Front door looks fine."

The wide oak doors had glass transom windows along the top, and two large brass knockers in the center of each. Going inside seemed like some sort of transgression, like I was pushing through the veil of my daydreams and entering the reality of the house. Would I be disappointed?

"Weren't we supposed to wait for Benton King?" Logan eyed the door.

"I told him when we'd be here. If he doesn't show up, that's on him. We can't sit around and wait while the case goes cold."

"You're the boss." He snapped the wristband of his glove. "The doctor is in."

The door opened with a low creak, and beyond lay a sunny foyer with dark wood floors and a chandelier hanging two stories overhead. I'd always imagined marble and overwrought woodwork, but instead the house was a bit simpler. Wood moldings and light gray walls matched with plain, and somewhat worn décor gave the house a casual air.

Logan peered into a sitting room off to the right. "I'll start here."

"Let's work from the front rooms to the back and then

head upstairs." I turned left and entered what seemed to be another sitting room along the front of the house, a piano in one corner and elegant—if uncomfortable-looking—furniture flanking a fireplace. A portrait hung on the back wall, and I paused to study it. A young Benton, his back straight and his unmistakable stoic gaze already dominating his young face, sat at the piano, his fingers poised on the keys. On the rug behind him, a boyish Porter played with a toddler girl with long dark hair.

Apparently, Benton King had always been a serious type. The portrait gave me some insight into his mannerisms and what I'd initially perceived as coldness. His refusal to turn over the files from his father's office made more sense as I studied the lines and curves of the painting. Benton played by the rules, and it seemed he always had.

I swept the rest of the room, flipping through the music books inside the piano bench and going through a writing table. Finding only pens and empty notepads, I closed the drawers and returned to the main hallway. "Logan?"

"In the dining room." His voice floated to me from a doorway down the hall on the right. "Do you have any idea how much this bourbon is worth?"

Peeking in the doorway, I found him standing with a bottle held up to the light. "Focus. We aren't here to raid the liquor cabinet."

"Speak for yourself." He smirked and replaced the bottle inside a wide buffet to the side of an even wider dining room table.

Sunlight filtered through high windows that gave a clear view of the side yard and a massive magnolia tree, its creamy blooms browned and withered. I continued down the hall and found the kitchen. Though well-maintained, the kitchen had a vintage flare, the double ovens on the wall a light blue with a matching refrigerator. Each room I visited readjusted my vision of the house. Instead of the grand mansion with stainless steel everything, granite everything else, and perfection around every corner, it was a well lived in home, not the showplace of my imagination.

I went through each drawer in the kitchen, methodically checking for any scrap of information that would assist in our investigation, not that I expected to find a smoking gun among the forks and whisks. Once satisfied, I moved on to the main living area at the back of the house. Logan and I searched together, combing through a wide bookcase along the wall, the magazine rack next to a well-worn recliner, and a chest full of keepsakes that included baby pictures of all three children, Porter's letterman jacket, a stack of awards with Benton's name on them, and Charlotte's diplomas.

"Nothing." I sighed as we re-entered the hall. "I'll take the office down here. You head upstairs."

"Alone?"

I arched a brow. "Scared, Detective?"

"Damn right." He faked a shiver. "Why do I get the feeling I'm about to discover a sex dungeon with tons of kinky costumes?" He waggled his fingers. "I'm going to be real glad that I'm wearing these gloves."

"There is something wrong with you." I fought my smile.

"I'm just saying. If I get up there and find some mannequins in BDSM gear or a suit made of human flesh, I want you to know that I already called it."

I pushed open the windowed French doors to Mr. King's office. "Just don't steal anything for your own collection. That's all I ask."

His grumbling faded as he headed for the stairs.

The office was neat with leather couches and chairs in front of a wide, dark desk. The smell reminded me of the library, which made sense given that the walls were lined with books, most of them legal reporters full of cases. The desk had a few neat stacks of paper, a laptop, and a photo of Randall King's Dancing with the Stars win from last year. He smiled in the picture, his arm around Lina Garvey's waist, her sparkling dancer's outfit glittering in the flash. I'd forgotten she'd won that year, and I brushed away the comparison of the Lina in the photo versus the broken girl I'd found at the bottom of a ravine a month ago. An accident. One that hit too close to home and had Chief Garvey spending more time at the hospital than he did at the station.

Sighing, I pulled the curtains back from two windows, letting light flood the room. Starting with the documents on top of the desk, I flipped through each piece of paper and thumbed through the books scattered on the edge of his desktop day planner. Bills, junk mail, and receipts from a recent trip to Tupelo constituted the majority of items.

"I thought I told you to wait for me." Benton strode in the doorway.

I jumped but tried to play it off as I flipped through some more mail. "You weren't here, and I had the key and permission to search." I shrugged. "So I searched."

"Find anything?" He sank down on the nearest couch and folded his hands in his lap. He'd ditched his suit coat, and was dressed in his black pants, light blue button-up shirt, and dark blue tie. I wondered if this was as casual as he got.

"Not yet." I opened the desk's top drawer and found several common office items—pens, stapler, scissors, paperclips. Nothing of interest. "Does anyone else have frequent access to this house or this room?"

"Other than my siblings and I, the only person who comes in here is Mrs. Denny, the cleaning lady." He let out a long breath and rubbed his eyes, the first intentional sign he'd given that his father's death was weighing on him. "Unless he has visitors. Sometimes Judge Ingles will stop by, Mayor Baker, Letty Cline, or the Reynolds."

"Your dad was quite popular."

"He was." The 's' sound lingered, as if he were tasting the past tense and finding it sour.

A fledgling burst of pity rose in my breast. I paused my search and met his gaze. "I really am sorry about your father. I didn't know him, but I did know of him. He seemed like a nice man who did a lot of good for Azalea."

"Thank you. I appreciate that." He shook his head. "None of this makes any sense. Dad didn't have any enemies. And no one would have known about the safe unless they worked at the firm, or possibly a client who saw him open it years ago. Not to mention, I have no idea what could've been in it." He seemed to be talking it out to himself instead of me.

My detective mode kicked back on, and I asked, "But it's possible that there was something of value in the safe that you didn't know about?"

He threw his hands up. "Sure, but I can't imagine what. I'm pretty sure he didn't have the Maltese Falcon tucked away in there. And like I said, all the firm money is in an account down at First Mississippian."

"The Maltese Falcon? I didn't peg you as a detective novel sort."

"I'm not, but I enjoy old movies, especially noir." The corner of his lips almost snuck up into a smirk. "Femme fatales and adventure, what's not to love?"

"I see." I realized that Benton King had a lot of layers underneath his unyielding exterior. As far as my investigation was concerned, I wasn't sure if that was a good thing or a bad thing.

Returning my focus to the desk, I closed the top drawer and checked the ones on the left side and then the right. After finding more of the same—bills and random documents—I closed the final drawer. As I pressed it all the way shut, something struck me as off. I pulled it out and examined the unused letterhead and envelopes inside. Nothing amiss. Pulling out the drawer above it, I discovered the difference. The top drawer was a few inches deeper. Not enough to notice unless you were truly paying attention.

The bottom drawer had a false back.

## 6

## BENTON

*S*he ducked behind the desk and made a "hmm" noise.

"What is it?" I'd been in this office, sitting in this very spot, thousands of times. Some of my earliest memories were of playing on the floor in front of my father's desk. If Detective Matthews crawled beneath the worn mahogany, she'd probably find crayon marks and dinosaur stickers, relics that only had special meaning for me.

"This bottom drawer has a false back." She pushed the desk chair away, and it rolled languidly until it hit the nearest bookcase.

"There's a small wooden lever at the very top of the drawer. Press down and pull out, and it will open right up."

She popped her head up from behind the desk. "You know about it? You could've said something."

"Maybe I was testing your detecting skills." Honestly, I'd forgotten about it. Perhaps some of my toy soldiers were still in there, patiently waiting for their chance at battle and glory. It was an easy hiding spot.

She grumbled and disappeared again before popping up with a handful of papers, each of them folded in a nice bundle with a shoestring keeping them together. "Have you ever seen these before?"

I leaned forward. "No. I had no idea they were in there." I'd given her permission to search the house because I was certain she wouldn't find anything. I'd been here too many times to let something important slip past me. The bundle of letters proved me wrong.

Setting them on the desk, she rolled the chair back over and sat. With nimble, gloved fingers, she untied the package and pulled the first letter from the top of the stack.

I stood and walked over to her side to get a better look, curiosity like a persistent scratch in the back of my throat.

She gave me a long look. "Logan is upstairs."

Distrust thickened the air between us. Was she afraid of me? The idea struck me as nearly comical, but for the hard look on her soft face.

"What do you think I'm going to do? Strangle you in my father's office and have Porter cover up the crime for me?" Now that I thought about it, maybe she had a point to be suspicious.

"You might try." She patted the gun on her hip. "But there would only be one murder victim in this house, and it wouldn't be me."

*Damn.* I didn't blame her. In fact, I rather liked her

directness. "Now that I know where I stand, can we please see what the letters are about?"

With one more wary glance, she returned her attention to the letter in her hand. The envelope had my father's name and address printed in even handwriting, but there was no return address. She slid her fingernail under the flap and flipped it open, then pulled out a hand-written letter on a piece of lined notebook paper.

Moving closer, I read over her shoulder.

*Randall,*

*I'm warning you. This is the last time I'm going to ask for what you owe me. If you don't pay up, I'm going to go to the judge and get this settled once and for all. I'll give you one more week. I've waited long enough for you to do right by me, and I refuse to waste any more time begging you to do the right thing. I know your reputation in town makes you think that you can push me around. But when they find out what a son of a bitch you are, I think they'll stop bowing down. And I'll make sure they all find out. Let me know your answer.*

*M*

She turned and looked up at me, a question in her eyes. Her hair smelled like some sort of berry shampoo. "Who's M?"

"I don't know for certain, but I can guess. Winston Morris."

"You told me that your father didn't have any enemies." She waved the letter before plucking the next one from the stack. "But you know about a Winston Morris who's been sending threats. Is there anything else you haven't told me?" Ire colored her words, the sound like glass breaking.

"I know Winston Morris, but I didn't know he was threatening my father. That's news to me." I leaned down so I could see her eyes. "I swear. I didn't know."

After a few awkward moments of staring, she gave me a slight nod, then flipped open the next letter, which held more vitriol and threats. The next three were the same. "Tell me everything you know about Winston Morris." She narrowed her eyes. "And don't leave a thing out. Start with how he's related to your firm, King and *Morris*."

"Caught that, did you?"

"I already have one smartass in my orbit," she deadpanned. "He doesn't need any competition."

As if on cue, a thump sounded from upstairs.

I retreated to my seat on the couch, putting some necessary space between detective Matthews and myself. Her hair smelled ridiculously good, and it was clouding my brain.

"Winston Morris is the last of the Morris line. As you've noticed, the law firm is named King and Morris. Ever since the firm was established, the King and Morris families were close and worked together. Until Winston. He went to law school with me, both of us in the same class at the University of Mississippi." I paused, trying to figure out the least offensive way to explain. "While he was there, he got involved in some questionable activities that culminated in his dismissal from law school."

"Questionable activities?"

I shifted and drummed my fingers on my thigh. "He and some of his fraternity brothers—all lowlifes as far as I'm concerned—were caught defacing university property and hanging nooses in the trees near black fraternities."

Revulsion flared across her face, and I couldn't blame her. I'd felt the same when I heard about what Winston had done. "At that time, Winston's father had already left the firm because of his Alzheimer's, though we kept him on as a partner—just an honorary roll since he was lucid less than half the time—and intended to hire Winston as soon as he graduated from law school."

"I take it that didn't happen?" She rifled through some more papers as I spoke.

"Not a chance. When Winston's father discovered what his son had done, he agreed with my father that Winston was no longer welcome at the firm. They wound up the Morris side of the business and put the money from his share in trust for Winston's mother and sisters. Winston raised a stink about it at the time, claiming his father was too far gone to make decisions about his money, but Judge Ingles sided with Winston's father and issued a court order to that effect. After that, Winston left town."

"Where is he now?" She tapped the stack of letters. "These were sent local, looks like."

"There have been rumors that he's holed up in a cabin on the far edge of his family property."

"So, you're telling me the racist Unabomber had beef with your father and lives nearby?"

"He had beef ten years ago maybe. Sure. But we haven't heard a peep from him in all that time." I stared at the stack of letters. "Or at least I thought we hadn't heard a peep."

Logan appeared in the doorway, his expression souring as he spotted me. "I heard voices."

49

"How close are you to being done upstairs?" she asked.

"There is a spare bedroom full of papers and all sorts of stuff. It's going to be a while." He wiped a fine sheen of sweat from his brow with the back of his forearm. "Doesn't help that it's hot as hell up there."

She pointed to the stack of envelopes. "I've got a lead. Randall King had been receiving threatening letters from Winston Morris."

"That guy? I didn't know he was still around."

She cocked her head to the side. "You know him?"

Logan rolled his shoulders. "We had a little run-in several years ago. He saw me at the bar making time with some pretty little blonde thing. Things got...heated. I asked him to step outside." He paused and shot a furtive glance at me, perhaps trying to decide how much to share in mixed company.

She waved a hand. "You've never met a fight you didn't like. I get the gist."

He nodded, a satisfied smile creeping across his lips. "Never saw him at the bar after that night."

Walking over to him, she grabbed an evidence bag that he'd stuffed in the waistband of his jeans. Placing the letters inside, she said, "I need to get out to his place and question him."

He let out a relieved sigh. "Thank god. It's a sauna up there. I'm ready to go."

"Not a chance. You two have history. All bad. I can't have you turning him off the second we roll up. Stay here, and keep going through the upstairs. Call me if you find anything big."

Logan peeled a glove off his hand. "Now wait just a

minute. This guy is some grade-A level psycho. You shouldn't be going out there by yourself. He and I may have some history, but that doesn't mean I can't—"

"That's exactly what it means, Logan. What if he confesses to me? Any good defense attorney would be able to get it thrown out simply based on your presence. If you beat his ass a few years ago, that's plenty of reason for a judge to find his current confession coerced. I can't risk it."

I found myself nodding along with her reasoning. Though I doubted Winston would be foolish enough to confess to anything, she was right to plan ahead.

Logan placed a hand on her shoulder. Something streaked through me, a foreign sensation that I barely recognized. Why was Logan so familiar with Arabella? That level of touching certainly wasn't professional. I wouldn't allow it at my firm. In fact, I might even go so far as to discipline somebody for touching another employee in such a direct fashion.

"He's dangerous, Arabella. Especially to people with the wrong skin tone." He plucked a dark lock of hair from her shoulder and rubbed it between his fingers. "And that includes you."

"I'll go with her." I wanted to knock his hand away, but instead I stood and crossed my arms over my chest. "I don't have any direct dispute with him, and maybe my familiar presence will put him at ease enough that he'll talk."

Logan cut his eyes to me. "Not a chance. You aren't even law enforcement. And we haven't cleared you as a suspect yet."

"Neither of you are going." Arabella pulled off her gloves. "I don't need an escort to do my job."

"You're being unreasonable. Listen..." I pulled my phone from my pocket and dialed Porter while Logan and Arabella continued their argument.

"This is Porter. I mean, this is Sheriff King. How can I...help you?"

I barely stifled my eye roll. "It's me, idiot. I need you to deputize me."

Arabella and Logan stopped talking and gawked at me.

"Say what now?" I could imagine the dumb look gracing my little brother's face.

"As the sheriff, you have the ability to deputize people. Deputize me so that I can assist with finding our father's killer."

"Okay, so how exactly do I do that?"

I pinched the bridge of my nose. "I'm honestly beginning to think I would make a better sheriff than you."

A huff whistled through the earpiece. "You don't have to be a dick about it."

"Meet me down at the courthouse in ten minutes. You can swear me in with the county clerk. All you have to do is say that you have asked for my assistance and that I am properly deputized."

"Okay. Sounds simple enough. See you there."

I ended the call and met two pairs of incredulous eyes.

Arabella kicked her chin up. "I never said you could come with me."

"Once I'm deputized, I can investigate all I want. The Morris property is out in the county, which will be in my jurisdiction, not yours." I loosened my tie and pulled it off, then released my top button. "So really, it's you who's coming with me."

Logan shook his head. "Don't listen to this guy. I'll go with you. I can—I don't know—sit in the car or something."

She looked at me and then back to Logan, considering each of our offers. After a few moments of tense silence, she gave me a nod. "You can come, but I'm taking the lead on this. Understand?"

"Arabella, come on. This guy—"

"I made my decision. Stay here and finish searching. I also need you to bag the laptop. See what's on it." Her tone was clipped, all business.

I stepped closer to her. "If there are case files on there or attorney work product, then I won't allow—"

She held up a hand. "Logan, if you see anything related to client case files, pass over that for now. We'll wait for our court order." She glared at me. "Which we will get, I can assure you."

"Hang on." Logan took her by the elbow and pulled her into the hallway.

What was worse, she let him. Their hushed voices didn't carry far enough for me to hear, but every second that passed had me itching to grab her other elbow and lead her away from that asshole Logan. He was unprofessional at best.

They finally finished their discussion, though Logan gave her a wary look. "Be careful out there."

"Don't worry. I'll check back in with you as soon as we're finished with Winston." She strode toward the foyer, the evidence bag with the letters in her hand.

I followed her, but Logan stepped into my path.

"You do anything to hurt her or hinder this investigation, and I will personally fuck you up."

I had a few more inches of height than he did, which was satisfying when I was able to stare down my nose at him. "I really should have a talk with Chief Garvey about professionalism among his detectives. It's clearly lacking."

He smiled, though there was nothing friendly about it. "You've been warned, smart guy."

"Thanks for the advice." I pushed past him and into the hall.

Arabella had already walked out, her dark hair disappearing down the front steps. Logan followed me to the foyer, then slowly ascended the stairs to the second floor.

I paused next to the thermostat and kicked the temperature up a few notches and slammed the door on my way out.

## 7

ARABELLA

"Is Judge Ingles in?" I leaned on the clerk's counter, baskets for incoming warrants, certified documents, and case filings lined up neatly to my left, and an ancient computer terminal with a green screen to my right.

"Let me see." Gail plucked her receiver and hit a button.

"Ready for this?" Porter strode in, his hat cocked back on his head, giving him the appearance of a boy playing at being sheriff.

"Let's get it over with." Benton stood next to the attorney mail boxes—one for each lawyer in the county. Several of them were overflowing with notices and letters. Benton's was meticulously neat and empty.

Porter lowered his voice. "Forensics left the firm. Coroner Stapleton arrived for the um, for…"

"The body." Benton matched his hushed tone.

"Right. I guess we need to make arrangements."

"Get in touch with Margaret. She'll know what to do."

Benton rubbed the bridge of his nose. "You talked to Charlotte?"

"Yeah, told her to come home. Didn't tell her why. She said she'd call when she got back into town."

Gail hung up. "The judge is in, Detective. Want me to let him know you're coming?"

"Seeing the judge?" Benton stepped to my elbow. "If this is about the files—"

"No, I just want to ask him a few questions about your father."

"I'm coming with you."

"Don't you have to get sworn in?" I turned on my heel and headed down the hall to the judge's chambers. My interview would go smoother without Benton gumming up the works.

"Porter, get it done!" Benton barked.

I turned the corner and almost knocked over an older woman, both of us in a hurry. "I'm sorry, ma'am." I gripped her shoulders to keep her from toppling over.

She steadied herself with one hand on the wall. "Sorry about that. I guess I wasn't looking where I was going."

"You okay?"

"I'm fine." She straightened and brushed some iron-gray strands from her face.

I hadn't recognized her at first, but she owned the florist shop over on the square. I'd bought flowers from her for special occasions, even though Mom pitched a fit whenever I brought home lilies: "*Smells like a funeral parlor, Belly, and I ain't even dead yet!*"

She knelt and picked up a manila folder she'd dropped.

"Let me help you with that." Though I was in a hurry, I

snagged a few papers that had escaped—documents that looked like some sort of deed.

"Thank you." She took the papers, a slight shake in her hands. "Sorry again."

"It was my fault. No worries. Have a good one." I stepped away from her and continued down the hall.

"You too," she called.

With quick steps, I pushed the heavy wooden door with "The Honorable Bradley Ingles" on it in gold lettering.

His secretary waved me back through another door, and I entered his office. Judge Ingles sat with his back to me, his gaze on the oak tree outside his wide windows. The scene echoed back to the one I'd witnessed this morning, though I was glad to see a clean desk and floor instead of pooled blood.

"Judge?"

He spun slowly, his watery blue eyes dim despite the sunny windows. "Miss Matthews, what can I do for you?"

I let the "Miss" slide. "I assume you've heard about Randall King."

He dipped his chin, but kept his eyes on me. "Word travels, especially word like that." With one gnarled hand, he pointed at the leather chair across from his desk. "Please, have a seat, young lady."

"Thank you." I perched on the edge of the chair, my notepad and pen in my hands. "I know you and Randall were good friends. Do you know of anyone who wanted to hurt him?"

"Randall? No. Of course not."

"Can't think of any enemies he may have had?"

He opened his eyes wide, as if shocked at the very suggestion. "Not a one."

Acting wasn't his strong suit. His lies were like a biting insect in my brain, burrowing in. I glued my lips together. Letting the silence stretch until the room was full of it, bursting at the seams, had always been a good tactic. But Judge Ingles settled back in his chair, his eyes drawn to the windows again. Whatever pressure I'd hoped for didn't seem to bear down on him at all.

"Judge?"

"Yes?" He dragged his gaze away from the tree and back to me.

"Is there anything you can tell me? Anything at all?"

A spark flashed in his eyes, but quickly died down. He was playing possum. Something told me there was a whirlwind of thoughts in his mind, but none of them wanted to pass his lips.

"I could tell you plenty of things, Miss Matthews, but none of them would be of any help." He shrugged. "It's too late for that."

I leaned forward, trying to keep his attention. "What do you mean?"

"I mean—"

A brief knock, and then the door opened. The moment broke, and Judge Ingles swallowed, likely beginning the slow digestion of whatever secret he was about to spill.

Benton strode in and took the seat next to me. "Judge." He gave him a quick nod.

"I'm sorry about your dad." The judge's shiny pate wobbled back and forth as he shook his head. "Such a shame."

"Judge, when you said 'it's too late,' what did you mean?" I pressed.

He waved a hand and glanced at Benton. "Just that it's too late for Randall. May God have mercy on his soul. That's all I meant."

*Dammit.* I stowed my notebook. Judge Ingles wasn't giving me anything, not now that Benton was in the room.

"Do you know of anyone who'd do this?" Benton leaned forward, his elbows on his thighs.

"No, son. And who knows why people do anything these days?" He sighed, the sound one of bone-deep tired, the sort you can't simply sleep off in one night.

"There was a note." I took a chance and dangled the carrot in front of him, hoping he'd bite.

"A note?" The judge clasped his hands on his desk top, the age-spotted fingers gripping each other. "What did it say?"

"The words 'You're next'."

"Oh." His eyebrows dropped, the bushy gray slashes almost covering his eyes. "Goodness."

"Any idea who the note could be referring to?"

He spun away again, his gaze focused outside the room.

I knew his answer before he gave it.

"No idea."

\* \* \*

WE HEADED out of town along Route 42. The houses became less frequent until the forest took over entirely on either side of the road. Logging trucks flew by, only slowing when they saw my cruiser and no doubt speeding up as soon as they crested the next hill and disappeared from my rearview.

"Do you give out tickets?" Benton craned his head as another truck, it's trailer empty, sped past.

"Not anymore." Though I certainly had the itch to flip on my lights and give a trucker an earful.

"Too important now that you're a detective?"

I shot him a glance. "I have other duties."

"Not too many bigtime capers going on in Azalea, are there?"

His flippant tone rankled, but I kept my voice even. "Maybe not. But there are still plenty of thefts, domestic disputes, and meth labs."

"Sounds about right. I bet you spend a lot of time over on Razor Row trying to get the lowlifes straightened out."

My hands tightened on the steering wheel. "Does your clientele know how you feel about them?"

"My clientele?"

"The people of Azalea. The *lowlifes* you mentioned."

"Ah." He gave me a sardonic smile. "My clientele isn't *your* clientele."

"Is that so? I'm pretty sure I spotted Lucas Kitston sitting in your waiting room when I arrived at the firm."

He gestured to the trees along the right-hand side. "This is the edge of the Morris property. And what does Mr. Kitston have to do with anything?"

"I busted him six months ago for soliciting prostitution."

His brows knit together. "Lucas Kitston? Twice-decorated veteran and deacon at First Presbyterian?"

"That's the one. He lucked up that the girl was eighteen. Though she'd told him she was fifteen. That was why he'd picked her." I shouldn't have taken so much pleasure in watching his superiority bubble deflate with a wheeze, but I did.

He scrubbed a hand down his jaw. "I never heard a word about it. How did it not get into the Gazette, or around the courthouse at the—"

"Judge Ingles is a close friend of Mr. Kitston, and so was your father." I slowed as I rounded a curve. "That was pretty much the long and the short of it. Thanks to them, Kitston got deferred prosecution and the whole thing was hushed up."

"I didn't know." His words were genuine, the confused surprise etched on his face real.

"No offense, but it seems like there's a lot about your father—and this town—that you don't know."

He opened his mouth, then closed it—as if his snappy comeback couldn't wrestle its way into existence. "It's here." He pointed to a gravel and dirt road leading between the pines.

I turned, steeling myself for the bumps. The suspension on my old cruiser would make sure we felt every one of them. "Hang on."

He gripped the oh-shit handle above the door as we wound our way through the woods, the highway a distant memory as the ruts bounced us and the deep hollows dragged us down. Silence reigned between us, the tense kind that felt like a third person in the car. I needed to ask more questions about his father, to dig down until I hit the bedrock of the truth. But I couldn't ignore the fact that Benton was obviously in pain. His snarky exterior couldn't hide it. His father's passing was still sinking in, like dark paint through light cracks. So, I let the silence stay intact, him alone with his thoughts and me in an ongoing tug-of-war with the steering wheel.

After ten minutes of jostling, I broke down and asked, "How much farther?"

"Probably a quarter of a mile," he said through gritted teeth.

When we hit a particularly bad series of ruts, the car began to jog sideways, sliding toward the edge of a steep hollow.

"Whoa." Benton leaned toward me and away from the approaching drop off.

I hit the brakes, the tires crunching over the gravel as we skidded to a stop near the edge.

He let out a breath and ran a hand through his hair, mussing it. "Holy shit, that was close."

I caught the scent of his aftershave, some sort of expensive, sophisticated mix. It could have been unicorn tears and rainbow drops as far as I knew, but it smelled good. With his dark hair and wide shoulders, he was a nice-looking man. His nose was too sharp, his eyebrows somewhat severe, but all that gave him a unique air, setting him apart from his more traditionally handsome younger brother.

"It's safe. We can go," he offered, settling back into his seat. "Maybe just a little slower this time?" He grabbed the handle and assumed the position again.

I gave him points for not freaking out and demanding to drive. That's something Logan would have done. I would have told him to shut the hell up and sit down, of course, but the difference was noted.

"I'll keep us on the road." I pressed on the gas and maneuvered us into the center of the lane, if it could be called that. The deeper we crept into the woods, the more tall grass appeared between the tire tracks, the stalks tickling along the underbelly of the cruiser.

"It should be just—"

The sharp crack of a rifle cut through his words.

8

BENTON

*I* yanked Arabella down and leaned over, hoping that the car gave us enough cover to stop any bullets.

"Hey!" She unsnapped her service pistol and pulled it free. "Stay put."

"No way." I kept my grip on her arm.

"Let me go, Benton." Her face was close to mine, both of us hunkered down. "This is my job."

"I told you he's a psycho!" I whisper-yelled. "You can't go out there with him shooting at us."

"Benton, I'm warning you. Let me go or—"

"You can't be out here!" A hoarse yell came from the woods on the driver's side. "I got rights. You can't be on my property without my permission!"

"Winston?" she asked, her warm breath fanning across my cheek.

I gave her a slight nod, aware of how close we were, how it would only take one more movement for us to touch.

"I have to talk to him. So you have to let me go."

"What if he shoots you?"

"If he wanted to shoot me, he would have already done it. He's got a high-powered rifle, but he didn't shoot the car. Warning shot."

"What if he's just a shit shot?" I couldn't let her go out there.

"This is my job, Benton. Trust me." She straightened and cracked open her car door. "Sit tight."

Like hell I would. I sat up, too, and scanned the woods nearby.

"Mr. Morris," she called.

"You need to turn around and get on out of here."

"Winston, stop being a prick," I yelled. "We need to talk."

A rough guffaw erupted from behind one of the trees about twenty feet away. "If it's not the high and mighty Benton Goddamn King."

"Mr. Morris, I'm Detective Matthews, Azalea PD." She kept her gun down, hidden behind the door. "I'd like to ask you a few questions."

"I don't think so." He moved out from behind the tree.

I barely recognized him. He'd grown a full, shaggy beard and wore camouflage coveralls and a camo ball cap. It was as if he'd aged thirty years in the space of ten.

He slung his rifle over his shoulder and walked toward us. Arabella holstered her gun, but kept her hand near it as she closed her car door. I joined her on the driver's side.

Winston stepped onto the road, his muddy boots a perfect fit with the rutted surface. "I may not have gotten my law degree." He spat a stream of dark tobacco juice, several droplets remaining on his unkempt beard. "But I know this is out of your jurisdiction, girl."

"I'm Detective Matthews. I have a few questions for you about Randall King."

Though she ignored the "girl" slight, I ached to give Winston a lesson on manners.

"What about that son-of-a-bitch?" His beady eyes narrowed on me. "Did poor old Daddy send you out here?"

"Mr. King was found dead at his office this morning." Arabella didn't waste any time.

He shifted his gaze back to Arabella. "Come again?"

"You heard me. During my investigation, I found a stack of threatening letters from you. Care to explain yourself?"

He spat again, the dark liquid perilously close to Arabella's shoe. She didn't back down, just pinned him with a direct stare.

"Nothing to explain. He owed me." He turned to me. "So, I guess that means *you* owe me now, since he's dead."

Arabella snapped her fingers. "Hey, either you talk to me and tell me where you were last night, or I take you in right now on suspicion of murder."

He glowered and ran his fingers down the leather strap of his gun. "I'm not saying shit. Not to some half-breed whore—"

I reached forward, grabbed him by the beard, and yanked him toward me. He stumbled, the rifle sliding off his shoulder and clattering to the ground as I maneuvered behind him and wrapped my arm around his neck.

"Just like old times, Winnie." I closed the choke hold by grabbing my wrist and squeezing. "Now you're going to learn some manners." He tried to throw an elbow, but I had him pulled in too tight.

We'd done this a hundred times when we were kids. Porter, Winston, and I all rough-housing while our fathers drank, and our mothers shook their heads. Though I'd outgrown the wrestling phase long before Porter and Winston, I still remembered the submission moves, the easy way to beat an opponent without any unruly fists flying.

"Benton!" Arabella held a hand out. "Let him go."

I squeezed tighter. "Where were you last night?"

"Asshole," he sputtered and tried to grab for my hair. The stench of body odor nearly bowled me over, but I held tight.

I leaned forward until his forehead pressed to the hood of the cruiser, and then I leaned harder. "Where were you?"

"Benton, you can't do this." Arabella didn't move to stop me, but her tone was icy.

"Not ... jurisdiction," Winston gasped.

"She has reasonable suspicion that you committed a crime." I bounced his forehead on the metal with a thump. "That means she can arrest you outside of her jurisdiction." *Thump.* "Leave the lawyering to me, you halfwit." *Thump.*

He gurgled, a line of dark spit leaking from his mouth. "All right, all right!" He gripped my forearm. "I was at the cabin with Vera."

"Vera Lincoln?" Arabella asked.

Even I'd heard of Vera, Azalea's priciest prostitute.

"Yes. We have an arrangement. She was here last night. I swear. Ask her."

I released him and backed off. He sputtered and coughed, his eyes bulging as he turned to me with his hands fisted.

"Not a chance." Arabella placed her foot on the rifle and rested her hand on the butt of her pistol. "Everyone calm down. Take a breath."

"You saw what he just did!" Winston pointed at me. "That's assault! You should arrest him!"

"You'll have to take that up with the sheriff."

"The sheriff?" Winston wiped his mouth with the back of his arm.

"Benton is a deputy sheriff. Any disciplinary complaints need to be directed to the sheriff. Not the Azalea PD. As you pointed out—" she smiled, "—this isn't my jurisdiction."

"But you saw what—"

"I saw a deputy doing his job. Now, if you'll excuse me, I need to do mine." She plucked the rifle from the ground and opened the driver's side door. "I'll leave this about a mile up the road against a tree. Come and get it once we're gone."

"You can't take that. The second amendment says it's my right to have that!"

She sat and closed the door.

"You fucking nig—" His vile word cut off on a yell as I feinted toward him as if I were going for his beard again. He stumbled back, tripped over his own feet, and landed on his ass.

"Stay down, asshole." I retreated, but didn't turn my back on him, and eased into the car. For the first time in my life, I wanted to do real, physical damage. Kicking him while he was down seemed like a great idea. The filth that streamed from his mouth demanded it. But we'd gotten what we came for.

Arabella put the cruiser in reverse and backed a ways down the road before doing a three-point turn.

Once Winston disappeared from the rearview, she took a deep breath. "Benton, you can't do that."

"I know."

"That's not how I run my investigations. And you can't rise to every taunt that—"

"But he was saying—"

She held up a hand. To my faint horror, it worked. I shut up.

"I'll tell you just like I tell my daughter. Just because someone says something you don't like doesn't mean that you can put your hands on them. You have to keep a level head."

I turned to her. "Wait. You have a daughter?"

"I do." Slowing to a stop, she grabbed Winston's rifle, trotted to a tree near the road, and leaned it there as she promised.

A daughter. I'd been under the impression Arabella was single, especially since she didn't wear a ring and made no mention of a husband. I ignored the disappointment that made my stomach sink. Did her husband know about Logan? He was a little too over-protective of her, too free with how he touched her.

She returned to her seat, and we braced ourselves for

the bumpy ride out to the highway.

"How old is she? Your daughter?"

"Four." She swerved to avoid a pothole the size of a bathtub. "Once we get back on the highway, I should have enough of a signal to call Logan. He can check with Vera. See if Morris was telling the truth."

Hint taken. No more questions about her family.

"If you could drop me back at my father's place, I'd appreciate it." Or was it my place now? I hadn't thought about what happens after. After he was in the ground. After I'd become the eldest living King. The loss tugged me down, memories of my father flashing through my mind. But I couldn't let nostalgia overcome the need to find his killer. And there was too much to do already.

Breaking the news to Charlotte would be one of the hardest things I'd ever done. She was strong, but not strong enough to withstand this without cracking, maybe even breaking. I hated when she cried, always had. And I would do anything to keep the hurt from her, but there was nothing for it. No way to make the pain disappear. My baby sister—though no longer a baby—would have to suffer right along with Porter and me.

But I wouldn't wallow in my grief, not when my father's killer was walking free. After speaking with Charlotte, I needed to get back to the office. I had files to go through. The thought of walking through the front door again drained the blood from my face. It would look the same, feel the same, but the entire place was irrevocably changed. It occurred to me that the body would be gone, but what about everything else? My stomach lurched as I thought about all the blood. My father's blood. Staining the floor and seeping through the wooden slats, dropping onto the plumbing underneath in crimson dots.

"You okay?"

I swallowed hard to keep the bile from rising. "Fine."

"Maybe you should call it quits for the day." Concern colored her tone.

"Not until we know who did this."

She slowed and stopped, turning to me until I met her gaze. "Logan and I will be working on this case night and day. I'm going to do everything in my power to find the person who killed your father."

"I appreciate that, but—"

"You need to let us work. And you need to grieve. Make arrangements. Take care of your family."

Her soft voice was almost enough to wrench away my control. Emotion tried to bubble up, but I tamped it down, pushing and pushing until it was buried inside me. I was practiced at it—hiding any weakness. My father was dead, and the most important thing to me was finding out why. I could grieve later. Alone. And in my own time.

She seemed to have sensed my thoughts, because she sighed and continued the hard slog toward the highway.

Once we hit pavement, she lifted her phone and peered at the screen. With a frown, she gassed it to the top of the next rise, then slowed. Both of our phones went off with a series of dings and notifications.

Mine were automated court notices of filings and scheduling details as well as the first few sets of condolences from the few local lawyers. A text from Porter popped up: "Charlotte's in town. I sent her to your place so I can meet her there. Come when you can." God. I didn't know how I was going to look my little sister in the eye and tell her Dad was dead. The selfish part of me hoped that Porter got there before I did to break the news.

"A restraining order? Against who?" She held the phone to her ear, but I could make out a deep voice on the other end. Had to be Logan. "When?"

I strained to hear what he said, but couldn't make it out over the hum of the engine. "I'm on my way." She ended the call. "Looks like your father had a restraining order against an ex-con."

"What?" I shook my head. "That can't be right." My father had never had any trouble. Especially not the sort that warranted a restraining order. And no way he had dealings with a convicted felon.

"Got it five years ago against a violent felon with two murder counts and numerous assaults to his name. Name is Theodore Brand."

"Never heard of him." And how could that be? My view of Dad was changing by the second. Secrets. So many secrets. What else didn't I know? I gave in and ran my fingers through my hair, then yanked at the strands a few times before dropping my hands in my lap.

She flipped on her lights and siren as she burned rubber toward Azalea with a hard look of determination in her eyes. "This could be our guy."

9

ARABELLA

*I* wolfed down what was left of my burger and dialed May Bell on speaker phone. Logan cruised down the highway to the east of town toward the last known address of Theodore Brand.

"You coming home anytime?" May Bell cut right to the heart of the matter, as usual.

"Not for a while. How's Vivi?"

"Ask her yourself. Hang on. Here, it's your mommy..." A clatter followed by some muffled sounds, and then, "Hi, Mommy!"

"Hey, baby!" I drained my soft drink. "How are you feeling?"

"Better." Her voice still carried a touch of scratchiness. "I painted."

"Yeah?" I poured all the enthusiasm I had left for the day into my questions. "What did you paint?"

"A rainbow and a dead bat."

Logan shot me a bemused look.

"A dead bat?"

"Yeah." Her tone didn't change from the sweet, high-pitched tinkle. "When you come home?"

"Hopefully soon."

"Soon?"

"Hopefully."

"Okay."

"Listen to Meemaw, okay? Be my good girl."

"I'm good." A sneeze rattled down the line.

"Go blow your nose. Love you, baby."

"Love you." The call ended after a bit of snuffling.

"She all right?" Logan flipped on the headlights in the deepening gloom.

"Yeah, still has the cold."

"May Bell on top of everything?"

"As much as she can be." I stuffed the burger wrapper into the white paper bag and shoved it onto the floorboard.

"What do you make of Benton?" He chewed on his straw.

I shrugged. "He's stuffy, particular, and oddly good in a jam."

"Really?" He stopped chewing for a moment, then restarted with extra vigor.

"I don't think I would have gotten anything out of Morris if it weren't for him. Not that I agree with his methods."

"He doesn't seem like the 'rough stuff' type, but I guess I'm wrong on that one."

"No, he doesn't." Benton King had plenty of layers, and

only the very topmost one was well-starched and straight-laced. The rest of him was a mystery.

"How do you like him for a suspect?"

"Not at all." I picked back through the facts I'd gleaned from him and about him. He and his father were on good terms, no money issues at the firm, no personal issues outside of it. Same with his brother, Porter. But I was still going to check their alibis, all the same. "How about you?"

"I don't like the guy." He flipped his visor down to combat the low sun on the horizon. "He looks at you too much. And it's out of more than just professional interest."

My cheeks warmed, but I cut my eyes at him. "That's the dumbest thing you've said all day, and you say plenty of dumb things. Trust me." I'd felt Benton's curiosity about me during our ride to and from Morris's property. But that didn't mean anything. He was reeling from his father's death, and I was the one tasked with finding the killer. It made sense for him to want to know more about me, to know whether I was capable.

"Burn. And you're mad because I'm right."

I smirked. "You aren't even right as often as a broken clo—"

My phone rang, Chief Garvey's name across the screen. Shit, I should have called him already. "Hello, Chief."

"Where are you two?" His gruff voice was like a bear paw to the face.

"Headed out Highway 45 toward Polktown. We have a possible suspect living on the county line."

"You need to keep me informed, Arabella. I just went

by to speak with Benton. Charlotte was there. She's not taking the news well. Porter doesn't know his ass from a hole in the ground, and Benton looked about ready to blow. You need to find the perp and fast."

"We're following every lead we ha—"

"What about the firm? All those files of Randall's. You need to—"

"Get a warrant. Benton won't let us touch them until I get a court order."

"The hell you say?" he barked, making me pull the phone away from my ear.

"He's claiming privilege on them."

"What a load of horse shit."

"I couldn't agree more. For the time being, we have two suspects—Winston Morris and Theodore Brand. Winston felt disgruntled about his inheritance from his father's half of the firm. We've got threatening letters as proof. But Winston claimed he was with Vera on the night Randall King was killed. Logan spoke to Vera, and his story checks out, though we'll need to do a little more digging to make sure."

"What about this Brand character?"

"Randall got a restraining order against Brand about five years ago. The pleadings at the courthouse aren't clear as to why, except for the boilerplate harassment language that's in every complaint. Judge Ingles granted it. Everything else was oral argument, and there's no official record of what was said."

"That's it?"

I'd been under the impression that my investigation

was moving at a swift clip. Chief Garvey's tone disputed that impression.

"It's a start. I still need to get in touch with Pauline about her findings, get the law firm files, and interview Randall's closest friends."

"But instead, you're on a wild goose chase in the country." His words took a bite out of me. "I've got Mayor Baker calling nonstop, and that prick Norcross from the DA's office wants to know what's going on, too. Shit."

"Chief—"

"Talk to this Brand character, then get your ass back here and do your job." The line went silent, and I dropped the phone in my lap.

"Tough love?" Logan shot me a smirk.

"Shut up."

"At least he's back to his usual self, right? Maybe Lina's getting better."

Ass chewings weren't frequent, but they still didn't feel too good. It was all part of the job, and the buck stopped with me. My investigation, my responsibility.

I retrieved the phone from my lap and dialed Pauline.

"Dr. Monroe." Her voice was crisp and efficient, just like her.

"It's Detective Matthews. Any news?"

"Hang on. Honey, put that down for me, would you?"

I waited as a child mumbled some cute gibberish in the background.

After a few moments, I heard a door shut. "Sorry about that. I just got home, and my son has needed all my attention."

A pang of guilt reverberated in my chest. Vivi was at

home. I hadn't seen her since this morning, and if I were being honest, I wouldn't see her before her bedtime.

"Sorry to interrupt, Pauline. I just wanted to know if you found anything of interest?"

"I'm sitting in on the autopsy in the morning, but I didn't find any other obvious injuries other than the single gunshot wound, likely fired at close range, but not close enough for any major stippling or scorching around the entry point. I'd say whoever it was stood on the other side of the desk when they pulled the trigger. Death was instant."

"Time of death?"

"Given the rigor, I'd say late last night, but with a window of maybe six hours."

"Anything else?"

"The only other item of interest was the note in his back. The wound barely bled, so it was definitely done post mortem. Of course, I saved the note for handwriting analysis in case we ever get a sample worth comparing it to. There was no shell casing, so whoever did it cleaned up behind themselves. I took—" Clanging erupted in the background. "Scotty baby, Mommy's on the phone."

"It's fine. If you think of anything else, or if the autopsy turns up anything, please give me a call."

"Will do. I should have the"—*clang*— "preliminary report ready for you late tomorrow."

"Thanks." I ended the call with no more information than when it started. I wanted to bang my head on the dash.

"Nothing?" Logan slowed as the woods began to clear back from the road.

"Nope."

On either side, trailers sat on wide plots of acreage, many of them abandoned with long grass growing in the yards. A tarpaper shack had fallen in on itself, and a single wide trailer right next to it had done the same. Junk cars rusted in the southern heat, and lightning bugs blinked in the deepening night.

Logan's phone claimed we'd arrived at our destination, but he eased forward, his eyes trained on the mailboxes to the right.

After about another hundred feet, I pointed. "1209. Right there."

The mailbox had no door to it, and the numbers on the side had been sloppily done in green, the paint running down from the bottom tips of the numbers. A dirt drive led up and over a small rise.

"Let's do this." Logan turned, the cruiser jumping as we left the smooth pavement. The suspension whined, the earlier rough ride still fresh.

We didn't have to go far. Once we crested the hill, we found a trailer sitting at the edge of a stand of pines. The front yard was overgrown and littered with children's toys and bits of garbage. A dog lumbered around the side of the rusted structure, its nose in the air as it approached our car.

"Isn't this how Cujo starts?" Logan killed the engine.

"I don't think they had one of these." I patted the shotgun locked between the two front seats.

Light flickered through the front blinds, as if a TV were on inside. A beat-up Chevy pickup sat off to the side.

"Someone's home." Logan pointed as a shadow passed behind the blinds.

The dog, apparently disinterested in the visitors, wandered back the way he'd come, disappearing around the side of the trailer.

Logan whistled. "Did you see the balls on that thing? Jesus."

"Yes, Logan." I didn't even bother shaking my head. "Thanks for pointing that out."

We opened our doors and stepped into the tall grass. I took the lead, walking toward the cinderblock steps rising to the metal front door. The dog came trotting from the other side of the house, his hair standing on end and his teeth bared. His low growl cut through the hum of frogs in the trees.

"Shit." Logan pulled his pistol.

"Wait." I held a hand out toward him and crouched to get on the same level as the dog.

"Not smart."

"Come here." I clucked my tongue and gently patted my knee. "It's okay."

The dog crept closer, its teeth still bared, the hair on its nape like porcupine quills.

"Up, Arabella."

"We aren't going to hurt you." I patted my knee again.

The dog snapped its teeth. I realized that maybe this wasn't my best idea. I slowly rose. The dog increased its pace, heading right for me.

"Shit," Logan spat.

The metal door opened and slammed against the metal side of the trailer. "Beans, get out of here!" A large man stood on the top set of cinder blocks, his head buzz cut and tattoos snaking up his arms and disappearing behind his gray wife beater. His face bore more ink, prison tattoos from the looks of them.

The dog stopped its advance and looked up, its head cocked to the side.

"Go!" The man gestured toward the woods, and the dog took off running.

Logan holstered his pistol and let out a deep breath. "I think it would have been easier to shoot a human. Damn, I didn't realize I was a dog person till right then."

"What are you two doing out here?" The menace in the man's voice matched the dog's.

Shaking off the close encounter of the canine kind, I strode to the bottom of the steps. "I'm Detective Matthews and this is Detective Dearborn. We're looking for Theodore Brand."

"Found him." He stared down at us, his face in shadow. "What do you want?"

"I have a few questions about a restraining order that Randall King got against you about five years ago."

Even in the dark, I could see the frown deepening the lines of his weathered face. "What about it?"

"The court file isn't clear on the events leading up to it. I was hoping you could explain to me what happened."

"Ask King." He crossed his arms over his chest. "He's the one that got it."

I listened for the lie in his tone, for something to tell me that he knew King was dead because he was the one who killed him. It was absent.

Logan cleared his throat. "Look, we know about your

record. More violent crimes than I can count on my fingers and toes and—"

Brand snorted. "The fuck are you? The bad cop?"

I held a hand behind me, silently begging Logan to shut his trap.

"Mr. Brand."

He switched his attention back to me.

"We aren't here about any of those things." I glanced around at the well-used toys. "Huh. My daughter has the exact same one." I pointed to a motorized pink scooter lying near the Chevy pickup.

His posture changed slightly, his shoulders lowering. "That's my Brynn's. She loves that scooter. She only gets to come every other weekend, but when she does, she rides that thing like there's no tomorrow."

"Mine does too. Did you get the extra battery pack for it? Ours goes dead in no time."

"Yep, had to. I keep one on charge at all times, just in case her mom ever decides to drop by with her." The sad note in his words told me that her mom never brought Brynn by more than necessary.

He shifted from one foot to the next, his gaze on me. After a few moments of quiet, only interrupted by the frogs and the cicadas, he tossed a glance behind him. "Look, I know I'm not supposed to invite cops into my house. I'm not stupid. But you can come in."

"Thanks. I promise this won't take long." I climbed the first step.

"Just her." He pointed at Logan who'd moved to follow me. "You can stay out here."

"No way." Logan bristled.

"It's fine." I shot him a hard look over my shoulder. "Just watch out for the dog."

"Seriously?"

I didn't answer as I followed Brand into his house and shut the door behind me.

## 10

### BENTON

*I* left the house once Charlotte fell asleep on my couch—the cocktail of Xanax and wine strong enough to dull her misery so she could fall into oblivion. Porter's idea, and one that I agreed with after I witnessed Charlotte coming apart, her grief like a physical knife through her chest.

She'd been the closest to Dad. The youngest, the only girl, and the sibling that had heart like Porter and brains like me. Scrubbing a hand down my face, I got into my car and simply sank for a minute. Blood roared in my ears along with the echo of my sister's anguished cries. Her horror served as a reminder that it hadn't truly hit me yet. My father was dead. I repeated the phrase over in my mind, trying to get the sense of finality in the words. But it wasn't there. Not yet. My mind knew he was gone, but I didn't *know* it. Grief isn't linear.

But I had to keep moving. The only thing that would bring some sort of end to this mess was to find out what happened to Dad. I turned the key in the ignition.

Brody Elliot, the youngest cop in town, sat in an unmarked car across the street from my house. Arabella had ignored my request for no police presence. I wasn't surprised in the least. I gave the kid a small wave as I drove away, leaving him and Porter to watch over Charlotte.

My knuckles turned white as I gripped the steering wheel and maneuvered through Azalea's quiet streets. Frustration welled inside me. Anger, too. All of it aimed at my father. How could he have done this? My thoughts didn't make sense, and I knew it. Blaming the murder victim for his own demise, but the thoughts and emotions were there, all the same. His loss was a betrayal—the things I didn't know about him were proof of it. What else had I missed? What else had he failed to tell me, or covered over, or hid from my view?

"Fuck!" I slammed my hand on the wheel. Something tickled my face, and I swiped at it. My hand came away wet. Tears. I hadn't cried since Mom died. That was what, ten years ago?

The burden fell on me. I was the oldest. And I'd already decided to keep certain cards close to my vest. The less Porter and Charlotte knew, the better. Maybe I could shield them from whatever it was our father had gotten mixed up in.

I pulled into the firm's parking lot. The ends of yellow police tape rippled in the small breeze, the rest of it secured in an 'x' across the front door. My father's life work—and mine—was now nothing more than a crime scene. I sat for a moment, fatigue weighing me down, my stomach on empty and my mind a mess of memories and worry.

On heavy legs, I got out and walked to the rear entrance, finding the same yellow tape there. I gripped the center of the 'x' and yanked it away, tossing it on the porch behind me. The firm was silent as I entered, the air stuffy. I used to enjoy working in the dead quiet, not a sound but my thoughts as I read over case files or the scratch of my pen on paper. Now, the silence oozed around me, filthy and dark.

Flipping on the hall switch, I headed toward the file room as the lights overhead flickered to life. My eyes were drawn to my father's office, the doors closed, even more crime scene tape blocking entry. I swallowed hard. Going in was a necessity. I'd need all his files, and there had to be some inside.

First, I turned into the file room, the long rows and high shelves filled with the last ten years of cases. I ignored the back two rows—those files were done, the layer of dust on them attesting to their disuse. The front two sets of shelves contained our active files. I swiped my fingers across a series of banker's boxes. I knew most of the cases already, having worked on them right along with my father.

A few boxes perched along the top of the shelves caught my eye, so I pulled over the rolling ladder and climbed up to take a look. The neat labels had been done in Margaret's practiced hand, the letters almost square in their perfection. The old Michaels Accounting files, nothing of interest. I climbed down and kept walking along the row, recognizing case names as I went. The domestic relations section, probate, land deals, insurance litigation—nothing seemed out of place. But there was something missing. I stopped in front of the land deals section, the banker's boxes lined up neatly, but not quite as neatly as the rest of the room. There was too much space. A box was missing, and someone had spread the others to make it less obvious. A cold bead of sweat trickled down my spine. Maybe it was in my father's office.

After one more perusal of the rows, I headed back into the hallway. The light at the very end near the reception desk flickered the slightest bit, as if a moth was caught in the glass.

I pushed down the tide of emotions that threatened to rise inside me as I approached my father's doors. This had to be done. And it had to be done by me. Though I'd been somewhat heartened by Arabella's investigative skills so far, I wasn't going to trust her to root through my father's work.

Hesitation wasn't getting me anywhere, so I grabbed the tape and yanked. It came free easily and ribboned to the floor with a faint *schick* sound. I braced myself for the blood, not that there was a way to do that. Not really.

Pushing through into the room, I felt a slight surge of relief to see his body was truly gone. Remnants of blood remained, but the pool of it on the desk and floor had been wiped away. It didn't stop me from gagging, from leaning forward and bracing my hands on my knees as my stomach tried to eject its contents onto the wood floor. But there was nothing inside me.

After a few moments, I straightened and trained my

gaze on the bookcases, searching for any hint of a clue about what happened. It was the same old books—unchanged ever since we began to use an online legal database for all our case law needs.

"Benton?"

I jumped and whirled in a move reminiscent of my basketball days, though the ache in my ankle was new.

"Sorry." Arabella held up her hands. "I'm sorry. I thought you heard me come in."

"No." I ran my fingers through my hair and narrowly avoided the urge to yank on the strands. "I didn't." At least I hadn't pissed myself.

"Sorry." She glanced around. "What are you doing in here?"

"Files, remember? What are you doing here?"

"Saw the light on." She cocked her thumb over her shoulder toward the hallway. "Figured I'd check it out."

I shrugged, not exactly enjoying the suspicious tone of her voice. "I just wanted to take a look and see what he was working on."

"You should have contacted me before entering the scene." She plucked at what was left of the yellow crime scene tape on the door frame. "Find anything?"

I ignored the scolding. "Not yet."

She chewed on her bottom lip, then sighed. "I guess it's fine. Pauline and her tech got everything they needed."

My fatigue drew out a temper I didn't even know I had. "I don't need your permission to be in my own law firm."

Her brows drew together, two storm clouds about to thunder all over the place, but then a thoughtful look crossed her face and she relaxed. "I know it's been a long, hard day for you. But you need to believe I'm on your side here. I'm going to do everything in my power to find out what happened to him." She moved closer, her eyes plaintive, though still sharp enough to catch every detail. "And I don't think I've had a chance to tell you that I'm sorry for your loss." She raised one hand, as if she were going to pat my arm, but then dropped it. "I really am."

My throat seemed to close up momentarily. "Thank you." It came out strangled. Something in her demeanor threatened to crack the wall I'd built to keep my grief at bay. I stepped back, and turned to face the window. Somehow, her warmth was far more daunting than the cold office splashed with my father's blood.

I cleared my throat. "What about your trip to see the ex-con? Any leads there?"

"Not what I'd hoped. Brand has a solid alibi. He had his little girl with him until early this morning. I've checked in with the girl's mother and at the restaurant where all three of them ate dinner as well as the church where they went for service. He's covered."

"Why did my dad have a restraining order against him?"

"That's a bit more difficult." She walked over to the nearest bookcase.

I was finally able to move once her eyes were off me. Skirting around the desk, I opened the nearest cabinet, intentionally keeping my eyes off the blood smears along the top. "What do you mean?"

"Brand definitely had a checkered past. The charges and convictions on his rap sheet are pretty heavy stuff.

But the thing with your dad was about a piece of property."

I pushed aside firm letterhead and dug around in the cabinet. "What property?"

"Some tract out in the pulp woods. About four hundred acres that had belonged to Brand's family for the past hundred years or so. When he went to prison the last time, it was for five years. While he was in the clink, the taxes came due on the land. He claimed he was never notified about the taxes. Anyway, he didn't pay, the county took the property, and then sold it at an auction to your father for pennies on the dollar."

"What about his redemption rights?" I peered at her over the desk.

"Brand still had two years to serve when your father bought his land. His right of redemption expired before he even got out and knew what had happened."

I wracked my brain for any memory of new timber land my father had purchased. Nothing came to mind. Another secret. *Fuck.* I sat back on my heels, spots swimming in my vision.

"Hey." She hurried over and hooked a hand around my elbow, helping me to my feet. "Are you all right?"

"I'm fine." I felt like shit on burned toast.

"When was the last time you ate something?"

I didn't remember. "I'm okay, really."

She peered up at me, her green gaze following the lines of my face. "You don't look okay. Pale as a sheet." Her warmth felt good on my clammy skin, and I could have sworn she leaned into me the slightest bit.

"When I'm done here, I'll head back to my place. Charlotte and Porter are there."

"How did Charlotte take the news?"

"About as well as you'd expect." I blinked hard to dislodge the image of Charlotte crying in a heap on the floor.

"Oh."

I disentangled myself from her and knelt again to go through the desk drawers.

She sighed. "We can do this tomorrow. Together."

"I'd rather do it now."

"Are you looking for something in particular?" She opened the cabinets along the credenza.

I should have told her not to touch my father's attorney work product based on privilege, but the truth was, I didn't have the will to protest. Not with Dad's lifeblood in darkening crimson drops all around me. "Just anything out of place I guess. Any files." I thumbed through a collection of insurance defense litigation cases that I had worked on right alongside Dad. They weren't helpful. After searching the desk, I turned to the credenza and went back over the areas Arabella had searched. Other than another handful of files I was already acquainted with, there was nothing. So where was the banker's box from the real estate section of the file room?

"Something wrong?" She didn't miss a thing.

"No." It wasn't a lie. I couldn't tell if something was wrong. Not yet.

"Then why can I practically see the cogs turning inside your head right now?"

My poker face had faded with the last of my energy. I

struggled to get it back into place. "Just trying to put together what happened."

She tensed like a spider on a web, her gaze focusing on me with an intensity any trial lawyer could appreciate. "If you're holding out on me—"

"I'm not, all right?" I rubbed my eyes, thankful for the brief darkness the motion provided. "I just need to, I don't know, think. To try and figure out all the things he was hiding. Things I should have known. Maybe if I'd paid more attention. Maybe if I'd—"

"It's not your fault, Benton." Her quiet voice tried to quell the tempest that raged in my mind. "What happened here, it wasn't your fault."

"I'm not a suspect?" I dropped my arms to my sides and let the poker face disappear again. Let her see me.

"In any investigation like this, I'm going to look to family members or people who were close to the victim first." Her gaze never wavered. "So, yes, I considered you a suspect when I arrived here this morning—right along with Porter and everyone else."

"And now?"

With one hand resting on her hip, she pointed at me. "You aren't a suspect, but that doesn't mean I believe you've been entirely straight with me."

I wanted to argue. To tell her I hadn't been holding anything back. It would just be another lie. And I was too tired to tell it.

She shook her head, not pressing any further, but not letting it go either. "I think we're done here for the night."

"I need to keep looking. There has to be some clue."

"You shouldn't be here." Her eyes softened. "Give

yourself a moment. You need it. If you keep going like this, it won't be pretty."

I let a sigh leak out, defeat in the sound.

"Besides, I want to take up the file issue with Judge Ingles first thing in the morning. You'll need to be there to make all your legally dazzling arguments against it, remember?"

"You're not wasting any time." I shot one more look around the room, trying to find whatever was hiding in the cracks. I *had* to be missing something.

"Not on a case like this, no." She waved me over. "Come on. You can come back tomorrow—with me or with Logan—and turn this place upside down as far as I'm concerned. But right now? You need a break."

She was right. Not that I would have admitted it to her. But I was running on fumes, all of them toxic.

"What about you?" I followed her into the hallway and closed the doors behind me.

"Me?"

"Yeah. You're working late."

"It's the job. And I'm not the one who lost a parent today." We walked to the back door, and I flipped off the lights as I went.

"Your husband doesn't mind you working late hours?"

She cut her gaze to me as I locked the outside door. "Excuse me?"

*Shit.* "I didn't mean to imply that you have to answer to your husband. I was just saying that, since you have a family and all, do they mind your job?" I tried to climb out of the hole I'd dug.

She didn't shovel any more dirt on top of me, at least.

"My family understands I have a job to do." Her words were careful. "I'm the one who misses out, really." She shrugged. "Like tonight. I was out interviewing a witness, so I missed my daughter's bedtime. It's not something I enjoy, but it's just one of the sacrifices I have to make if I want to do my job and do it well. And I do. So…"

We took the few short steps to the parking lot.

"I understand." My short relationship with my last girlfriend—if you could call her that—consisted of her seeking my attention while I buried my nose in my law books or forced her to listen to me practicing my opening statements.

"Do you need me to follow you home?"

"No, Brody is sitting outside. I'm sure he'll report to you if I don't make it back." I cast her my best withering look. "I suspect Brody is the reason you showed up here. Is he there for protection or spying?"

She smiled, the light reaching her eyes. "Six one way, half a dozen the other."

A beautiful woman by any standard, when bathed in moonlight, she seemed almost ethereal.

"I'll check in with you first thing." She opened the driver's side door of her cruiser. "And I'm serious, go home. And if you come to the office tomorrow, let me know."

"Will do." I sank into my car and cranked it up.

She waited for me to leave the lot, then pulled out and followed for a while. When I lost her headlights in my rearview, I took a hard left, driving in the opposite direction of my house.

## 11

## ARABELLA

"Wake up, baby doll." I flipped on the light in Vivi's room. She had one thumb in her mouth, her rump in the air, and a giant stuffed tiger as her pillow.

I should have started pulling her clothes for the day from her dresser or herding her to the bathroom so I could brush her teeth. Instead, I crawled onto the bed next to her and pulled her close.

She patted my cheek, leaving a wet smear from her thumb. "Mommy."

"Yeah." I kissed her forehead.

"Where you been?"

"I had to work late. Did you have fun playing with Meemaw?"

"Mmhmm. I was a mermaid who ate peanut butter." She popped her thumb back in her mouth.

I promised her I'd break her of the habit once she lost her first tooth. She didn't even have a loose baby tooth yet

—apparently, her brand of stubborn also applied to her teeth.

"I didn't know mermaids were into peanut butter."

"I got a shark for a boyfriend."

"A boyfriend?" I opened my eyes wide. Maybe she wouldn't notice the bags under them. "That seems positively illegal."

"What's eagle mean?"

"*Illegal* means it's against the law."

"What's the law?"

"We don't have enough time to even begin to explore that subject." I dropped a kiss on her forehead. No fever. "How's your nose? Better?"

She sniffed, the congestion still there but not as bad. "Better."

May Bell scuffled through the hallway, her tried and true house robe with the pink kittens on it swamping her small frame. "Rise and shine, girls."

I wanted to stay right where I was, warm and snuggled up with Vivi. Her dark, wavy hair tickling my nose, her snuffles and smiles—all of it was like a siren song to me. But she was four, and the lights were on, so she crawled out of my arms and bounded to her feet, then threw herself at May Bell. "Can I have Cocoa Poofs?"

I stretched and sat up, then bent over to pull out some pants and a shirt for her. My phone rang from my bedroom next door, but I ignored it.

"Your phone." Vivi turned her dark blue eyes to me.

"Later." I motioned her over. "Let Meemaw fix your cereal, and I'll get you dressed."

"Your phone!" She disappeared.

"You don't have to—"

She jumped past May Bell and stuck the phone in my face, Chief Garvey's name on the caller ID.

"Thanks, baby doll." I took the phone and answered the call as Vivi put the clothes back that I'd picked, then selected a ruffled skirt and a sleep t-shirt from her drawer.

"Where are you?"

"Getting Vivi ready for preschool." I covered the mouthpiece. "You have to wear pants. It's going to be kind of cooler out there today."

She wrinkled her nose and shook her head.

"I need you to get over to Walnut Drive." The rough edge to Garvey's voice had my antenna twitching.

"What's going on?"

"Letty Cline's dead."

At first, shock silenced me. Then, something jostled in my memory. "The florist?"

"Do you know of any other Letty Cline in Azalea?"

"I'll be there in ten."

"Make it five." The line went silent.

"What's going on?" May Bell hovered in the hallway, her hearing just as good as it had always been.

"We've got another…" I glanced at Vivi who was wrangling her skirt on backwards. "M-u-r-d-e-r."

She canted her head to the side, disbelief painting her bleary brown eyes. "Who?"

"Letty Cline. I've got to head over to her house." I knelt and pulled the skirt off a protesting Vivi, then had her step into some pants.

"Mommy!" She stamped her foot.

"You can wear the skirt on top." I pulled up the pants, then held out the skirt.

Vivi's nose un-crinkled and she petted the ruffles. "I'm a princess."

"Can you drop her?" I stood. "I've got to go."

"Sure." May Bell waved Vivi over to her. "Cocoa Poofs."

"Yay!" Vivi bounced down the hall to the kitchen, her dark hair flying behind her.

By the time I'd dressed and kissed Vivi goodbye, twenty minutes had passed, and Chief Garvey had called twice, Logan once.

I dialed Logan as I turned the cruiser toward one of the nicer residential areas just off Main.

"Hey, where are you?" Some voices in the background told me he was already at the scene.

"On my way. Five minutes out. Garvey there?"

"Yeah, and half the neighbors are out in the street over here. I'm setting up the tape perimeter to keep the gawkers at bay."

"What happened?"

"Lead poisoning, Garvey said. But I haven't set foot inside yet."

"You call Pauline?"

"Garvey did. She'll be here shortl—hey, back it up. Back it up. This is an active crime scene. And put those damn camera phones away!"

I turned onto Rose Avenue, the morning sun hidden behind a cloud bank that didn't bode well. "I'm almost there."

"All right, bye." He cut off in the middle of another

scolding.

I rolled down the residential street and caught sight of a school bus making its rounds. The rest of the town continued on even though we had two dead bodies and an ever-deepening mystery on our hands.

By the time I arrived on Walnut, the crowd had gathered off to one side. A camera crew began setting up on the edge of the tape.

"Shit." Media attention was the last thing I needed.

I parked behind Logan's Jeep and climbed out. He stood on the porch of a modest craftsman-style home, his arms crossed over his chest and a surly expression on his face. We both needed coffee.

A brisk wind promised a change in the muggy weather as it swept past. I walked up the stairs, the residents in their robes and pajama pants eyeing me.

"Detective?" A blonde with a microphone tried to call me over to the camera.

I kept walking, and followed Logan into the house.

Chief Garvey stood at the foot of the stairs, his fingers tapping on the heavy wood bannister. "About time, Detective."

"Sorry." I glanced around, taking in the wood paneling, gleaming floors, and the huge arrangement of flowers sitting on a dining room table to my right.

"In here." Chief pointed to the room on the other side of the stairs, the wide entryway and the back of a leather couch hinting at a living room. I strode in, the tang of blood hitting me in the face as soon as I stepped into the room. The couch sat in front of me, the wide front window to my left, and a lounge chair with a body in it to my right.

"Jeez." I pulled some gloves from my jacket and slipped them on. "Anyone touch anything?"

"No." Garvey hovered at the entryway. He could be gruff, could be a total asshole sometimes, but he let me do my job. He didn't step on my toes or try to take over my investigations. And this one was mine.

"Who found the body?"

"Cleaning lady. She only comes once a month. I guess she lucked up today."

"Where is she?"

"Kitchen. She wasn't looking too good, so I sent Trevor out to get her a coffee."

I bit back my question about whether Trevor was getting me a coffee, too, and eased around the couch.

Garvey turned to Logan. "Go check on her, will you? It's Inez from the Shop & Go. I guess she cleans houses part time."

"Sure." Logan disappeared beyond the stairs.

The hint of a throwaway memory turned into a full-on clue as I got a better look at the body. "You know, I saw her at the courthouse yesterday."

Garvey scratched his balding head. "Inez?"

"No, Letty Cline. When I went by to see Judge Ingles, she was in the hallway with some papers."

"That'll help with time of death, at least."

"Yeah, she was alive yesterday around noon." I eased closer and stopped.

She was slumped over the arm of a chintz chair, her gray hair obscuring her face. Dressed for bed, she was wearing slippers, an oversized t-shirt, and pajama pants.

"I need to know what the hell is going on, Arabella." Chief Garvey's deep grumble resonated through the house. "This shouldn't be happening. Not in my town."

"I know." I eased around behind her. "There's another note." Written on floral print paper, the familiar scrawl of "you're next" had been stabbed into her with a pencil. The back of her head was a mess, the blood matting her hair and coating the chair back. Though I couldn't see her face, I suspected I'd find an entry wound in her forehead, the same as Randall King.

"Is this a serial killer? Is that what this is?" Chief Garvey beat the side of his fist on the door frame.

I moved back around to her front and dropped into a crouch. Her hands were balled in her lap, and a sliver of paper peeked through the fingers on her left hand. "She's holding something."

"What?"

"Can't tell."

The front door opened.

"Doc, welcome to the circus." Chief Garvey shook Pauline's hand as she and her tech entered the room.

She raised a brow. "Something in the water?"

"Not sure." I rose. "Thanks for coming."

"It's my job." Her no-nonsense demeanor was on full blast.

"Ready." The tech lifted a heavy-duty camera and began taking photos while he used his other hand to sweep a camcorder around the room.

"She's got something in her hand I want to see." I pointed. "Go ahead and video that as well as snap some pics."

The tech obliged, moving all around Cline's body and taking photo after photo before filming it all. "Okay, you're good." He stepped back and kept the camera focused on her hands as I knelt and tried to snag the piece of paper from between her stiff fingers.

"Here." Pauline handed me a pair of tweezers from her kit. "See if that'll get it."

"Thanks." I gingerly worked the tweezers inside her fist and closed them on the paper. With a few steady tugs, the small white card pulled free. I turned the crumpled mess over in my hand.

"What is it?" Garvey asked over my shoulder.

I recognized it, but not the writing on the back. "It's Benton King's business card."

BENTON

*J* awoke from my fitful sleep, my sheet tangled around me. My dreams were soaked in blood, and my father appeared in each one.

"Jesus." I took a breath, then another, the nightmares receding a little more each time.

The water was running in the bathroom across the hall, and the scent of coffee wafted up the stairs. It was odd having people in my house. It was odder that my father was dead.

Sitting up, I dug the heels of my palms into my eyes, trying to erase the images of gore.

The water turned off and, after a few minutes, the door opened. Porter emerged in a haze of steam, a towel around his waist. "You up?"

I looked down at myself. "Seems so."

"Charlotte's making breakfast."

"That's a first."

He shrugged. "It's food. I'll take it. And I won't even complain about the eggshells."

I stood, the shock of the past twenty-four hours still lurking inside me, weighing me down. The steamy bathroom gave a slight reprieve, and instead of going downstairs for coffee, I jumped in the shower. By the time I made it to the kitchen, Porter was finishing up a bacon and egg biscuit, crumbs all over his uniform.

Charlotte's eyes were red-rimmed, and I could feel the tears just waiting to be set free. At least she'd slept.

She scooped an overdone egg onto a plate, threw some bacon and a biscuit next to it, and slid it down the counter to me. "Eat."

I perched on a bar stool next to Porter and forced the food down despite my stomach's protest.

"We need to come up with some sort of plan of attack." She slapped the spatula on the counter next to the stove and turned to us, an uncharacteristic steeliness in her tone. "Whoever did this needs to pay. I want to find—"

A brisk knock at the door interrupted my sister's fiery sermon. She stared past me as the knock came again.

"Coming!" I grabbed my cup of coffee and walked to the foyer.

Arabella stood on the porch, her green eyes tired but still bright. "Morning." Her breath puffed in the chill air, the late summer turning to fall with all the ceremony of taking out the garbage in the dead of night.

I stepped back. "Come in."

"Thanks." She walked past me, and I shut the door behind her.

Her lack of hesitation warmed me more than the coffee.

Porter strode in from the kitchen. "Howdy, Arabella." He opened his arms for a hug.

She eyed him, then pulled out a notepad from her pocket.

*Denied*. I shot him a smug glance.

"Sorry, Porter, but I need to speak with Benton. Alone."

"Not a chance." Charlotte barreled past Porter, her dark brown hair whipping as she shook her head. "I'm his attorney, and unless you are arresting him, you aren't going to—"

"Charlotte." I put my hand on her shoulder. "Arabella is here to help."

She shrugged me off. "If she were helping, she'd be out finding who did this to Daddy..." Her voice cracked on the last word, and I squeezed her shoulder.

"I'm sorry for your loss." Arabella kept a steady gaze on Charlotte. "And I can assure you I'm doing everything in my power to figure this out. But what I need right now is a moment to speak to your brother." Even in rumpled clothes and a messy bun, Arabella still had the presence of a hardboiled detective.

"Charlotte, I can handle myself here, okay? Go eat some breakfast." I turned to Porter. "Make sure she eats."

He nodded. "Come on, sis. I'll show you the right way to cook eggs."

Charlotte crossed her arms over her stomach. "Let me know if you need me." With one more suspicious look at Arabella, she followed Porter into the kitchen.

"She's a tough customer." Arabella's lips hinted at a smile.

"She can be." I gestured toward the living room. "I think she's still in shock, honestly. But she wants answers. We all do."

She walked into the sunny living area and sank onto the tufted couch near the fireplace.

"Would you like some coffee?"

"I'd love some, but let's talk first."

I sat across from her and leaned forward with my elbows on my knees, anxious for any information. "Must be important if it comes before coffee."

Another hint of a smile ghosted across her face until she pulled a small evidence bag from her jacket pocket. She held it up to the light.

"My business card." I could see the stark lines of my name through the baggie. I wanted to ask why it was evidence, but the queasy feeling in my stomach told me I was about to find out anyway.

"We found this." She spoke carefully, her gaze on the card. "This morning."

"Where?"

"Letty Cline's house." Her gaze shot to me and focused, as if she were recording every minute movement of my face.

"Why were you in the florist's house?"

"Because she was found dead this morning."

My breakfast sloshed around inside me, threatening to erupt. "Letty Cline is dead?"

"Gunshot wound, much like your father's."

"Jesus." I rubbed my eyes with my thumb and forefinger. "And my card?"

"Clutched in her hand."

Maybe I should have let Charlotte stay after all. "Are you saying I'm a suspect?"

"I'd like to know if you've seen this card before." She flipped it around and showed me the back. "If these numbers mean anything to you."

I took the baggie and smoothed the plastic over the card. Scrawled on the back was a series of numbers. "No clue."

"Recognize the handwriting?"

I peered closely at it. Something was familiar, but I couldn't place it. "Not Dad's, not mine, not Porter's, not Charlotte's." I wracked my brain. "Was it Letty's?"

"Don't think so. I found some examples of her writing in her house. Nothing like this." She flipped open her pad and poised her pen over the paper. "How did you know Letty?"

A brief image of her in a yellow dress at one of my mom's parties flitted through my mind. My mom had been the town socialite when I was little, having get-togethers and charity projects at our house all the time. Letty had been one of her close friends, always around, always bringing fresh flowers for the white vase in the hall. "I've known her since I was a kid. She was close with my parents."

"Was she still on good terms with your dad?"

"As far as I know." I tried to think of the last time I'd seen her. "She was one of the Dancing with the Stars contestants last year."

She raised a brow. "I'd only heard about it in passing until I got involved in this case. Apparently, I've been missing out."

"Not at all." I sighed. "I mean, the competition is held at the senior citizens' center, if that tells you anything. It's just a way to raise money for charity and to give the older folks something to look forward to every year."

"So you saw her last year?"

"Yeah. Dad tried to talk me into being her dance partner." I'd laughed at him and returned to the case file I was working on.

"You don't dance?"

"Not if I can help it. Besides, she partnered with Vaughn Somers, the one who owns that brand new studio just off the square. He's a pro."

"Your dad won last year, right?"

"Yeah." I could still hear him in my head, bragging about how he was the best dancer, not just in Azalea, but in the state.

"Was that the last time you saw her?" She scribbled a few notes.

"As far as I know, yeah."

"What about your dad? Did you know if they were still close?"

I shifted in my chair. The way she watched me told me she already knew about the rumors. "Yeah, I think so."

"How close?" Her pen still moved as she glanced at her notepad.

"*Close.*" I put enough inflection in the word to get my point across.

"That's what I heard." She clicked her pen. "A casual sort of arrangement."

"Right." I knew he'd been seeing Letty for years. I

didn't begrudge him the relationship, not since Mom had passed so long ago.

Inspecting the card, I tried to decipher what the numbers meant. "It's too long to be a security code. I know it isn't the law firm safe's combination."

"It could be an account number." She sat forward and peered at the card.

"Yeah, maybe. It's far too long to be at First Bank of Azalea, though." I handed the card back to her.

"Logan's running it through a web search right now, trying to figure out what it could be." She stuffed it back in her pocket. "Why do you think she wrote it on your card?"

I laced my fingers together. They were clammy, slick. "I don't know."

"Any reason you can think of why she'd have it?"

"My card?"

"Yeah."

"No."

She clicked her pen. "Nothing at all comes to mind?"

"No." I wiped my palms on my pants. "I wasn't her attorney. Dad was. Maybe she grabbed it when she dropped by the law firm at some point."

"Wouldn't you have seen her if she'd come by?"

I shrugged. "Not necessarily. If I was in my office or at court, I could have missed her."

"Did she come by often?"

"Not sure." I shrugged. "Dad met with a lot of people at the office, at Shady's, at his house. I mean, he was an alderman, could have been mayor if he'd wanted to. Hang on. I have an idea." I rose and hurried into the kitchen.

"What's going on in there?" Charlotte cocked one fist on her hip.

"Letty Cline's been murdered."

Her mouth actually dropped open.

"You shitting me?" Porter slurped down a cup of coffee.

I grabbed one of the travel cups stamped with King & Morris on the side and filled it up, tossed in a couple of sugar cubes, and splashed a few spoons of creamer inside before snapping on the lid. "Hand me my phone." I jerked my chin at it on the counter.

"Are you full service now?" Porter grinned—the first time I'd seen him smile since the previous day—as he stuffed my phone in my back pocket.

"I'm just being hospitable."

"She doesn't think you had anything to do with Letty, does she?" Charlotte tensed. "If she's trying to drum up some sort of charges—"

"No. She's just trying to piece it together. Letty had my business card in her hand when she was killed, so Arabella is—"

"What?" Charlotte's eyes widened.

"Yeah." I know it sounded bad, but I couldn't change it. "I don't know why."

"Where are you going?" She pointed at the travel mug.

"That's a good question." Arabella strode in, looking around the kitchen before settling her gaze on me. "Looks like you're halfway out the door." She glanced at the travel cup in my hand.

"This is for you." I handed it to her.

"Oh." She wrapped both hands around the cup, as if

she needed to warm up. "Got cream and sugar?"

"I already put some in." I hustled into the hall and grabbed my jacket.

"Where are you going?" Charlotte's voice rose.

"We need to see Margaret."

"Margaret?" Porter and Charlotte asked in unison.

Arabella just nodded and took a sip of coffee. She gave me an appreciative nod. "Perfect, thanks. I needed this."

"Why Margaret?" Porter scratched his head.

"Because her memory is a steel trap. Not a speck of rust on it." Charlotte's tone was thoughtful.

"Right," I said. "She knows everything about the firm. Who comes and who goes. Maybe she can tell us if anything was up between Letty and Dad."

Porter coughed into his hand. "I think you know that Dad was porkin—"

Charlotte held her hand up. "Stop."

"Sorry." Porter shrugged.

"I'm aware." Arabella's voice was back to all-business, not the conspiratorial tone she'd used with me. Was she playing good cop, or did she genuinely like me? I shouldn't have cared, but I did. She continued, "I need to find out what other links they had between them. There has to be something—other than Dancing with the Stars —that they had in common. And I need to find out fast." She opened the door. "Margaret sounds like a good start."

"Don't move too fast." Charlotte's hackles were still up. "You'll miss something."

"I'm afraid I don't have time to waste. Another note was pinned to Ms. Cline's back." She walked out onto the porch. "Someone else is next."

## ARABELLA

"There are people stealing my okra, I'm telling you! They come at night. They steal it and then they go in my garage and eat it, or maybe they—I don't know—maybe they do some kind of experiments in there? I don't rightly know, but I *do* know my okra is missing, and I hear noises in my garage!" Millie Lagner's shrill voice was like a needle in my ear.

"I understand, Mrs. Lagner. But we have two murders in town, and—"

"It's gone! I even had my son go out there with me and look, and *he* said there was okra missing. I can't be making this up if Lenny saw it too, okay? So I need you to take this seriously..."

I took a right toward the old mill while Mrs. Lagner continued her tirade against okra thieves.

Benton must have been able to hear her through the phone's speaker, because an amused expression pulled up one side of his mouth. Handsome. Even though he was unshaved, tired, and beaten down from his father's death, he was still an attractive man, and that little smile of his made something flutter inside me. Something I hadn't felt in a long time, and something I would never trust. Not again. Not after Dale.

"Did you hear me?" Mrs. Lagner finally took a breath.

"Yes, ma'am. I'll send Detective Dearborn over when he's done with his current assignment, all right?"

"Chief Garvey has been promising me for a week—"

"I know. Today, okay? Either Detective Dearborn or I will be out at your place this afternoon. I give you my word."

"I'll be waiting. Bye." The line went dead.

"Okra theft, is it?"

I rolled my eyes. "Don't get me started."

"A bit late in the season for okra, no?"

I imitated Mrs. Lagner's high, angry voice. "Well, my papa always told me to plant okra late. Cooler weather will keep the aphids off. And if the aphids are off, then so are the ants. And if the ants aren't there, other pests won't be drawn to the okra."

"I had no idea okra was such a serious business." His genuine smile reached his eyes where it crinkled at the corners in laugh lines I hadn't realized were there.

"More serious than murder, according to Millie Lagner."

His smile faded, and I wished I hadn't said it.

"It's the yellow one." He pointed to a small bungalow, the flower boxes neat, the grass neater, and not a blade or a petal out of place.

"This definitely screams Margaret." I pulled up to the

curb, and we got out. The cool wind swirled the newly fallen oak leaves pooling in a neighbor's yard.

The door opened before I could ring the bell. Margaret's gray hair was in the same no-nonsense style as she wore at the office, but instead of professional attire, she wore a navy track suit.

"Benton." She smiled at him, then lowered her brows at me. "Detective."

"Can we come in?" I tried my warmest tone. "I have a few follow-up questions."

She was already motioning Benton inside. "Get out of the weather." It was more of an admonition for me than an invitation, but I treated it the same.

"Thanks." I glanced around at the neat little house—a few old photos on the wall and a vase of silk flowers to greet visitors. I caught the scent of something that reminded me of my grandmother's face cream.

Margaret led us to a small sitting room, the furniture pristine and the white carpet a little too white. The low hum of voices came from a back room, likely the TV in her den.

We all sat, the firm couch promising that my ass would fall asleep if we stayed too long.

"What can I do for you?" She clasped Benton's hand in her own weathered ones.

"Can you tell us if Letty Cline came to visit Dad anytime recently?"

"Letty? Sure." She looked up. "Let me see here. The last time I saw her would have been…" She pulled her hands back and tapped her index finger on her chin. "A month ago, on a Wednesday."

I made a note on my pad.

"She came in at about 10:30 that morning."

"Where was I?" Benton asked.

"Up in Tupelo for that school bus case."

"Right." He nodded. "Okay, so do you know why she stopped by?"

Margaret cut her eyes to me. "I don't have any idea."

"You can tell her everything you know." Benton grabbed her hand and squeezed. "She's trying to find out what happened to him, and we need your help."

Her eyes watered a bit, and I hoped that meant her guard was coming down.

"I don't know exactly."

The way she said "exactly" had me leaning forward.

She continued, "Letty had been by off and on, you know." She swallowed, color creeping into her papery cheeks. "Because she and Mr. King were…"

"We know about that." I bit my tongue when she gave me a sharp look.

"Anyway, on that Wednesday, she came in on a tear. Didn't stop at the desk, just stomped on down to Mr. King's office and slammed his door. After that, I heard them arguing."

I was like a hound dog with a scent. Instead of broaching her for more, I let her tell it in her own time, though her dramatic pause was a bit…dramatic.

After a few moments, she broke. "Letty was doing most of the yelling. Every so often, Mr. King would raise his voice, but it was Letty who was on fire."

"What about?" Benton's brows were furrowed.

"From what I was able to hear, it sounded like Mr.

King had been…" Her chin trembled as she glanced at me. "I don't want to speak ill of the dead. And especially not of Mr. King."

I wanted to yell "out with it!" Instead, I sat with my pen poised over my pad.

"Your father was always so good to me, you see?" A single tear escaped her right eye and meandered down her face.

"I know." Benton's voice was gentle, but there was a strain to it. "And you aren't speaking ill of him. You're helping get justice for him." He gentled his tone even more. "It's okay. Tell me what they were fighting about."

She took a deep breath. "Your father had been seeing… another woman. Or, at least that's what Letty was accusing him of."

I gripped my pen a little too tight as Margaret melted into full-on tears. I'd spent half an hour interviewing her at the law firm, and not once did she say a word about Letty Cline having beef with Randall King. "Why didn't you mention that yesterday?"

Benton shot me a warning look.

I fumed. Silently.

"It's all right, Margaret." He patted the back of her hand and kept holding it.

"No." She blubbered something unintelligible. "I'm sorry. I should have said something, but I didn't think it mattered. It's not like Letty would have done something like that to him, especially not after they made up."

"They made up?" I tried to keep the reproach from my tone.

She nodded. "He had me book a stay for them at a

hotel in New Orleans for the next weekend. They left together."

"I remember that." Benton gave her hand one more pat, then pulled back.

"So I figured they'd worked through everything, you know? Letty didn't come busting down the door again or anything. She called for him every so often, but she was normal—not angry."

"Who was the other woman?" I clicked my pen.

"I don't know."

"Margaret, I need the truth." My patience was wearing thin.

"That is the truth. I really don't know. I wasn't aware of another woman until Letty came bursting in that day." She didn't meet my gaze, a red flag.

I tried another tack. "When was the last time she called?" Logan would be pulling her phone records, but it would take a while to get them.

She sniffed. "Friday afternoon."

"She called him the Friday before he was killed?" I made a note.

"Yes."

"How did she sound?"

"Fine." She blinked, clearly not keen to offer any more information.

"Did she say anything to you? Did you know why she was calling?" Benton coaxed.

"She sounded normal. I put her straight through to his phone. He was still talking to her when I left. The light was lit up on my phone."

I made a note to check Letty's call log, though Logan

had probably already gotten to that at the scene. "Is there anything else you haven't told me? Anything at all that has to do with Randall King and possible enemies or problems?"

"That's all I can think of."

"Who came to see Randall last week? Anyone stick out in your mind?"

"Just the usual clients. No one I didn't know." She wrung her hands. "The mayor and Judge Ingles both stopped by on Tuesday for an hour or two—all three of them shut up in Mr. King's office. I think it was an appointment to talk about some sort of tax law issue with that new hamburger place on the square."

"The mayor or the judge owns that?" I jotted down another note.

"I'm not sure which, to be honest. I tried to eat there once. After a night spent on my knees in my bathroom, I've stayed away. Sad what it's become, really. When I was a kid, that place was a fancy makeup shop."

"It closed when I was in high school. I remember." My mother had taken me in there one time so she could buy a lipstick. The sales staff had treated us like trash. In Azalea, everyone knew what side of town you were from, who your parents were, and likely what days the garbage ran on your street.

Margaret nodded at me. "Right, and then the place was abandoned till someone bought it a few years back. Spent a potful of money to get the burger place going. Shame."

"Okay, so other than those people, who came to see Mr. King? Anyone unusual?"

"Not that I recall. Other than maybe…" She pressed her lips together.

"Other than who, Margaret?" Benton urged.

"Other than, well…" She shot me another look, then took a deep breath. "Chief Garvey."

*W*e sat at the counter of Shady's Diner, the familiar sizzle of the griddle and the scent of greasy cooking swirling through the air. Arabella stared at her notes, the words written in clean block letters, as June took our orders. Arabella had argued with me about getting lunch at all, but I was beginning to flag, and she didn't look much better. I needed somewhere to sit and think. It seemed I wasn't the only one, as Arabella had been studying her notebook from the moment we sat down.

"Things aren't connecting." She pressed her pen to each bullet point. "Not in a way that makes sense, anyway. Did your father's new lover kill both he and Letty Cline in some sort of jealous rage or a revenge plot? I don't think so. The murders were too far apart. These were methodical executions, not crimes of passion. Why would Chief Garvey visit your dad? And what's with the—" She cut herself off and glanced over at me. "Sorry. I guess I'm just used to talking things out with Logan."

"Don't be sorry. I've been thinking the same things. Trying to figure out the thread that links the two of them besides the obvious." I'd jumped to a million conclusions as we left Margaret's house. None of them even remotely made sense. A niggling feeling tickled the back of my mind. I should have told Arabella my suspicion that a file was missing from the firm. But what good would that do if I didn't know what file it was? Not to mention, I wanted to find it first.

I poured some sugar into my cup and handed the container to her. "I suppose we have an appointment with Judge Ingles today?"

"Yeah, I had to push it back because of Letty." She added sugar and cream to her cup. "But we can go straight to the courthouse after lunch. Get in the ring for a few rounds. See who gets the TKO or the warrant. Whichever." The fatigue in her voice made me want to give in, to let her win this one. But I couldn't. I'd meant what I'd said about keeping my clients' information private if at all possible. That's what Dad would have done. At least that's what the Randall King I thought I knew would have done.

"And then I have a few more people to talk to." She meant Garvey. I would have pressed to go with her if I didn't know it would have been futile. No way was she going to let me sit in on that conversation.

Instead of kicking that wound, I cleared my throat and changed the subject. "So, Logan."

She gave me a quizzical expression. "Was that a question?"

"I was just wondering why he's so, you know...possessive of you."

"Possessive?" She shook her head. "It's not like that."

"Seems like it."

"I'm not discussing this with you." She took a big gulp of her coffee.

"I think if your husband saw the way he looks at you, he'd take issue."

She set her coffee down, the saucer clattering. "You don't know me. And that's none of your business."

The warning tone didn't stop me, even though it should have. "I'm just pointing out the obvious. Logan clearly has a thing for you, and—"

Her phone rang, and she answered quickly, though the storm clouds that had gathered in her eyes remained. I couldn't hear anything over the low hum of customers talking in the booths along the windowed wall plus the kitchen noise, so I drank my coffee slowly. Whoever was on the other end of the line seemed to do all the talking, because Arabella only got in a few affirmations here and there.

I replayed my words over again in my mind. What the hell was wrong with me? I had no right to say a word to her about Logan—or about her life, really. I didn't know her. The fact that I wanted to didn't justify anything.

When she hung up, I spoke before she had a chance to. "I'm sorry."

Her eyebrows shot up.

"Seriously. That was out of line, and I apologize. I guess I'm just not dealing with all this very well, but that's no excuse for me to act like an unmitigated ass. So, I apologize."

The tension in her ebbed, and she gave me a slight

quirk of her lips. "'Unmitigated ass'. I like that. I'll have to use it sometime."

I smiled. She had that effect on me. Or maybe I was still out of my mind with grief and shock. It was all a wash at that point.

"Look." She stirred her mashed potatoes and gravy. "Just so you know—even though it's none of your business—" I couldn't tell if she was reproaching me or herself, but she continued, "I'm not married. I live with my mom and my little girl, Vivienne. Logan is like a brother to me and an uncle to Vivi."

"So Vivi's father…"

She took a big bite of country-fried steak and washed it down with the coffee. "Long gone."

"I'm sorry."

"It is what it is." She shrugged. "Dale was never meant to be a father, a husband, or anything like that. Depending on him was impossible. But I was too foolish to see that at first. It all became crystal clear when Vivi was born. Dale went on a bender for weeks. He stopped by the house once afterwards, gathered his things, and left. Haven't seen him since."

"Shit." I hesitated, but then reached over and grabbed her hand, giving it a squeeze before letting go. "I'm sorry. I shouldn't have brought it up."

She glanced at her hand where I'd touched her, then said, "Why? Worried you'd dampen our jovial mood?"

I had to smile at that. "Gallows humor. Always in fashion."

We ate in silence for a while—me, contemplating her

single motherhood, and her, probably thinking what an ass I was.

I broke the awkward impasse. "Who called?"

"Pauline, the forensics doc."

"She find anything?" I didn't particularly want to hear any grisly details, but if it would help us solve the case, I was all for it.

"Nothing other than it looks like Letty was killed late last night, early this morning. Everything was consistent with what happened to your father. Except, of course, the business card in her—"

"Excuse me, can I get this to-go?" A man stood at the end of the bar, his accent jarring against the southern lilts all around. If Arabella had antennae, they'd be pointing straight toward him.

He glanced at us, and I was struck by his light eyes that verged on creepy. Blond hair, thin build, sallow skin—he could have been terminally ill or just cursed with bad genes. One thing was for certain, his Jersey accent didn't mesh. Usually, it wouldn't have raised an eyebrow, but with two murders in town and no answers...Arabella had zeroed in on him.

June delivered the man's coffee and made change for him. Arabella began to rise from her seat, her food forgotten. "Excuse me, sir. I'm—"

Her phone rang again. She pulled it from her pocket, cursed, and answered it. The man took his coffee from June and walked away as if Arabella hadn't spoken to him.

I tossed a ten down for June and walked toward the man's retreating back.

Arabella gasped and grabbed my arm. "You're shitting me!"

The wail of a siren cut through the diner sounds, and the man disappeared out the door. My stomach lurched as Arabella stared up at me, her eyes wide. Something was wrong. Bad wrong.

"What?" I sent up a silent prayer that Charlotte and Porter were all right.

"Let's go." She dashed toward the door and pocketed her phone.

"What's wrong?" I followed.

"Your law firm's on fire!"

ARABELLA

*W*e pulled up as the fire department sprayed the building, the flames already shooting through the windows and licking the siding.

Benton jumped from the car and dashed across the lawn.

"Hey!" I chased him and grabbed a handful of the back of his polo. "It's too late!" The inferno put off enough heat to singe, and deep cracking noises inside didn't bode well for the structure.

He let me pull him backwards until we stood at the curb, the firemen spraying sheets of water that created rainbows above the rampaging flames. He sank to his knees in the grass as Logan hurried over to me from his cruiser.

"Fucking hell." Logan stared at the inferno as the fire chief yelled instructions at his crew.

"I don't think this is a coincidence. None of it is." The heat came in waves as black smoke rose in a plume overhead. "Someone set this fire."

"The killer?" Logan shielded his eyes.

"Maybe. But it seems like they would've torched the place when they killed Randall King. Why wait?"

"Good question. I'll find out if they know anything." He struck off toward the fire chief.

I knelt beside Benton. "Hey."

He couldn't tear his eyes away from the firm, the ferns on the front porch wilted and sizzling.

"Hey." I took his hand in mine. It wasn't professional, but it was what he needed.

He blinked and turned to me. "It's gone. First Dad and then…"

"I know." I wanted to hug him, to do something that would erase the anguish that radiated from him like the heat from the fire. Instead, I gave his hand a squeeze. "I'm sorry."

He linked his fingers through mine, an intimate touch that I didn't expect. "We're going to find out all the secrets. All the lies."

Porter's SUV rolled up behind us, and Charlotte jumped out of the passenger side and rushed over to Benton. "You weren't inside, were you?" She checked his face, then her eyes darted to where our hands were joined.

"No." He stared at the firm as a chunk of roof collapsed.

I pulled my hand away and stepped back.

"How?" Porter stood next to Benton, the last of the Kings all watching as their namesake burned to the ground.

Logan hurried toward us, a grim look on his face.

"Arson. The chief would put money on it. We won't know for sure until the fire burns out, but he said the pattern of the burn was irregular to the point that he thinks someone doused the inside with gas before striking a match."

"So much for the warrant on the files." I put my hands on my hips and let my head loll back on my shoulders. "Shit."

A thunderous shudder shook the building as an even bigger chunk of the roof collapsed and sent sparks cascading upward.

Logan grabbed my elbow. "Move back. It's not safe."

Benton got to his feet, and he, Charlotte, and Porter followed us to the other side of the road. A few cars had stopped on either side, their occupants taking pictures of the fire or filming it with their phones. Waiting for the place to burn down wasn't getting us anywhere, and my frustration was building with each second I spent chasing my tail. I grabbed my keys and turned toward my cruiser.

"Where you headed?" Logan turned to me.

"I'm going to the courthouse. I saw Letty there yesterday. I want to know what she was doing."

"I'll come with you." Logan started toward my passenger side at the same time as Benton, both men almost bumping into each other.

"I'll go." Benton looked down his nose at Logan in that maddening way of his.

"I don't think so." Logan launched himself at my hood, sliding across the front corner and landing on the passenger side. He gave Benton a triumphant smirk.

I didn't have time for their pissing contest. Before I

closed my door and started the engine, Benton barked at Porter to take him to the courthouse.

All three Kings loaded into the sheriff's SUV as Logan gave me an eye roll. "Looks like you've got yourself a new puppy."

I weaved through the cars and gawkers along the road. "Don't be an ass."

"I'm just calling it like I see it. He can't take his eyes off you. Not even when his precious law firm is turning to cinders."

I sighed and headed toward the square, the sheriff's cruiser right behind me. A subject change was in order. "Please tell me you've gone out to Millie Lagner's place."

He scratched his jaw. "Not yet."

I slapped my hand on the steering wheel. "Chief is going to chew my ass over the fire *and* the okra. Not good, Logan."

"You couldn't have stopped the fire."

"I should have had Brody staking out the place instead of watching over the Kings." Hindsight always had a way of biting me right in the ass.

"Limited resources, Arabella. You had to choose between protecting people or protecting a building. You made the right call."

"I'm not so sure." Not when the biggest pile of evidence I had was now smoldering into ash. "When we're done at the courthouse, I want you to canvas all the businesses around the firm. Someone had to have seen something. It was broad daylight. Then pull the video from Sal's Gas Mart. It's the closest station. If someone used gas, they might be on the surveillance cam filling up some containers."

"Yes, ma'am." He pulled out his phone and dialed Sal as I parked in front of the courthouse. While he directed Sal to pull the recordings, I hurried up the front steps and into the main entrance. I waved at the security guard when the metal detector pinged as I walked through, then turned toward Judge Ingles' office. I'd seen Letty on his hallway, and it was a good bet that she'd been visiting him.

"Wait up." Logan fell into step beside me. "Sal should have the tapes ready for me when I get there."

"Good."

More footsteps behind us told me the Kings had arrived.

I turned and held up a hand. "I'll need you all to wait out here."

"Not a chance." Benton crossed his arms over his chest.

"I can't conduct my investigation with every King in the county looking over my shoulder. Just wait here and let me do my job."

Benton's jaw tightened, and he glanced from me to Logan. "Shouldn't he be at Millie Lagner's house?"

Logan stiffened and took a step forward. "I don't take orders from jumped up little boys who hide behind their names."

"Logan." I put a hand on his arm, but Benton's glower only deepened. The situation in the hall had turned into a powder keg in the space of seconds. "Everyone, let's calm down."

135

Logan shrugged. "I'm calm. How about you, *Benny boy*. You calm?"

"How about you and I walk outside, and I'll show you just how calm I can be." Benton dropped his arms to his sides and took a step toward Logan.

"Whoa!" I hurried around Logan and stood between them, holding my hands out toward them to keep them apart. "A little help here, Porter?"

Porter's amused grin reminded me of why he was voted 'class clown' in high school. "I'd love to see Benton kick this guy's ass."

Logan scoffed, but Charlotte stormed past all of us. "Get a grip! Daddy is dead, the firm is gone, and you assholes are trying to start a brawl in the courthouse!"

Charlotte was right. I dropped my hands and followed her around the corner. If those idiots wanted to wrestle while the firm burned, that was on them.

"—isn't here, I'm afraid." Judge Ingles' secretary sat at her desk, reading glasses perched on the end of her nose.

"Where is he?" Charlotte asked.

"I'm not sure, dear. He called this morning and said he had things to do today. Usually, that means he's at the farm or maybe hunting."

"Can you call him? We need to speak with him." I peeked into his office just to make sure. The light was off, and he wasn't there.

The secretary frowned at me. "I assure you he isn't hiding in a closet. Give me a moment, and I'll ring him." She picked up her phone and hit a speed dial button.

Low voices floated in from the hall. The men must have taken it down a notch.

Charlotte shook her head, her dark hair flowing down her back. "My brothers are such idiots sometimes."

I shrugged. "Logan is too. How are you holding up?"

She turned her blue eyes to me, the dark circles under them giving me my answer. "I just want this to be over. Whoever did this needs to pay."

The secretary hung up. "He's not answering, hon. I'll try him again in a bit and tell him to call you."

"Can I get his number?" I pulled out my notepad.

"We aren't supposed to give that out." She blinked.

"This is a murder investigation. Double homicide, and now an arson. I think he'd be okay with letting me have the number." I held my pen at the ready and stared her down.

She swallowed hard. "All right." She rattled off the number and seemed relieved when we turned to go.

Out in the hallway, Porter and Benton whispered to each other while Logan stood a few feet away, leaning against the wall.

"Judge isn't in." I walked to Logan as Benton burned holes in my back with his eyes. "We'll have to find him out and about. I'll drive over to his town house and then his farm. Go ahead and start that canvass and go see what Sal has on tape. Oh, and send Brody over to Letty Cline's house. We can't have any more evidence going up in flames."

"Will do. You heard from Chief?"

Something inside me pinched at the thought of questioning Garvey about his visit to Randall King. "Not yet."

I turned on my heel and marched down the hall, Benton right behind me.

"Where do you think you're going?" Logan elbowed his way past Benton.

"With Arabella."

"No. You're going home." Logan turned even gruffer. "You're still a suspect as far as I'm concerned."

"Slow your roll, Logan." Porter's warning tone reverberated.

"This isn't a county matter, *Sheriff*," Logan shot back.

I whirled. "I'm going *alone*. Logan, you've got your marching orders. Porter, if you want to help, send one of your deputies over to the firm and have them salvage anything they can. And give Logan a ride while you're at it." With that, I hurried down the steps and to my cruiser. The wind had picked up, a cloud bank on the western horizon.

"Wait, Arabella." Benton followed close at my heels. "Let me come with you."

"You've helped me as much as you can, all right? I can handle it from here on out. Go on home and get some rest. You're beat. I'll call you if I find anything." I sank into the car and closed the door.

Benton opened the passenger door and plopped down.

"Hey!" I turned to him. "Boundaries!"

"I've known Judge Ingles my whole life. He'll be more likely to talk if I'm there."

"Benton, I know you've—"

"Let me help, okay?" His earnest gaze melted me a little. "I can't sit at home knowing my father's killer is out there. I won't get in your way. I swear."

Logan knocked on my window and pointed at Benton. I rolled it down. "It's fine. He may be able to help loosen up the Judge."

"I don't like it." Logan narrowed his eyes. "Not at all."

"You don't have to. Get to work." I rolled the window up and backed out of my parking spot as a rumble of thunder shook the air.

Logan scowled but piled into the Sheriff's SUV with the rest of the Kings.

"You're pushy." I turned onto Main Street from the square.

"I'm desperate." He clasped his hands in his lap.

We passed the hospital, and I spied Chief Garvey's cruiser sitting in the lot. He must have been with Lina during the fire at the firm. I needed to confront him, but I didn't mind back-burnering it until after I spoke with Judge Ingles.

An alarm went off on my phone. "Shit. Is it three already?"

Benton tapped the silver watch on his wrist. "Yeah. What's up?"

"I have to pick up my daughter from preschool." *I don't have time for this.* Guilt hit me in the gut at the thought. I always had time for Vivi. Always. "I hope you don't mind."

"Not at all." He scratched the scruff along his chin. "Though I'd hoped I'd be a little more cleaned up when I met your kid."

I stopped hard at the four-way just past the hospital and gave him a "what the hell?" expression.

"I mean." He coughed into his palm. "Not that I was thinking about meeting your family, just that I thought maybe I would meet your daughter at some point, that's all..."

"Way to make it weird." Despite my words, I thought it was sweet that he wanted to meet Vivi. Most men ran far away when they found out I was a single mom with a spirited four-year-old. Then again, Benton wasn't like most men. He was straight-laced and haughty on the outside, but beneath that, he was sensitive. His father's death had laid that part of him bare to me, though he didn't seem to show it to anyone else.

"I just meant—" He shook his head. "Never mind."

"It's okay." I smiled and followed the side streets until I got close to her preschool. "But she's shy, so don't expect a lot. The only man she really knows is Logan, so she might take a while to warm up to you."

"I think I can handle that." His lips quirked into an ironic smile. "You aren't the first who's told me I'm tough to warm up to."

"I'm certain that's the truth." I flashed my blue lights and cut to the front of the pickup line.

"That won't make you any friends." He glanced at the stopped cars.

"This is the only time I've used my lights to cut in line. I think they'll forgive me, especially since everyone in town is talking about the murders and looking to me to solve them." I pulled to the curb.

Vivi ran toward my car, then seemed to remember the school rules and stopped, then forced herself into a cautious walk as a teacher scolded her lightly.

"She looks just like you." He waved at her as she approached.

"Vivi, baby," I called. "Go ahead and get in the back."

Benton got out and opened the door for her, and she

climbed in. He snapped her seatbelt on without being asked.

"Who that?" Vivi stared at him as he got back into the front seat and we pulled away.

"This is Mr. King."

"Benton." He turned around and smiled at her.

"He in trouble?" Her eyes were wide.

"No. What makes you say that?"

She pointed to the roof of the car.

"Oh, no, honey. The lights were just so I could pick you up first."

"First?"

"Yep. Didn't have time to wait in line." I smiled at her in the rearview, but she kept her gaze on the stranger in the front seat.

"Did you have a good day?" I turned back onto Main Street and cruised toward Razor Row. We'd moved off the Row several years back, but we didn't go far.

"I don't like Sarah Ellen."

"Aww, honey. You say that every day, but every day you play with her the most. Your teacher always tells me so. Why can't you two get along?"

She wrinkled her nose. "She's mean."

"Is she a frenemy?" Benton turned his head, but didn't give her his full attention. Smart. She'd get spooked if he looked at her straight on.

"Fremmy?" Vivi squinted. She still had baby-like features, her chubby cheeks reminding me of when she was still small enough to carry around everywhere. But she was clever for her age, sharp enough for her teachers to recommend she start reading early.

"A frenemy." Benton shrugged. "You know, someone you play with every day, but sometimes you feel like they're not being nice to you. You still play with them, though."

"I play with her, but she takes all the money." She let out a frustrated huff.

"The money?" Benton asked.

"They're learning how to count money at school," I explained.

"She takes it all. I can't count it. She takes it. She mean." Vivi huffed again.

"When I get home tonight, we'll practice counting, okay?"

"You don't come home last night." Her pout verged on heartbreaking.

"I know, baby. Mommy was busy. But I'll see you tonight before bedtime."

"Promise?" She finally looked at me in the mirror.

"I promise."

A smile broke across her face and she kicked her legs. "Bennon too?" She returned her gaze to Benton.

"I, um—"

"Benton has to go to his house for bedtime, baby." I stole another glance at her. "If you keep doing your nose like that, you'll get wrinkles."

"Bennon?" She'd dismissed me and was staring at him expectantly.

"I, um." He looked at me with something that could have been hopefulness.

I shook my head. No way was I inviting him into my home. It didn't matter that he was good-looking, intelligent, and clearly good with kids. He was a King, and also a snob, and also maybe a suspect.

"Bennon?" She kicked the back of his seat.

I cooed, "Baby—"

"Sure. I can come for bedtime. Sure." He nodded.

She squeed and clapped. "Bennon!"

* * *

I DROPPED her off at home. May Bell was just finishing up her breathing treatment, the nurse packing the medical equipment.

"Who's that in your car?" May Bell peered through the front window.

"Bennon." Vivi plopped down on the couch and grabbed her tablet.

"Benton King."

"A King?" May Bell coughed into her palm.

"He's riding along on the investigation. It's a long story."

"Shame about Letty Cline." She turned to me, her eyes grave. "I need you to be careful out there, all right?"

I hadn't heard worry like that in her voice in years. "I'm fine."

"Keep it that way. I'm too old to chase this little devil around for much longer." She looked at Vivi, unmistakable love in her eyes.

"I'm careful. I'm also striking out, but I think Judge Ingles knows something he hasn't told me. I'm going to see him next."

"I bet he does. That old coot has his fingers in half the pies in the county." She sat down next to Vivi.

"What do you mean?" I dashed down the short hall to the bathroom to relieve myself while she talked.

"Just that he seems to have come into some money a few years back. He's the one that invested in the square renovations. The burger place, the antique shop, even Letty Cline's place. You know that big, new sign and all the fancy coolers and flowery crap inside? They say he paid for it." She snickered as I washed my hands. "I mean, Letty paid him back if you know what I mean."

"I thought Letty was with Randall King," I called.

"She was. And Judge Ingles. And the mayor. And god knows who else. You might want to check with the fellas at the retirement home over on Spring Court."

I walked back into the living room, trying not to seem bewildered. "How do you know all this?"

"Belly, I go to dialysis once a week. I sit there for four hours with all the other sick old ladies in this town. Our eyesight is too bad to read our—" she covered Vivi's ears, "—s-e-x novels anymore, so we spend that time talking. About everyone and everything in this town. The real question is, what *don't* we know?" She coughed again, but it sounded a little clearer than usual. The breathing treatments helped keep her airways open.

"Any idea who's been killing Azalea's citizens?"

"Not yet, but maybe I'll find out in my quilting circle tomorrow night." She grinned, the light brown skin next to her eyes crinkling.

I bent over and kissed Vivi on the forehead. She was busy playing one of her math games on her tablet.

"I'll be back for bedtime."

"Bennon."

"Yeah, maybe him, too."

"You're bringing a man home? A King, no less?" Mom's eyes brightened.

"No, it's not like that."

"Bennon's coming to bedtime," Vivi said with finality.

"I've got to go." I ducked the curious look in Mom's eyes and opened the front door. "And go easy on the juice before bed, all right? I think you know what happens when you don't."

"We'll be fine." Mom cuddled Vivi into her side.

"There's a storm coming." The wind was whipping through the tops of the old oaks scattered throughout the neighborhood.

"Just go. And be careful!" Mom shooed me away with a wave of her hand.

"Love you." I pulled the door shut and hustled to the car.

Benton shot a glance to the small house on the dumpy street. "Vivi's cute."

"Trust me, she knows it." I pulled into the street and headed back to the more affluent part of town.

"I didn't realize you lived over here." He cast a glance down a few blocks to Razor Row. "I didn't mean to insul—"

"Don't sweat it."

He smoothed his palms down the tops of his thighs. "You know, my father and Judge Ingles always said I had a knack for public speaking. They thought that's why I'd make a good trial lawyer. And, turns out, they were right.

I've always been able to get a jury into the palm of my hand and push them whichever way I wanted them to go. But with you, all I seem to be able to do is jam my foot into my mouth until I get the full flavor of my shoelaces."

I fought my smile, but it won. "How do they taste?"

"Not so good." He frowned. "Could we sort of start over?"

"You mean could we pretend we didn't meet while I was investigating your father's murder and you were a suspect?"

"Yeah, well no. That part doesn't bother me since I know I didn't do it. I just mean that over the past couple of days, I've been kind of a…"

*Dick.*

"Jerk." He pointed to the next street. "Faster if we get onto Pecan Street."

"Sure."

"Anyway, I just wanted to say that I'm not as big of an asshole as I seem. At least I hope I'm not."

"You're under a lot of pressure. It's barely been twenty-four hours since this whole mess got started." I turned onto Pecan Street, the namesake trees dropping nuts onto the car's hood in the wind, each crack reminiscent of a gunshot.

"Thanks." He sighed and ran a hand through his hair. "Thanks for understanding."

"I do have a question, though." I took another right and caught sight of Judge Ingles' house up ahead on the left, the front façade a stark white Victorian.

"What's that?"

"Where did you go last night after you left the firm?"

BENTON

*T*he word "shit" lit up my mind in bright neon as she nonchalantly asked me where I'd been when I was *supposed* to have been at home.

"I know you didn't go straight home. Brody finally checked in with me a couple of hours ago. We compared notes. You should have been home an hour earlier than you were. Where were you?"

I swallowed hard and weighed the value of the truth versus the damage I'd do if I lied. One hard glance from her told me that coming clean was the right answer.

"I went to my dad's house."

She nodded, as if she already knew that little tidbit. "Why?"

"To see if we'd missed something."

"Like what?" She pulled past a beat-up pickup truck parked at the curb and into Judge Ingles' drive as the first fat drops of rain plopped on the windshield.

She put the car in park and faced me, one eyebrow slightly raised and her lips pressed into a thin line.

I angled my body toward her so she could look me in the eye. "I should have told you this before."

Her eyebrow lifted even more. "What?"

"When I was going through the files at the firm, I noticed that something was missing."

She dug her notepad from her pocket and clicked her pen. "And you didn't find this important to tell me?"

"No, I did, but I…"

"But you what?" The blunt edge of her irritation hit me in the gut.

"I thought I could figure it out by myself."

"Oh, really?" She furiously made some notes. "Good to know that you should be lead detective instead of me. Go ahead and tell me the solution. Who's the murderer, Miss Marple?"

"I searched for about an hour last night." I swallowed hard and continued, "I suspected a file was missing, so I went to Dad's to see if I could find it."

"What file is missing?"

"I don't know. It was in the real estate section of the file room, but that's all I could tell."

"And now I guess we'll never know since the firm burned to the ground, right?" She stowed her notepad. "Pretty convenient for you."

"I didn't burn the firm. I was with you all day, remember?"

"I remember." She gripped her door handle. "I also remember you promising me that you wouldn't impede this investigation—"

"I didn't—"

"You did." She yanked on her door handle and stood quickly, slamming the door on my reply.

I jumped out after her. "I fucked up, okay? I'm sorry. I should have told you about the file. But I was hoping I'd find it at Dad's. Then I would have shared it." I followed her up the front steps as the rain began falling harder. "I didn't trust you. Not then, anyway. But now I know you're solid." I grabbed her arm, then let go just as quickly as she whirled on me. "I would have shared it, okay?"

"I'm just supposed to take your word for it?" She shook her head, water droplets soaking into the dark strands.

"Yes."

"Not a chance." She raised a hand to knock, but the door opened before she made contact.

"Oh." A man who looked to be in his early thirties, with shaggy red hair, a pot belly, and wearing a worn t-shirt and jeans, had almost walked right into Arabella.

"We're here to see Judge Ingles. You are?" Arabella's crisp tone cut through the man's surprise.

"Leonard was just leaving." Judge Ingles appeared behind the man.

The man didn't need any other prodding, because he hurried past us and down the steps.

"Come on in out of the storm." Ingles motioned us inside.

"Mind if I ask who that was?" Arabella hitched a thumb over her shoulder as Judge Ingles shuffled ahead of us and into a front sitting room.

"He does odd jobs for me around the house. Things I can't do anymore." He sank into a wingback chair with a groan as lightning hit nearby, the accompanying thunder rattling the window panes.

Arabella and I sat on a creaky loveseat. The furniture was dated, and everything was coated with a layer of dust.

"Odd jobs? Like what?" Arabella already had her notepad at the ready.

He gave a sort of amused frown. "I'm not sure where this is going, Officer, but I'll humor you. I've gotten too old to take care of the lawn or even do the cooking. Nancy from next door handles that for me now. About all I'm good for these days is listening to people argue and deciding who's in the right." He rubbed his right knee with one age-spotted hand. "What can I do for you?"

"As I'm sure you've heard, Letty Cline was killed last night."

His face remained impassive, but he nodded.

"I came here because I think you may know something about her death. Hers and Randall's."

"Why would I know anything about that?" He adopted a puzzled, sad tone. "We were friends. All of us. Have been for a long, long time."

"Are you certain you can't think of anyone who'd want to hurt them?"

A streak of lightning brightened the stuffy sitting room, illuminating his face, the splotchy skin pale and weathered. "No."

"Can you tell me anything about Letty's shop?"

"Her flower shop?"

"Yes. I'm specifically asking about the extensive renovations a few years ago."

He stopped rubbing his knee. "What do you mean?"

"I mean that Letty's flower shop isn't known to do a high-volume business, so all those renovations had to be financed by someone else." She clicked her pen. "A quick check with her bank and a look at her records would probably tell me that she didn't get a loan."

Judge Ingles had gone still, not even moving when another close lightning strike had thunder booming through the house. "What does this have to do with me?"

"If you financed those renovations—and the renovations of other spots on the square and along Main Street —and used Randall King as the attorney on the—"

"I'm sorry." He rose unsteadily. "But I'm afraid it's time for you two to go."

"What?" I stared up at him.

"I'm asking you to leave." He motioned toward the foyer.

"What do you know?" I rose, anger heating my blood as I peered at the old man as if it were the first time I'd ever seen him. "What happened to my dad?"

"Benton, please." He shook his head and looked past me toward the back of the house.

"No." I advanced on him. "Tell me what you know. What the hell is going on?"

Arabella put a hand on my arm, the pressure firm. "We'll go."

"No." I balled my hands into fists. "You need to talk."

Ingles' tone turned pleading. "Please—"

A creak sounded from the hallway.

My hackles rose, and Arabella pulled her pistol.

"No, don't." Ingles' voice cracked as he moved toward her. "It's probably just Nancy with my din—"

Arabella peeked around the corner. A shot cut through the stuffy air, and I grabbed her shirt and yanked her back into my arms. The sound had been muffled, but a chunk of the door frame was gone, shattered by a bullet. My blood rampaged through my veins, and I didn't want to let go of Arabella. That bullet had come too close. I clutched her to me, desperate to keep her safe, even though she was the one with the gun.

Heavy footsteps thundered through the house, followed by the unmistakable sound of a screen door slamming.

"Let go!" Arabella pulled from my grip.

She dashed down the hall with me at her heels, though we slowed at the kitchen door. Her gun at the ready, she peeked around, then darted inside. Past the butcher's block, the back door was open.

Rain poured outside, a breeze carrying an earthy scent on the air. Beyond, the back yard was a sodden mess, and the high wooden fence blocked our view of the alley. The shooter had disappeared into the coming night.

"Shit." She leaned against the counter and holstered her pistol.

I rushed to her and pushed her hair away from her face, inspecting for any damage. A thin trickle of blood ran from her right temple.

"Hey." She flinched as I ran my thumb over the source.

"I think you got a splinter."

"A splinter?" She looked up at me. That's when I noticed her breaths were shallow, her hands shaking.

"Yeah." I moved closer. "Just breathe."

"I'm fine."

"You almost took a bullet to the face." I wanted to kill whoever had shot at her. The emotion made me blink hard, both because it was foreign and because of how strongly I felt it. Refocusing on her, I ran my fingernail along the edge of the splinter. "I can get it. Hold still."

"It's just a splinter." Her breath caught as I flicked at the tip of it. "Ow." She rested her hands at my sides, her fingers clutching the material of my shirt.

"It's too big to ignore it. As my mom used to say, it's 'tetanus-sized.'" I'd never been this close to her. Slowly, I pressed the tip of my thumbnail beneath the piece of wood, lifting it a bit.

She hissed. The primal sound sent a rush through me, adding fuel to the adrenaline fire that already blazed through my bloodstream. Inappropriate, but undeniable. I took a steadying breath then pinched the splinter between by thumbnail and fingernail, pulling slowly until it was free.

I leaned over and grabbed a dishtowel from the butcher's block and pressed it to her temple. "It's a bleeder."

She took the towel from me, our hands brushing during the change in ownership. Swiping at it, she took a look at all the blood, then pressed it back into place.

"Does it hurt?"

"Not too bad." Her hands weren't shaking anymore, and she seemed steadier.

I didn't want to back off a step, but I did. Gaining her trust had moved right to the top of my list next to "find my father's killer."

She took a deep breath, then glanced down the hall. "Looks like I have a few more questions for Judge Ingles."

"He knows what's going on. He has to." What did he get my father into?

She swiped at the wound again, then tossed the towel down on the butcher's block. "None of this is a coinci—"

The sound of an engine starting had us turning toward the front of the house.

"Judge?" I bolted toward the hallway.

We made it to the front porch in time to see Judge Ingles speeding away in his Cadillac.

## 17

## ARABELLA

*I* speed-dialed Logan as Benton and I rushed to
my car. Judge Ingles had disappeared into the
deluge, his tail-lights long gone as I backed into the street
and headed the way he'd gone.

"Arabella?" Logan answered.

"Put out a BOLO on Judge Ingles."

"On the judge?"

"Yes!" I hung a hard right onto Main Street, and
Benton's head was on a swivel as we searched for the
white Cadillac. "Someone just shot at me at his house.
Then he high-tailed it out of there. He's involved."

"Shot at you?" He whistled. "Are you okay?"

"Fine. They missed me."

"Jesus, Arabella. We need to be working this case
together."

"What we need is to find Ingles."

"You think he killed King and Letty Cline?"

"No." I squinted as tail-lights appeared ahead of me,
but it was an older Chevy beater, not the Cadillac.

"Maybe. I need to think more on it, but for now, tell everyone to be on the lookout. I want him found. And can you ride out to his farm property? It's off old 34 near Cane Creek. See if he's holed up there."

"I'm on it. Let me go so I can tell everyone. Then I'll head out to his farm, see if he's there. I'll call you back in a bit."

"All right. Bye." I dropped the phone into the cupholder and sped past Shady's Diner, heading out of town.

"Shit." Benton turned and peered at the road behind us. "He could have gone the other direction."

"I know." I slammed my hand on the wheel, then pulled onto the shoulder and skidded to a stop. Why did it seem like this investigation had been haywire from the moment my phone rang with news of Randall King's death?

"We'll find him." Benton's voice, smooth and low, cut through the static in my mind.

"Could he have killed your father and Letty Cline?" I leaned my head back and stared at the roof of the car as the rain drummed on the metal. I tried to imagine Judge Ingles as the gunman, but I couldn't. "At his age, with the way he was moving? I don't see how he could've gotten the drop on your dad."

"Dad was still spry. I mean, he won a dancing competition not that long ago. But if the judge had walked in with a gun in his hand..." He shrugged.

"But Letty Cline, too?" I thought back to how she looked. "She was dressed in her pajamas. As if whoever killed her had woken her and walked her downstairs, talked to her, then shot her. I can't see Judge Ingles managing a gun, a staircase, and a woman like Letty. She was younger than your father. In shape, too."

"Right."

"Not to mention that someone *else* was in his house. The shooter. But Ingles seemed to know he was there. I can't be sure. Maybe Ingles hired the shooter to do his dirty work?"

He looked up, his mental gears turning the same as mine. "How fast can Pauline and her tech do a slug comparison on the projectiles that killed my dad and Letty, along with the slug that has to be embedded in Judge Ingles' wall?"

"That's a specialized sort of testing that's done up in Jackson. It would take weeks, at the very least."

"Shit." He drummed his fingers on his knee.

I checked my side mirror, then did a u-turn back toward town.

"Got an idea?"

"Let's search the judge's place. He invited us in, not to mention we have plenty of probable cause after I was shot at. No Fourth Amendment issues there."

"Agree." He shrugged. "It would stand up in court."

Maybe it wasn't so bad to have a lawyer riding along on this investigation. I just wished he'd come clean with me about the missing file when he discovered it. Going to his dad's house—I already knew about that—though I was interested to see if he'd tell me the truth. Logan had put Trevor, Brody's partner, on the house to see if anyone turned up.

"How's the—" He tapped his temple.

"It's fine." It stung, but I wasn't about to admit it. "Thanks."

He shrugged.

"I mean thanks for getting the splinter out."

"I'm a man of many talents." He shrugged as we pulled in to the judge's driveway again. The rain was letting up, but thunder still rolled across Azalea.

"Let's do a quick sweep." I chewed on my lip as I considered my options. I only had a handful of uniforms to work with, and Brody was stationed at Letty Cline's, Trevor at Randall King's. The other two were patrolling and keeping a lookout for the judge. They'd been in the field almost nonstop since this mess started. Pulling any of them wasn't a good move. I only had one option, though it pained me to use it.

"Crap." I grabbed my phone again.

"What?"

"I'm calling Porter."

"Why?"

Porter answered.

"Hey, it's Arabella."

"You find out who did it?"

"No, not yet." I gave him a quick rundown of events, then asked, "Could you send one of your deputies over to Judge Ingles' place to keep watch? I hate to ask, but my officers are already spread thin, and I—"

"Not a problem."

"He owns a farm out on the edge of the county where it bumps up against Carson. I sent Logan out there to check it out, but I'd feel better about it if he had some backup."

"Okay. I can send Carrigan. He lives just this side of Carson County, so he'll probably know where it is."

I sighed, feeling even more relief than I'd expected. "Thanks."

"Just let me know if you need anything else. How's Benton?"

"He's—" I gave him a side-eye,"—moderately useful."

Benton grimaced and crossed his arms over his chest. "Yep. Sounds like him."

"Thanks again."

"Anytime. I'll get Jake over to the house in town right now. Later." The line went silent.

"Moderately useful?" Benton pinned me with a hard stare.

I shrugged. "You'd be fully useful if you would tell me the truth."

"I *am* telling the truth." He huffed. "We are on the same page. I swear."

"We'll see." I opened my door, a raindrop splatting on my forehead as I retraced my steps to the front porch.

He followed and beat me to the door, pushing ahead of me. "Wait. Maybe the shooter came back."

"In that case, I should go first." I'd already pulled my pistol, holding it at the ready.

A rattling noise came from the back of the house. We shared a look. Going slow, we crept down the hallway as the faucet turned on and the familiar *tick-tick-tick* of a gas burner ended in the hiss of flames. I dropped my arm to my side and peeked into the kitchen. A woman who I presumed was Nancy the neighbor was slicing up some okra on a cutting board while a cast iron skillet heated on the stove behind her.

*Okra, shit.* I never had gone to Millie Lagner's house to investigate the okra theft.

"Nancy?" I eased into the kitchen.

She looked up, the knife poised in her hand as a confused look crossed her oval face. "Hi?"

"I'm Detective Matthews, and this is—"

"Deputy King," Benton supplied.

I let that pass and continued, "We're going to have to ask you to go on back home. The judge isn't in."

"Is everything all right?"

"It's fine." I tried to give her a reassuring smile. "But if you don't mind…" I gestured toward the door.

"Oh. All right. Sure." She set the knife down, then wiped her hands on her apron. "I'll just put this in the sink."

Benton touched my arm, and then his warm breath tickled my ear with a whisper. "I'll check the rest of the house." He ducked into the hallway.

I wanted to tell him to wait, but I had business with Nancy first. Keeping my tone light, I asked, "Do you happen to know Leonard?"

"Leonard?" She rinsed her hands.

"Yes. He was here earlier. Judge Ingles said he did odd jobs for him, cut his grass, things like that."

Her eyes rounded with recognition. "Oh, you mean *Lenny.*"

"Sure." Something pinged in my memory, but I couldn't get a bead on it before Nancy continued, "He comes around at least once a week. Does landscaping, burns the leaves every fall, helps Judge Ingles with his gun collection. Things like that."

"Do you happen to know his last name?"

She hung her apron on a peg next to the sink. "Can't say as I do. He doesn't talk much. But he's always nice enough to me." She put her hand on the door knob, but hesitated. "Are you sure everything's all right with the judge? All these murders lately, and the fire…" She shivered, though it was a bit too dramatic to be genuine, and grabbed a wet umbrella leaning by the door. "It gives me the creeps."

"Everything's fine. Thanks so much for your help. I'll let the judge know you came by."

"All right." Wariness filtered through her voice, but she shot a quick glance to the badge on my lanyard. Apparently, she decided I was legit, since she opened the back door and stepped out, opening her black umbrella and picking her way down the steps.

I closed the door and locked it, then ventured into the hallway. "Benton?"

"I'm upstairs. No one's here."

"Find anything?" I called.

"Not yet. I just checked the closets and peeked under the beds. Nothing in-depth."

"I'll start down here, then." I crossed the hallway and entered a small study. A writing desk stood against one wall, a weathered wooden chair with chintz cushions sitting in front of it. I opened the drawers, but they had some blank stationery, pens, and office items. Nothing of interest. Judge Ingles didn't have a computer.

A filing cabinet sat in a corner, so I went there next.

The top drawer was filled with receipts for the past five tax years. The middle drawer had all sorts of information on cars the judge had bought within the last couple of years—several of them high dollar sports models that he'd special ordered from out of state. I thought back to the house layout—the attached garage could only hold one car. Where were the rest of them? I made a note, then continued to the bottom drawer. It was mostly empty, only a few random documents concerning his ownership of this house and his farm. Maybe the cars were there.

I moved out of the study and gave the dining room a quick once-over, then stopped to inspect the wall where the slug had lodged. I couldn't see it, only the splintered bit of molding and the shattered drywall. Pulling out my phone, I sent Pauline a quick text and asked her to send her tech over to photograph the scene and retrieve the slug. She replied with a simple "10-4." I liked that she didn't ask any questions, just did her job.

Heading up the stairs, I met Benton on the landing. "Anything?" I asked.

"No." I could hear his frustration, though the light had faded away until I could barely see him. "I even used the pull-down to the attic. Nothing up there but Christmas decorations that may, in some bizarre time twist, even predate Christ." He descended the steps.

"Nothing downstairs either, except some files on Judge Ingles' luxury car habit."

"What?"

"He's the proud owner of half a dozen foreign sports cars."

"That…makes no sense. The man's driven a Cadillac

since I've known him. Always last year's model. Always white."

"Money. It's money." I ran my finger around the outline of my badge while I thought through what we'd discovered. "Judge Ingles came into money somehow. He spent it on cars, apparently, and revamping businesses on the square. But where did the money come from? And some of the cars were purchased as recently as a couple of months ago. He still has cash. How? And was that what was in your father's safe? The judge's money?"

"Dirty money, you mean." He sighed. "There's no way this is legal. Which means, whatever it is, my dad was caught up in it somehow, knew it was going on."

The dark gave me some cover, just enough for me to reach out and squeeze his upper arm. "That's my working theory at the moment, yes. I'm sorry."

When I began to drop my hand, he covered it with his own. His palm was warm, and his large hand engulfed the comfort I offered. We stood in silence for a moment, both of us peering at each other through the gloom.

My phone rang, making me jump. I dropped my hand and answered the call.

"Yeah, Logan?"

"Hey. Everyone's looking for the judge. Even Garvey said he'd—"

"Why hasn't he called to chew me out yet?" I stepped away from Benton as the spell between us broke.

Logan snorted. "Oh, it's coming. Trust me. He was on his way in to see Lina when I spoke to him, so look for a call in a little while. Might want to be sitting down for it."

My stomach churned. "Great."

"I'm out at the judge's farm. He's got a little house out here. And by little I mean a two-story stunner that's bigger than my house plus your house. Amazing on a district judge's salary, you know?"

I whistled. "That's not suspicious or anything."

"Yeah. It's over the line into Carson County, so I guess we'd have no reason to know about it. But this place is enormous."

"Anyone home?"

"Not that I can see, no. I rang the doorbell and peeped through the windows. Nothing's moving. Hang on…"

"What is it?"

"There's a sheriff's car coming up the drive."

"That'll be one of Porter's deputies. I asked for some reinforcements."

"Good. About time the sheriff's office does something worthwhile. I'll give our deputy pal some stakeout orders and head on back. I still haven't had a chance to get with Sal over those tapes yet, but it's my next stop."

"Have you drafted any subpoenas for Randall or Letty's cell phone records?"

"Shit, no. Haven't had a chance yet. But you know that'll take at least a month for the carrier to get back to us. And more likely than not they'll have an objection to it, so we'll have to fight it out in court."

"I know, but we still need to get them drafted and sent. Just add it to your list for the day. Then check up with the crime scene tech, see if he found anything. I'll also need you to take a look at King's laptop, then—"

He sighed. "Jesus, I don't get paid enough for this."

"Suck it up, buttercup. Anyway, we've searched the

judge's house, came up empty. But I'm going to sweep it one more time. After that, I guess I'll have to go see Garvey, and then I'll—"

"Don't forget bedtime."

"Shit!" I pulled the phone away from my face and saw that it was already seven o'clock. "Double shit."

"You can make it." Logan clucked his tongue. "If you don't, Vivi is going to tear you a new—"

"Let me know what you find at Sal's." I ended the call, then hustled down the hallway and into the first bedroom.

"What are you doing?"

"Just checking the place before we lock it up." I peered into a guest bedroom, the bed made and the curtains drawn.

"Then what?" He flipped on the lights for me as I walked around each room.

"Then bedtime."

## 18

BENTON

*A*rabella gave me a warning look as we entered the small bungalow. "Vivi can be demanding. But as a rule, we can only have *two* bedtime stories. If you go to three, she'll take that opening, and before you know it you'll be reading half a dozen stories, then acting them out for her."

"Got it." I didn't have much experience with children, but Arabella's daughter seemed like a sharp kid. And I wasn't lying when I'd said I wanted to get to know Arabella and her family better. Maybe I was suffering from some sort of post-trauma haze, but I couldn't discount my interest. And I'd always been the sort of person who went after what I wanted, sometimes to a fault.

The house smelled like cookies and shampoo. A high, sweet voice floated down the hall and mixed with a lower, scratchier voice.

Arabella let out a sigh of relief. "We made it. Bath time

saved us. Have a seat." She pointed to a worn sofa with sagging pillows. "I'll go check on Vivi and May Bell."

I sat as instructed, the well-loved couch just as comfortable as it looked.

"Hey baby, you have a good supper?" Arabella's voice seemed to climb an octave when she spoke to her child.

"Mommy! We had chocolate chip cooki—"

"We had vegetables." The scratchier voice interjected.

Arabella's laughter sent a wave of warmth through me. "Meemaw is lying."

"She's not a lion. I'm a bear!" A roar ricocheted down the hallway.

I found myself smiling, unable to stop. A hairdryer began to hum, obscuring the rest of their conversation. I studied the photos on the wall, most of them of Arabella, Vivi, or both. They seemed to have great fun together—at the zoo, at the pool, at somebody's backyard barbecue.

The house was tiny, the furniture threadbare, and the neighborhood questionable, but this little family had just as much love—or possibly more—than the King family in our antebellum mansion. If I had driven past this place last week, I would've assumed so many things about its occupants, none of them good. I shook my head. Porter was always telling me what a stuck-up asshole I'd become. Maybe he was right for once.

The hairdryer turned off. After a few more moments of chatter and what sounded like Vivi picking out her pajamas, the little girl called out, "Bennon!"

"Yes, ma'am." I rose and skirted around the edge of the sofa and into the hallway. Lullaby music came from the first door on the left.

Vivi's room was scarcely big enough for her twin size bed and massive collection of stuffed animals and toys, but it was cozy, and the flowery walls seemed to suit her.

"Bennon!" She patted the bed, her bright eyes wide. "Sit next to Mommy."

Arabella looked up at me, and I realized that this was the first time I'd seen her completely at ease. She seemed younger, the harsh façade she had to wear while performing her detective roll fallen away.

"I told you she was demanding."

"I not!" Vivi tossed her dark hair over her shoulder and patted the bright purple comforter even harder. "Bennon sit!"

A cough from down the hall told me that Arabella's mom wasn't far. I entered the room, careful not to tread on a lineup of unicorns near the foot of the bed, and sat where Vivi had instructed.

She grinned, one of her bottom teeth missing, and handed me a book. "You read." She snuggled back into her bed, a lion tucked next to her, and watched me expectantly.

"Just two," Arabella hissed in my ear.

"Mommy." Vivi glowered.

"What?" She leaned away from me and shrugged.

I started, "The sun has set not long ago…"

Vivi nodded and hugged her lion as I continued. She didn't seem to get any sleepier as I finished the book. Instead, she happily handed me a new one to read.

"In the great green room…" I showed her the pages as I read through the book, and her mouth moved along with my words. She probably knew the story better than I did, even though my mom used to read me the very same book when I was a child.

When I finished the last page, Arabella stood quickly. "All right, time to go to sleep. You've got preschool tomorrow."

Vivi didn't spare a glance to her mother and, instead, pulled a third book from beneath her pillow and handed it to me. "*Stella Luna*, Bennon."

"I *hate* that one." Arabella fielded a scowl from Vivi. "I mean, it's my least favorite. I don't hate it."

"Bennon, you read." Vivi smiled and leaned back, hugging the lion tight against her.

"Vivi, it's time to go to sleep now. Benton and I have to—"

"It's fine." I turned to Vivi and tapped the front of the book, which had a large bat on it. "I'll read *Stella Luna* if you promise this is the last one. That'll keep you and me both out of trouble with your mom."

Vivi scrunched her nose as she considered my offer. Her expression mirrored one I had seen on her mother's face a few times over the past couple of days.

"You read good, and okay." Vivi nodded.

"Better you than me." Arabella folded her arms across her stomach and leaned against the door frame as I began to read.

The story, about a bat who lost her mother, flowed smoothly. I dropped my voice lower and lower as I went, and Vivi's eyelids did the same. By the time I whispered "the end" and closed the book, she was drowsing off.

I chanced a look at Arabella, whose eyes were soft, a

faint smile on her lips. My heart seemed to forget its job for a moment, sputtering before finding its pace once more. She was beautiful, her dark hair spilling over her shoulders and love in her eyes as she watched her daughter. For a moment, I let myself believe that maybe I could have a place in a life like this, with a woman like Arabella, and a child like Vivi. Which was silly, really. I would have to spend all my time rebuilding the firm. That's what my father would have expected of me. Carrying on the family name and the family business. It's what I wanted, wasn't it?

"Goodnight, little devil." Arabella whispered and walked over, bending down to kiss Vivi's dark hair. She crooked a finger at me, and we both left the room, the soft lullaby still playing in the background as Arabella closed Vivi's bedroom door.

"You read pretty good for a stuffed shirt lawyer." A woman with medium brown skin and dark, piercing eyes stood just inside the living room.

"Thanks?"

"Mom, don't." Arabella scooted past and into the kitchen.

"Mrs. Matthews, I presume?"

She smiled, deep wrinkles forming next to her eyes. "Call me May Bell. Everyone does."

"Nice to meet you. I'm Benton."

"I know who you are." She dipped her chin toward the kitchen. "I keep tabs on anyone hanging around my Belly. Sorry about your dad."

"Thanks." I knew the word sounded hollow. But the wound was still too fresh for me to say much more.

She patted my arm with one bony but warm hand. "It'll get easier. I promise."

I could tell where Arabella got her warmth from.

"So, you like my Belly?"

"Mom!" Arabella hurried out of the kitchen with two travel mugs in her hands. "Don't."

"I was just making conversation is all." May Bell gave me a conspiratorial look.

"You were working on embarrassing me. Like you do." She handed me a cup, steam rising from the spout. "We have to get going."

"Where to?" May Bell put one hand on her hip. "You won't tell me what happened to your forehead, it's already dark, and there's a killer on the loose, so I think—"

"Right, that's why I have to go." Arabella placed a hasty kiss on May Bell's cheek and opened the front door.

"Come back anytime." May Bell gave my arm a squeeze before I joined Arabella on the front porch. The storm had brought even cooler weather, the air thick with chill.

Arabella paused, a pinched look on her face as she turned back to May Bell. "If I'm not back in the morning—"

"I'll take Vivi to school. My dance card is free tomorrow."

"Thanks, Mom." Arabella turned and hurried toward her car.

"Bye, Benton. See you again soon, I hope." May Bell shot me a knowing smile before closing the door against the cold.

We piled into the cruiser.

Arabella started the car, but didn't put it in drive. After a few moments, she turned to me. "Don't get any ideas."

"What?"

"Look, Vivi doesn't have any men in her life other than Logan. I've never wanted her to get attached to anyone who wasn't going to stick around. Her father is out of the picture, like I said. And I keep any other guys out of the picture, too."

"You don't date?" I was surprised.

"No. I mean, in the past, here and there. But nothing serious. I won't let Vivi get hurt." Her tone was serious, her eyes dark in the dim car. "Do you understand?"

Did I take offense? Yes. But I also understood where she was coming from. "I get it."

"Thank you." She started the car and reached for the gear shift.

"But you can trust me."

Her hand paused on the shifter. "Why? Why do you even care if I trust you? Aren't you the one who's too good to associate with people like me and my family?"

I wished I could suck up all the stupid things I'd said to her and poof them out of existence. But she was right. I'd been a prick. "I know. I did say those things. And I'm sorry for them. But—"

"I already forgave you for saying them. That's not the point. The point is that you come from a world where that's a normal train of thought." She didn't quite glare at me, but almost. "We aren't the same, or even similar. I have a child and a sick mother at home. I spend my paycheck on childcare and May Bell's medical bills. We lived on Razor Row while you were growing up at the

King house." She laughed, but it was sad. "You know, when I was a teenager, I used to sit in my car and stare at that house. I'd wish it was me who lived there, me who had a housekeeper, me who had money to do whatever I wanted—but not piss it away on girls and beer like Porter always did. I was always just looking, a bystander taking part in a life that wasn't mine and that could never be mine. You can't just walk into my life and fit, just like I couldn't do that to yours. We are pieces to entirely different puzzles."

Her words sank deep, the clear divide between us like a jagged crack through Azalea—one that I'd exacerbated with my foolish words. Was there a way to fix it?

"Look." She let out a long exhale. "I'm going to solve this case. So let's work together right now to—"

Her phone rang, the sound jarring in the tense air. She answered it. "Chief—"

What ensued was a one-sided conversation from Chief Garvey, while Arabella answered with a string of "yes," "no," and "I'm on it."

I replayed her words over in my mind and tried to think of a way to bridge the gap. Maybe she was right. Maybe I should have been backing away from her and her family. But I couldn't. From the first moment I saw her, I was curious. And the more I got to know her, the more I liked her. It was out of character, but also felt more right than anything I'd done in a long, long time. It was as if Dad's death had deconstructed me on some fundamental level, and when I looked back at myself, I realized how empty I'd been, how stuck, and how goddamn unhappy.

"Shit." She ended the call and pulled me from my thoughts.

"What?"

She put the car in drive. "You up to investigate an okra theft?"

## ARABELLA

*I* pulled into Mrs. Lagner's driveway behind an aging Buick. She lived in a one-story ranch home just on the outside of the residential area of Azalea. The big front yard was dotted with trees, and the backyard had a wide expanse of grass, a separate area with bean poles and other gardening items. A garage sat nearby, one door open, but the insides shadowy.

A light flicked on above the front porch, and the door swung open. An elderly woman, her robe clutched tightly around her round frame motioned for us to come on.

"I'm going to kill Logan," I muttered as I grabbed my heavy flashlight and exited the car to walk around to the porch.

Benton had been quiet on the short drive over here. I didn't blame him, especially after I dressed him down about any expectations he may have had regarding my family or me. Funny thing was, I expected him to deny that he was even thinking about me that way. But he didn't, which scared me and warmed me in equal parts.

"Get on in here."

"Mrs. Lagner?" I flashed her my badge, but the squad car seemed to be enough for her to welcome two complete strangers into her home. "I'm Detective Matthews and this is...Deputy King."

Benton followed as I stepped over the threshold and into a small hallway with a sitting room to the left and the dining room to the right. The air was stifling hot, to the point I wanted to fan my face.

She paused and gave us both a once-over. "Got a deputy out here and everything, huh? It's about gosh darn time!" She nodded hard, her short gray curls not moving a millimeter. "You can cut through here to the garden, and I'll show you what I've been telling Chief Garvey for what feels like days on end." Her exasperated tone covered an edge of excitement as she hustled down the hall, sprightly for her age. "I've been telling him and telling him, but he keeps telling me that there is no way..." Her high voice became muffled as she turned into what look like a den area with the TV blaring some nighttime game show.

Old family photos yellowed around the edges and covered the hall walls. Babies and kids who had long since grown up and moved away, or perhaps remained in Azalea and started families. Benton stayed a couple of steps behind me, which was a good thing. I didn't want to look him in the eye, not after my little confession in the car.

"This way." Mrs. Lagner crossed the hallway once more and entered a galley kitchen, the floor tiles old but clean, and the counters some sort of green Formica straight from the 70s. Pulling open the back door, she ushered us into the darkness beyond. "Watch your step. That big rain left the grass kind of mushy back here."

I clicked on my flashlight and took the few stairs down to the turf, then turned right and picked my steps toward the bean poles.

"Oh!" Mrs. Lagner exclaimed.

I turned around to find Benton helping her along as she glued herself to his side. He gave me a brief eye roll that I could barely see in the dark.

"Thank you, sugar," she purred. "I mean, Deputy." If I could have gotten a better look at her, I was certain she'd be blushing.

I came to the edge of the dirt marking a large square of tilled earth, though most of the area had sprouted winter weeds amongst the husks of decaying vegetable plants.

"The okra's along the back," she pointed.

I followed her direction and walked another dozen feet or so. My breath plumed in the cool air, winter seeming more like a promise than a hint.

"You see?" Mrs. Lagner and Benton caught up to me.

Training my flashlight on the tall stalks at the corner of the garden, I found four rows of okra, none of the plants looking too happy with this recent turn of weather. Their leaves were drooping, the stems already turning dark. Bending over, I inspected the closest plant. Just as Mrs. Lagner said, okra had been harvested from the stalk. The same was true for the surrounding plants, too.

"So, you're saying that someone came out here and cut the okra from your plants?"

"Yes, ma'am. That's exactly what I'm saying."

I made a show of turning around and staring into the

distance at the neighbors' houses. Outside of town like this, the plots of land were bigger, the homesteads farther apart. The nearest house was at least a quarter of a mile away, its lights faintly glowing through the trees. "You suspect a neighbor?"

"No."

God, I needed more coffee. "Let me back up. Do you have anyone in mind that you think could have done this?"

She finally let go of a relieved Benton. "I suspect it's the same people who have been messing around in my garage at night."

"And who might that be?"

"That's what I've been asking Chief Garvey to figure out." She latched onto Benton's arm again. "And now that I have this fine young deputy out here, maybe I'll get some answers."

I reminded myself that Chief Garvey told me that if I didn't get Millie Lagner off his ass that he would think about promoting Logan to lead detective and putting me back on traffic patrol with Brody. Was he kidding? Yes. Did he sound like he was kidding? No.

"Let's take a look at the garage." I skirted the mucky garden and stepped onto the worn gravel tire track leading to the white clapboard garage. Shining my light through the open door, the back of an old car, more rust than metal, appeared in the gloom. "Is there a light switch?"

"Not out here. No."

"Hang on." Benton disentangled himself from Mrs.

Lagner. "I'm going to head on in with Detective Matthews. Will you be all right out here?"

"I'd feel better if you were here with me." She added a slight shiver to her voice. "But I understand the importance of your investigation."

"Thank you so much, Mrs. Lagner." Though his words sounded too sweet to be real, Mrs. Lagner didn't seem to notice the difference because she gave a little giggle.

Benton walked past me and pulled open the other door. It creaked and groaned, but swung open to reveal the rest of the car along with a smattering of yard tools, a couple of dusty hay bales, plus several other rusted or discarded items.

"There's a path through all this beside the car." Benton moved along the side of the rust bucket as I followed, keeping the light ahead of us.

"I don't think anyone's bothered with the garage since this car got parked." I swung my flashlight to peer into the murky window. "Or maybe not."

"What?" Benton turned to look at what I had trained the light on—a blood smear on the glass.

I leaned closer. "It's on the outside. Someone's been in here. Recently, by the looks of it." I turned and yelled to Mrs. Lagner. "Go on inside. We're going to keep searching. Let you know if we find anything."

"Are you sure? I can stay—"

"We wouldn't want you to get cold. A pretty lady like you needs taking care of." Benton shrugged at me.

Another giggle filtered through the door. "It is chilly out here. I'll go in and wait for you, Deputy."

"Thank you, ma'am." He dropped his voice and bent

his head close to mine. "You think the okra thief accidentally cut himself during his pilfering and is hiding out in the garage?"

I couldn't help but smile. "Maybe his last okra caper didn't go the way he'd planned."

"Okra accidents happen all the time." His smile matched my own, and I elbowed him lightly in the ribs.

"What do you know about okra?" Before he could make a joke, I continued, "In any case, someone may be in here, and we don't need your new girlfriend getting hurt over some okra."

"My girlfriend? Hmm. Do you think she'll put out if I solve this okra thing for her?"

I smacked him in the arm. "There is something wrong with you, *Deputy* King."

"Jealous?" He leaned closer, his lips pressing against my hair. "Don't worry. She's not my type."

"Too young for you?"

He laughed, the sound too loud but also just right.

"Shhh." I shimmied past him and continued deeper into the dark garage. "Let's get this done so we can be on our way."

"Right behind you."

I turned sideways to edge my way past an overturned wheelbarrow, more pitchforks than a normal person should own, and a smattering of automobile parts. "There's a door back here."

"And a ladder." He pointed to my left.

A wooden ladder, the rungs promising splinters and tetanus, rose into the low rafters. There was a small landing up there, but I couldn't be sure the ladder would hold for me to even take a look.

"Let's try the door." I tested the handle. It turned easily and swung open to reveal a large shed—the sort you can buy at home improvement stores—with front windows, a door, and a light burning inside.

"Does someone live here?" Benton walked to the closest window and peered inside.

I was too short to look, so I tried the front door. Locked. "See anything?"

"A bed, one of those all-in-one stove, fridge, sink things. No one's home, but someone does live here."

I'd had enough of the okra chase. Just based on what I'd seen, I couldn't tell if Mrs. Lagner had picked the okra and forgotten she'd done it, or if whoever lived on her property…"Her son. She mentioned it on the phone. Her son must live here." I'd forgotten that fact, buried it under an avalanche of information on Randall King and Letty Cline.

Benton scratched his chin. "It seems to me that her son had a late-night hankering for some okra, took it, and didn't want to admit to his mom that he had done it. Or maybe he just likes watching her chase her tail about stolen okra. Some guys are assholes."

"You sure you're a lawyer? Maybe you missed your calling. Okra investigator is more your speed."

"I think you're right. I should've run for sheriff instead of Porter. I guess I'll have to chalk that up in my missed opportunities column."

Despite the teasing, he was right. There was zero evidence that someone else came onto the property and took any okra. "Come on. Let's give her the news and get out of here. I've got bigger fish to fry, and just coming out here for this should get Garvey off my ass." I struck off toward the house, but Benton gently grabbed my arm.

"Hey."

I turned to face him, our breaths mingling in the dark. Staring up into his eyes, standing too close—it was like he saw me. Not the detective. Not the single mother. Not the girl from Razor Row. Warmth spread through me, though I tried to will myself into discomfort.

"I just wanted to say thank you."

"For what?" The question came out too breathy, too interested.

"For letting me meet Vivi. For bringing me along. For trusting me enough to walk into a creepy garage with me. I know you didn't have to do any of those things. But I'm glad you did."

And just like that, I was utterly out of my depth.

\* \* \*

WE LEFT Mrs. Lagner's in a hurry after promising to look further into her okra matter. And I wasn't lying. I intended to pass the case off to Logan as soon as I could. He could look into it right after we solved the murders.

"Where to now?" Benton fiddled with the heat.

"I'm going to drop you off at your place and head by the station."

"Okay." The hint of disappointment in his tone cut me a little.

"It's just that I need to speak with Garvey and follow

up with Pauline and Logan. I'm not trying to…" What was I trying to say here?

"I understand." He turned one of the center vents toward me. "I need to check on Charlotte anyway. Porter is there with her, but she isn't in the right headspace at the moment."

"Are you afraid she'll break down?" The streets were dark and shiny from the earlier rain, and the icy wind had me fighting with the steering wheel every so often.

"She already did that. No, I'm more worried that she'll go off half-cocked or go out looking for trouble."

"I didn't take her for a scrapper."

He smirked. "That's one of her gifts. She seems so sweet and nice, but she's tenacious. If she finds out who did it before we do…" He trailed off and shook his head.

His sister had just moved up in my estimation. "Then definitely keep an eye on her. We don't want to add any more murders to our list."

His smirk faded.

"I'm sorry." I gripped the wheel tighter to keep myself from reaching for him. "That was bad wording on my part."

"No. You're right. I need to keep the family I have left safe. Losing Dad has been hard enough. And I still haven't really processed it. I keep trying to, but my brain seems to lock up whenever I think about his office or him in it." His voice broke at the end.

Though it was a mistake, I reached over and took his hand in mine. It was cold, so I gave it a squeeze and pulled in front of the vent. "It was a shock. It's going to take time. But you can get past it. You'd be amazed at how many things we're able to get past, no matter how bad they are." A mirror image of myself flitted through my memory, my left eye black, my lip split, my stomach swollen with Vivi. That had been one of the last times I'd seen Dale. "You'll be stronger in the end. And you can rebuild." I returned his hand to his lap, but he didn't let me pull mine away.

"One day I hope you'll tell me what made you so strong, what you had to get past." He grazed his thumb along the inside of my wrist, back and forth in slow arcs. Such a small touch, but one that resonated deeply.

I pulled away and cleared my throat. "Once I drop you off, I expect you to stay at your place. No late-night jaunts to your father's house or any of the crime scenes. Got it?"

He sighed. "I'll stay at my place. Unless something comes up."

"Nothing is going to come up that Logan or I can't handle." I turned onto his street. "So stay home."

"I promise… Unless there's an emergency."

"Do they teach you that in law school?" I pulled to a stop at the curb, behind Porter's SUV.

"No. I've been difficult since the day I was born." His lips twisted into a wry smile. "At least that's what my mother always told me. And Porter can attest that I haven't changed a bit."

I shook my head and reassured myself that this wasn't flirting. "I'm pretty sure I can attest to that too."

He leaned closer, his clean scent wafting to me. "I think you like that about me."

A dozen thoughts raced through my head, the loudest of which was that I did not need to get involved in anything like this during a murder investigation. Especially not with the victim's son. Even so, I couldn't resist his invitation to spar. "I'm pretty sure I don't like anything about you."

"You must be joking." He smiled. "I don't know if you noticed, but I was named Azalea's Most Eligible Bachelor last year by the Gazette."

"I didn't take you for the sort of guy who went for that kind of popularity contest nonsense."

He shrugged. "Maybe it was a practical joke by Porter, and maybe I got pissed off enough to stop talking to him for a month—but that doesn't mean it wasn't true."

He was too close and far too attractive for his own good. I shot a glance to Brody in his cruiser across the street. He looked away quickly. Damn. He had probably already radioed Logan about us talking and the windows beginning to fog.

I grabbed the gearshift and put the car into drive. "Well, thanks for your help with the okra investigation. It was one for the history books. Stay put, and I'll give you a call if I find out anything new." How quickly I'd gone from "I'm not telling you shit" to "let's share information" wasn't lost on me. But in our short time together, I'd built up a modicum of trust with Benton. My instincts told me that he wanted to find his father's killer just as much as I did.

He moved away, the mirth fading from his eyes. "Be careful out there, okay?"

"I will." I patted the grip of my gun. "Don't worry about me."

"I can't help it." He opened his door and got out. He

paused, as if he were going to say more, then thought better of it and closed the door gently.

With one last look at Benton, I pulled away and drove toward the police station. Though I wasn't looking forward to it, I needed answers from Chief Garvey about why he was visiting Randall King in the days before his murder.

## 20

### ARABELLA

*C*hief Garvey's cruiser was parked out front as I climbed from my car and entered the station. My stomach roiled, and I wiped my hands down my jacket to alleviate the cold sweat. I gave Helen, our dispatcher, a curt nod as I hurried past. She was on the phone with someone and waved in response.

Logan sat at his desk, his feet propped up and a VHS tape in his hands.

"That from Sal's?" I peeked toward Chief Garvey's office. His door was open, the light on.

"Yeah, I got it from him before he closed up for the night. Problem is, the last VHS player we have is busted." He cast a glance to a beaten-up TV/VCR combo that had been collecting dust in the storage room for the past decade. "We haven't needed it in forever. But Sal still depends on technology from 1985, so I'm going to have to rustle one up from somewhere. I'm just trying to figure out where."

"Call Porter. I'd be willing to bet the County Sheriff's

Department has a VHS player for tapes like this. If that doesn't work, get Sal on the phone and ask if we can stop by his store to use his VCR."

He chuckled. "Oh, I asked Sal if I could use his VCR. He says he doesn't have one. All he has is a recorder, and he religiously changes the tape every morning when he gets to work. But he's never had a reason to look at them."

"You've got to be shitting me right now."

Swinging his legs down from his desk, he said, "I wish I was."

"Call Porter. If he can't find one, get in touch with Lewis at the pawnshop. Surely he's got one sitting around somewhere in the back." I was just wasting time, trying to pull myself together before confronting Chief Garvey.

"I'm on it."

"You got anything else for me?"

"Nothing good. No one has seen hide nor hair of the judge—"

"That reminds me—tell the guys to be on the lookout for a man with a Jersey accent and light eyes."

He cocked his head, his tired eyes incredulous. "That's all you got?"

"For now. I saw him at the diner today, but got the call to go to the firm fire, so I missed him."

"Why is he a person of interest?"

"Just a feeling. He didn't do anything in particular, but his accent doesn't fit, and even Benton agreed that there was something off—"

He rolled his eyes. "Benton, huh?"

"Don't start."

"I'm not starting anything, but it seems like you have a new partner on this case, and it's not me."

"You're my partner. We've just been dividing and conquering today. Though we're pretty short on the conquering part."

"No shit!" Chief Garvey's gruff yell came from his office. "Quit stalling and get your ass in here, Arabella."

Logan tried to look amused, but I could sense the worry beneath the surface. We'd been too close for too long for me to miss it.

"Wish me luck." I adopted a swagger I didn't feel and walked into the lion's den.

Chief looked even more haggard than usual, his tired eyes perusing me, the dark circles beneath them like pools of unrest. "Sit down."

I closed the door behind me.

"You didn't have to do that. Logan would probably love to hear me go over all your fuckups of the past forty-eight hours."

Sitting, I crossed my legs at the knee and waited for the onslaught.

"How the hell did you manage to let someone burn down the law firm right under your nose? All that evidence, gone, with no way to retrieve it."

I wanted to argue my case, to tell him there was no way to stop the fire unless I was clairvoyant, but when he got a head of steam like this, it was better to let him go.

"And that." He pointed to my temple. "How the hell did you get hurt?"

"Just a scratch."

"I asked you a question!" He slammed his meaty palm

on his desk, the jolt knocking over a photo of him and Lina. "Damnit." With a gentle touch, he sat it back upright.

"The shooter at Judge Ingles' place. He aimed for me, missed, but I got a piece of wood from the doorframe right here." I tapped the spot where Benton had removed the splinter. "Not a big deal."

"You almost dying from a bullet to the head is a very big deal!" He leaned forward, his arms on the top of his desk, pushing into his unused keyboard. "What about Vivi? And May Bell?" His gaze travelled back to the photo of he and Lina—she was holding a trophy from when she won the high school 4H competition. "I'm already losing Lina…" He sat back, a deep sigh escaping from him as he rubbed the heels of his palm into his eyes.

"I'm being careful, Chief." I kept my voice low, trying to placate him before he got worked up again. "As careful as I can be. But I have to find this guy. There's something bigger going on here, something I'm only seeing bits and pieces of. I need more of the puzzle to surface before I'll know what it is. But I'm working on it."

"I know you are, but this deal with Judge Ingles fleeing town, the fire, the deaths—the phone's been ringing off the hook, and people want answers. Mayor Baker wants to talk to you, so does that jumped-up DA. I told them both to pound sand. We'll call them if we need two more bumbling idiots gumming up the works. Helen's been fielding calls from media outlets over in Columbus and all the way up to Tupelo. This sort of thing doesn't belong in Azalea. And each second that ticks by is a second lost. You need to get this case solved before it goes any colder."

His constant berating began to wear thin, cutting

through the layers of armor I'd built over the years—layers already weakened from too little sleep and not enough food.

"Chief, I'm doing everything I can. Maybe if you hadn't sent me out to the edge of town to investigate okra theft, I would have—"

"Don't give me that shit, Arabella. You need to do your job. *All* of your job, or I'll find someone else who will."

The armor cracked. "Bullshit! There's no one who would do this job with its shit pay and you constantly breathing down their neck. I'm beginning to think I was the only one dumb enough to accept the position."

He smirked. "Sounds about right." Some of the tension left him, and he leaned back in his chair. "You were definitely a fool to take a job working for me." He sighed again, the sound verging on creaky. "What a fucking mess." He pinched the bridge of his gin-blossomed nose.

"I'm going to investigate until it's solved." I took a deep breath and plunged ahead. "And on that note, I need to know why you went to see Randall King last week."

He opened his eyes, resting his sharp gaze on me. That look was probably the same one he wore when he was a detective like me twenty-five years ago, before the drinking and the sadness started eating away at him. I only hoped that wouldn't be me in twenty-five more years.

"Wh-What did you say?" His tone was the thin paper cover around a stick of dynamite.

"I know you went to his office last week. I want to know why."

"Oh, now *I'm* a suspect? That's what you call detective work?"

"Chief, I'm following every lead, just like you taught me." I pulled out my notebook and pen, clicking it for emphasis. "Why were you there?"

"Jesus, Arabella." He shook his head. "You really want to do this?"

"I have to."

He scratched his neck, his beard in need of more than just a trim. Dropping his hand, he went lethally still. "Yeah, I went to see that son of a bitch last week. And I'm glad he's dead."

## 21

## BENTON

*P*orter was on all fours, cursing and yanking on the cords that ran from the TV to a dusty VCR one of his deputies found in their evidence room.

"Where does this cable even go?" he muttered.

"Do you need me to do this?" Charlotte sniped. "You've been trying for all of five minutes, and you're having a meltdown like it's been two days."

"Anyone want coffee?" I walked into the kitchen to avoid the bickering. Two resounded "yeses" rang out from the living room as the VCR war continued.

It was late, already close to midnight, but Arabella had called Porter to say she and Logan were coming by with the VHS tape. Did it irk me that she hadn't called *me*? No, not at all. I slammed the coffee canister into the Keurig and jabbed the button to start the brew.

Since she'd dropped me off, I'd given the rundown of what happened to Letty Cline to both Porter and Charlotte. I'd skimmed over the Great Okra Caper. My thoughts continued to stray back to both my father's death and Arabella. Two incongruous topics that seemed to take up all the free space in my head.

A sharp rap at the door told me she was here. Charlotte opened it before I could get there and invited Arabella and Logan inside.

The latter gave my sister a warm smile—too warm. "We've only met in passing, I'm afraid. I'm Logan."

She took his outstretched hand and shook. "Charlotte."

"Nice to meet you." He smiled.

She blushed.

Arabella pinched him in the side, and he hustled into the living room. She turned to me, her expression hopeful. "Do I smell coffee?"

"Definitely." She followed me to the kitchen and perched on a stool at the bar as I fixed her a cup.

"Any news?"

"Some." She stripped off her navy jacket, leaving her in the simple white button-down she'd been wearing earlier. No real jewelry, just a simple sort of beauty that shone more than metal ever could.

"Care to share?" I stirred, then set her cup down in front of her.

"No, but I guess I will. Did you know that Lina was—how to put this—in a *relationship*—" she used air quotes,"—with your father?"

I stopped in the middle of the kitchen and turned to her. "Are you kidding?"

"Nope, not even a little bit."

"Dad and Lina Garvey?" I couldn't even do the math, but he had to have been 45 years older than her. "No way."

"Yes." She took a sip and wrapped her hands around

the mug. "They were together." Her cheeks colored a little, but I couldn't tell if it was from the coffee or from what she was trying to imply with as much tact as possible.

I reset the coffeemaker as her revelation sank in. "That's who Margaret was talking about? The other woman?"

She nodded. "I think so. Unless there was someone else I don't know about."

"A third?" I wanted to say that wasn't possible, but what did I know? Nothing. My father had more secrets than I could have ever guessed at.

"Seems unlikely, but I can't be certain. Though, from what Chief Garvey said, Letty had major beef with Lina over Randall. Lina was definitely the reason Letty went on a tear at the law firm that day Margaret told us about."

The image of Dad dancing with Lina flashed through my mind, her dress sparkling, his smile pasted on. Or was it? I supposed their cha-cha had a little extra flair, more heat than had been necessary to win the trophy. How had I missed it? I took the cup, added cream and sugar, then plopped down next to her at the bar. "This is just so...so far-fetched."

"I thought so, too. But Chief Garvey found out about it. That's why he went to see your father last week. Well, let me back up. Chief admitted he threatened Randall when he found out about the relationship about three months ago. He thought Lina and Randall had broken it off after that. But last week, Randall visited Lina at the hospital. When Chief heard about it, he blew a gasket and went to your dad's office to confront him. It got heated, but he left before it came to blows."

"Do you believe him?" I cradled my head in my hands and tried to sift the truth from the lies.

She paused for a moment, then said, "I do. I mean, I've known Garvey for a decade, and he's been a decent man all that time. He doesn't fit as the killer."

I pictured Garvey in Dad's office, his service pistol pointed at Dad's head. My blood ran cold. "I've known him a long time, too. But I've been wrong before." It wasn't lost on me that my father had been fooling me for years. "I think Garvey could have done it. Killed Dad."

"I don't think so." She took a slow sip. "That's not to say that he couldn't have snapped or something, but the way Randall was killed, the safe, and then Letty's murder the next day. It seems like—"

"Does he have an alibi?" My mind was firing through all the possibilities of Garvey killing Dad and Letty, then torching the firm.

"He was in Lina's room Sunday afternoon, fell asleep there, and hadn't left yet when we got the call about your dad. I phoned the nurse's station to make sure. It checks out. He didn't do it."

"Who didn't do it?" Charlotte had walked up behind us.

Arabella turned to her. "Suffice it to say, we don't know who the killer is. But we're working on it."

Charlotte raised a brow. "Work on it in the living room. Porter finally got the VCR on."

"I am the golden god of ancient technology!" Porter's yawp rang through the house.

Charlotte rolled her eyes. "I swear he's not related to us."

"No such luck." I rose and followed Charlotte and Arabella back into the living room.

Logan sat on the couch, his head propped on his hand, his eyelids drooping. We were all at the bottom of our tanks, scraping for a last bit of energy to get us through.

"What the hell is 'tracking'?" Porter stared up at the TV from his vantage point on the floor with the VCR.

Arabella sat next to Logan and offered him her coffee cup. He took it and drank, his lips touching the same spot where hers had just been. An ugly surge of jealousy rocketed through my system, but I turned my attention to the TV in an effort to seem uninterested.

The video was black and white, grainy, and had a questionable timestamp at the bottom right corner. But the pumps outside of Sal's were within view for the most part.

"Fast-forward." Logan drained the rest of the coffee I'd made for Arabella. "This looks like the morning rush, probably 8 AM or so. The fire happened after noon, so unless our arsonist was an early bird, we need to look later in the day."

"Thanks, Logan." Porter shot him a smartass grin. "We'd never be able to crack this case without your Johnny-on-the-spot instincts and crackerjack wit."

"Don't be a dick, *Sheriff.*" Logan made clear he didn't put much stock in the title.

Porter held up his left hand, his middle finger at attention, while he fast forwarded through a couple hours of tape. I sat next to Arabella, our thighs and arms lightly touching.

"Hang on." Charlotte pointed to the screen. "There's a

truck on pump four that's out of the frame, but it looks like the bed has a bunch of gas cans in it."

Porter backed up the tape then pressed play. We all leaned forward, doing our best to ignore the lines running across the screen and the jumpy movement of the images.

"Yeah, I see it too." Arabella stood and approached the TV. When she bent over slightly, I was not enough of a gentleman to look away. Neither was Logan, which irritated the hell out of me.

"There." She pointed to a figure at the pump. "He's definitely filling up gas cans. Just let it play. Maybe he'll show up better in a second."

"Of course the asshole that we're looking for is right outside of the frame. Can't even get a license plate on the truck. Black and white video, can't tell what color it is. Horse shit." Porter leaned back, propping himself on his elbows the same way he did when we were kids watching cartoons. Dressed in a white T-shirt and pajama pants, he'd made himself at home.

"That's what? Four containers so far?" Charlotte tapped her finger on her chin. "That has to be the guy. But nothing about him seems familiar. I can't see his face, but he doesn't ring any bells—not the way he moves or anything."

Arabella asked, "Benton, do you think that could be Winston Morris?"

Porter made a pffft noise. "That kook would have to leave his shack in the woods to do something like this. No way. He doesn't have anything to do with the firm anymore, either."

Arabella and I exchanged a look. I hadn't told Porter

and Charlotte about the threatening letters. It was part of my sad attempt at "Dad Damage Control." But even I could see that keeping them in the dark had a limited shelf life.

We watched for about thirty more seconds, everyone in the room squinting at the screen.

"That's it. He's pulling away," Porter said. "I can see a license plate, but this piece of shit VHS is way too blurry." He looked back at Arabella. "Don't y'all have some CSI shit that can like, enhance it or something?"

"That's only on TV." She shook her head and reclaimed her seat next to me.

"Oh." A crestfallen Porter stopped the tape.

Logan rubbed his eyes again. "I'll call Sal first thing. Go over it with him again, see if he remembers anything about this guy."

"Maybe he paid with a credit card. See if Sal can get us a list of all transactions for that morning." Arabella let her head fall back on the top of the couch, her eyes closed. "It's all connected, but I just can't find the thread that links it all." She seemed to be talking more to herself than anyone else.

"Your guy see any movement at the judge's place out in the country?" Logan asked.

"Not a thing. The judge went to ground somewhere or left entirely. But if he turns up anywhere in the county, we'll know. Y'all find anything at Letty's house?"

Logan glanced at Arabella. She didn't open her eyes but seemed to sense his stare. "You can share what we know. Everybody here has skin in the game."

"Nothing that amounted to anything. We searched her

computer, turned the house upside down, and searched her shop, but nothing seemed out of order. Other than her relationship with Randall King and the judge, we don't know why she was targeted."

"The money. It all goes back to the money," Arabella mumbled, perhaps to herself.

"You mean the judge's money?" Charlotte chewed her thumbnail. "It's not like Dad was driving around in a Maserati all of a sudden, so I'm not sure what he has to do with whatever dirt Judge Ingles was up to."

"Charlotte, you know they were thick as thieves." I tried to keep the bitter note from my voice. Failed. "Whatever Judge Ingles was into, Dad knew about it."

She shook her head. "There's no reason to believe Dad did anything wrong."

My shield began to crumble, the damage control façade fading into vapor. I was still loath to tarnish the version of our father that lived in her memory. She wasn't a child anymore, but she'd always be the baby of the family. It was time to come clean. Maybe if we all put our heads together—once all the pieces were laid out—we'd be able to figure it out. So I told them about everything Dad had been hiding—the Theodore Brand land grab, the missing file, the letters from Winston Morris, the lies.

When I got to the part about Lina, Charlotte put a hand to her mouth, shock in her eyes. "She's younger than I am."

"They got close when they were doing that Dancing with the Stars thing. But the affair didn't last long. Letty Cline put a stop to it."

"Do you think what happened to Lina has anything to do with the murders?" Charlotte asked.

Arabella sighed. "I've been considering it. Can't say for sure just yet. That day when we were all out searching, I found her at the bottom of a ravine. She was a mess. Looked like she had more bones broken than were intact. But if she had been at the top, standing along the tree line, and lost her footing, then those injuries would make sense. We recovered her camera—well the memory card was still intact, and she'd been taking nature shots. Her computer at the paper office had half an article about outdoor recreation when the weather turns cooler. It all fit—she was out there taking pics to go with her story; her fall was an accident. I didn't look into it any farther. But maybe there's more to it."

"Too many moving parts." Porter lay all the way back on the rug, tucking his hands under his head.

"I brought one more." Logan leaned over the arm of the couch and pulled a laptop from his bag. I recognized it from Dad's office.

"I've tried a bunch of password combinations. No luck. I could send it off to the crime lab in Columbus, and they could hack into it there. But that'll take time. Given the 'you're next' note on Letty, I think the sooner we access this, the better." He placed it on the glass coffee table. "Anyone here happen to know the password?"

Porter and Charlotte looked at each other while I weighed the pros and cons of helping with the laptop. Time wasn't on our side. I could feel the chances of solving this mess slipping away like blades of summer grass between my fingers. It was an easy decision. I slid the computer down to my side of the coffee table and flipped it open.

"Are you seriously going to break into Dad's computer?" Charlotte perched beside me on the arm of the sofa.

"Do you have any better ideas?"

"No. It just seems so…"

Porter rose and stood next to her, placing a gentle hand on her shoulder. "It doesn't matter anymore. He won't mind. And maybe it'll help us figure out what happened."

Her eyes watered. "You're right. I'm still just not in step with this new reality where he isn't here."

"None of us are." I clicked in the password box. "Any guesses?"

"I tried combinations of all of your names and birth dates, with upper and lowercase, and weird symbols instead of certain letters." Logan threw up his hands. "I got nothing."

"Did you try Letty's name?" Arabella pressed close to stare at the screen.

"Yep."

"But you wouldn't have tried Lina's." Charlotte spoke my thought before I had a chance.

I typed in her name. No dice. "Anyone know her birthday?"

"Yeah, hang on." Arabella pulled out her phone and accessed her calendar. After a few moments of scrolling, she said, "March 10. Don't know the year."

I tried Lina10. Didn't work. L1na10. Nope. Lin@10. Still nothing.

"Shit." The blinking cursor mocked me.

"Try this year at the end," Arabella suggested.

Denied.

"What about Royal?" Porter piped up.

"What's that?" Arabella asked.

"We had a dog for the longest time. Dad named him Royal. It's a good guess." I tried the name capitalized and lowercase. Neither worked.

"He died in 2016, right? Dad was devastated. He treated that dog like one of us. Maybe it's Royal and the ye—"

I'd already typed it in. "That's it." The desktop loaded, though it was sparse. He had an Internet browser, a program that functioned as a Rolodex, and a download folder. "I'm going to keep my objection to any possible client files that are in—"

"Just get on with it," Charlotte barked.

"I like your sister." Arabella pointed at the downloads folder. "Let's start there."

The downloads folder had a smattering of things—memes that would've been amusing to my father, a few pleadings that he must've downloaded from the court's online system, and not much else. I scrolled through all of them, noting that there was nothing special in the pleadings. I'd seen them all before. I clicked over to the finder program and opened his documents. He only had one. It was a draft of a letter in one of our creditor cases that had already settled.

Next I moved to the photos folder. "Got something." There were at least 50 files inside.

"What are they?" Arabella leaned closer, and everyone in the room focused on the screen.

I clicked the first file.

Arabella let out a choked gasp. Porter said, "Damn, Dad." And Charlotte slapped a hand to her face, covering her eyes. It was an image of a smiling Lina Garvey, nude, her legs spread, lying on my father's bed.

"Jeez." Logan didn't look away.

I clicked off the image and selected thumbnail view for the rest of them. A quick rundown showed me that each one was an explicit image of Lina. A few included a nude man, which I knew was my father, but I refused to look closer.

"I think I'm going to be sick." Charlotte hurtled out of the living room and into the powder room in the hall.

I backed out of that folder, the overwhelming need to escape what I'd seen trumping any desire to find out more.

"Let me." Arabella slid the laptop over to her and turned it away from Porter and me. "I'm looking through the web browser to see what websites he's visited," she narrated. "He's been to the state court filing system, Cabela's, news websites, oh." Her cheeks heated to the point she looked feverish.

"What?" I shouldn't have asked.

"Just some other websites. You know. Stuff."

Porter snorted and mouthed "porn" at me. *Jesus.*

She kept going. "He visited the county property register within the last few weeks. Any idea why he'd go to the GIS database to look at properties?"

"No." I stood and walked to the kitchen. "I take that back," I called. "He'd go there to maybe do a title search on disputed property or if one of his clients wanted him to double check a closing for them." I returned to the living room with a bottle of whiskey and a handful of glasses.

"Thank god." Porter snagged the first glass I poured, downed it, and held it out for more.

"There's no way for me to see his search history inside the tax mapping program." She clicked a few more times. "And he didn't save anything."

Porter glugged some more whiskey as I passed glasses to Arabella and Logan. "All this laptop search has done is made Charlotte lose her lunch."

"I'm fine!" she yelled from the other room.

I took a large swallow of whiskey, relishing the burn as it sloshed down my throat. "I needed that."

Arabella sipped hers and continued her examination. "Me too." After a few more minutes of clicking, drinking, and comments on anything but the Lina photos, she sat back. "There's nothing else there. Not even emails. Seems like he only used the laptop for..." She took a bigger drink.

"Yeah." Porter stood and stretched. "I follow."

Charlotte walked back in, her face pale.

"You okay?"

"As okay as I can be." She took the last glass from the coffee table. With a grimace, she raised it. "To Dad."

"To Dad." I clinked my glass with hers, and Porter grabbed the bottle as I took a drink.

"To Dad." Porter chugged the whiskey, then added, "the old pervert."

## 22

### ARABELLA

*I* awoke with a start, unsure of my surroundings. "Vivi?" I turned my head. This wasn't my house.

Sitting up, I put my hand to my head. A stampede of bulls raced through my gray matter. "Shit."

"You're up." Benton appeared in the living room doorway, his hair wet, his face clean shaven.

"What happened?"

He walked over and knelt next to me, his fresh, clean scent at war with my stale whiskey breath. "We drank too much—you on an empty stomach. And you fell asleep."

A few flashes of memory ignited in my mind—Logan drinking, Charlotte drinking more, and Porter cracking jokes that had us all howling with laughter. A light snore caught my attention for a moment—Logan was passed out on the rug.

"Hey." Benton smiled at me. He was attractive with scruff, but with a clean jaw, he was the epitome of handsome.

CELIA AARON

I felt a blush bloom from my head to my toes. "Yeah?"

"There's a full bath at the top of the stairs. I'm making breakfast and should have it ready in about ten minutes. If you want to get washed up and fed, you're more than welcome." He didn't seem the least bit put-off by my hangover.

I knew I must have looked like ass. Glancing at the clock over the mantle, I realized I had enough time to get Vivi to school, even if I showered and ate first. The good news had me swinging my feet over the side of the couch. Benton offered his hand, and I took it.

For a moment, I simply stood as the room swayed.

He rested his hands at my waist, steadying me. "I've got some ibuprofen for you on the kitchen counter. How about you take that first, then shower?"

How long had it been since I'd let a man get this close to me? I honestly couldn't remember. But it felt good, so much so that I wanted to lean into him, wanted to know what it would feel like if he wrapped his arms around me.

"Arabella?"

"Hm?" I realized I'd been standing silent for a beat too long. "Oh, sorry. Yes, pills." I had to get my head straight before starting over again for the day. The investigation needed me running on all cylinders, not nursing a hangover like a lightweight. "Okay."

He wrapped his arm around my waist, pressing me to his side, and walked me into the kitchen. I could have done it myself, but he was warm and sturdy, and he smelled like an expensive bar of soap. No Irish Spring for Mr. Benton King.

A bowl full of cracked eggs sat on the counter, a whisk to the side, and a cast iron griddle rested on the stove top.

I swiped the pills from the granite countertop and downed them with a gulp of ice water. "Thank you."

"Don't mention it." He stayed at my side. "Let me help you up the stairs."

"I think I can manage." I ignored the thrill that shot through me when I thought of the two of us together in the bathroom, him undressing me for a shower. Jesus, the hangover seemed to be short-circuiting everything in my noggin.

"Okay. Holler if you need anything. I laid out a towel, washcloth, and some of Charlotte's girly soap stuff. She won't mind. She'll be even worse off than you when she wakes."

"Why aren't you hungover?"

He shrugged. "Iron constitution?"

"I don't think so." I pinned him with a stare.

"I may have thrown up last night." His nonchalant tone made a laugh bubble up from my gut.

"Lightweight." I giggled, but stopped when it felt like an ice pick in my temple.

"Maybe, but at least I'll be able to make you breakfast." He grabbed the whisk, whirled it in his palm, and began beating the eggs.

"Good point." I turned and made it up the stairs, barely.

A hallway ran to my right. There were a few doors along it and one at the end. Snores to rival Logan's came from the closest room. I peeked in and found Porter on his back, shirtless, and fast asleep despite all his noise.

Turning quickly—almost too quickly—I stumbled into the bathroom.

As Benton had promised, a towel and toiletries were laid out on the marble vanity next to the walk-in shower. His house was nice, far nicer than anywhere I'd ever lived. It was a newer development of what my mother called "McMansions" on a few acres in town that used to belong to a small cotton farm. I stripped and got into the shower, though it took me a minute to figure out how to set the water temperature just right.

Standing under the spray, I thought back through the events of the last couple of days. After I'd washed my hair with Charlotte's fancy shampoo, I soaped up. The shower had white marble tiles with a gray vein running through them. Everything was modern. The place had only been built in the past few years. I stopped mid-wash. *In the past few years.* This subdivision, the renovations at the florist, the burger joint, the other cash businesses on the square.

I almost fell out of the shower in my soapy haste, jumped back in and rinsed off, then grabbed a towel, wrapped it around me and pounded down the stairs. Benton was flipping pancakes in the kitchen as I rushed past and landed on the couch, pulling the laptop close to me and entering his dad's password.

Pulling up the Morrison County property search, I entered Randall's name. A few properties came up—the firm and his residence. But not the property in the county, and none of the other businesses, either. I did the same for Judge Ingles. He owned a few houses in town. Some were even on Razor Row, but nothing on the square. A search for Letty Cline was another dead end.

*Damn.* I sat back, chewing on my lip as my wet hair turned cold, the drips of water down my back sending goosebumps along my arms.

"This is the best morning I think I've ever had." Logan sat up and grinned, his eyes pinned to where my towel was bunched around my thighs.

I smoothed it out. "Knock it off or I'll write you up for sexual harassment."

"What's going on?" He winced at the morning light filtering through the front windows.

"I was just thinking about how things on the square have been sort of rebuilding lately, even though we haven't had much of an economic upturn to support it."

He clenched his eyes shut against the sun, but peeked at me as much as he could. "So?"

"So." I wasn't sure where I was going with this. Maybe I needed to get through my hangover before concocting theories. "I'm just thinking that maybe that has something to do with this. The judge was, I don't know—" I waved at the computer, "—involved in funneling money or something."

"From where, for what?"

"I don't know." I leaned back but made sure my thighs stayed glued together. "I had this thought in the shower, like a Eureka sort of moment, but it didn't pan out. Not all the way. Though there is something interesting. That plot of land Randall bought out from under Theodore Brand—"

"Your favorite felon." He smirked.

"Shut up. He was actually a decent guy, except for that whole rap sheet. *Anyway—*" the adrenaline was draining from me, leaving me even more irritable, "—as I was saying, that piece of property doesn't belong to King anymore."

"Maybe he sold it." Logan stared at my legs.

"Stop!"

"What?"

"Look away, asshole!"

"Fine." He turned his head, but not far enough that I wasn't still in his peripheral vision.

"Never mind. I'm going to get dressed. You are too damn juvenile to even listen to me right now." I rose and headed toward the stairs.

"Oh, come on, Arabella. I'm sorry. I won't—"

I flipped him off, then ran into Benton so hard that my towel came loose. I snatched it back together at my breasts.

He gripped my upper arms, his warm palms smooth against my cool skin. "You're naked." He swallowed hard, his Adam's apple bobbing.

"Sorry. I had an idea, so I—"

"Naked." He ran his wide palms up my arms and rested them on my shoulders.

When I looked into his eyes, I couldn't mistake the heat in them. Jesus, what was I thinking coming down here in just a towel? Suddenly, I wasn't cold anymore. It was hot, and I needed to escape. But I didn't move, just stared up at him, my lips slightly parted as my mind tried to get its footing on what to say.

"Hey." Logan's low voice sounded from behind me. "Get your hands off my boss."

I stepped back, and Benton let his hands drop. But our

gazes were still locked, and I couldn't look away no matter how badly I needed to.

"Arabella?" Logan said my name like a question, though I wasn't sure what he was asking. Benton broke eye contact to glare at him, his jaw tightening.

"I'll um, I'll go get dressed." I darted away and up the stairs. Their low voices followed me up, but I didn't want to know what they were saying. I'd just made a fool out of myself over a property search and managed to undermine myself with both Logan and Benton at the same time.

"Great," I muttered. Head down, I walked into the bathroom and grabbed my shirt from the vanity.

"Did I miss the group shower?" Porter's voice rumbled behind me.

"Oh, fuck off." I turned and slammed the door in his face.

"Guess so." He laughed.

Someone—must have been Charlotte —groaned next door. At least I wasn't the only one with a hangover.

I dressed quickly, then paused in front of the mirror, giving myself a once-over. Though my clothes were rumpled, I smelled better, and my hair was clean. I ran Charlotte's brush through it a few more times. Stalling. A quick check of my watch gave me a little relief. I didn't have time to stay for breakfast and make it to Vivi's carpool on time, so I'd have to skip the food. No awkward looks, and no need to get involved in a pissing match between Benton and Logan.

After a deep breath, I opened the door and hustled down the stairs. Logan stepped into the hall, his phone at his ear.

"What?" I pulled my phone out and stared at the screen. Blank. I'd have to charge it in the car.

Logan covered the receiver. "On the phone with Sal."

"He know the guy?"

He shook his head.

"Of course not." We couldn't catch a break. "I'm going to head out. Take Vivi to school."

"*Okay,*" he mouthed, Sal's tinny voice floating from the phone.

I hurried into the foyer, the front door within my grasp.

"Hey." Benton's voice slid down around me like silk.

I didn't turn around. "I've got to get Vivi—"

"I figured. Here, I made it for you to-go." He handed me a coffee cup and a breakfast burrito wrapped in aluminum foil.

"That's so…" I took both items, the scent of the coffee giving me life.

"You're welcome." He opened the door for me, letting an unseasonably chill breeze into the house. "Be safe, and tell Vivi I said hi."

"I will." I don't know what I expected, but a hot breakfast from Benton King wasn't it. "Thank you."

"Catch up later, okay? I kind of liked our good cop/bad cop routine." He pulled the lapels of my blazer together against the cold, the movement far too presumptuous, but sweet all the same.

I peeked behind him. "Don't let Logan hear you saying that."

"I rather think I'd like for him to hear." He stepped

even closer so that I had to tilt my head up to meet his eyes.

"I know this will sound nuts, and it's the worst possible time—for both of us—but would it be forward of me to ask if I could—"

A sharp whistle sounded from the hallway behind Benton, and Logan came barreling into the foyer.

"What?" I stepped back so fast I almost lost my footing on the threshold, but Benton caught my arm and kept me upright.

Logan arched an eyebrow but didn't say anything about what he'd walked in on. "Just got off the phone with Sal."

"And?"

"And he didn't know the guy." He grabbed his coat from a peg next to the door.

"You already told me that." Time was ticking for me to get Vivi before Mom loaded her up and took her to school.

"Yeah, but he asked his mechanic who was working yesterday morning. He knew the guy from school. Saw him filling up gas cans, but just figured he was doing yard work or something, needed it for lawnmowers."

"Who was it?"

"Name's Leonard Lagner."

"You've got to be shitting me." Benton grabbed his coat.

"Is that the same Lagner that's been calling about her okra being mis—"

"Yes." Benton and I said at the same time.

"Leonard is her son!" I almost did a palm-to-forehead.

"The okra on the judge's counter. The guy—Leonard, aka Lenny—working for the judge. Doing his *dirty work!*"

"Where do you think you're going?" Logan turned to Benton.

"With Arabella."

"Like hell you are." Logan put one hand on his hip. "You're staying here. You're a suspect, not a goddamn detective."

"No, I'm a deputy, and I've been helping with this investigation from day one while you've been twiddling your thumbs doing fuck all."

"You might want to shut your college boy mouth before I do it for you." Logan's voice dripped with menace as Benton stepped onto the porch, both men nearly toe to toe.

"I don't care who stays and who goes, but we need to get out to Millie Lagner's house now!"

"He's staying, and I'm coming with you." Logan moved aside as I hurried down the steps, the low sun doing nothing to warm the frigid air.

"I'm coming." Benton followed.

"No, you fucking aren't."

A scuffling sound erupted behind me. I turned to find both men on the ground rolling and trying to pin the other one.

"I don't have time for this shit." I threw my hands up and dashed to my car. When I started the engine, they stopped wrestling.

And when I pulled away from the curb, they both glared at me in my rearview.

## 23

*L*ogan flipped the heat on, then gingerly touched his jaw. "You're a dick."

My eye was still watering from the blow he'd landed there. "Just drive."

"I would have left your sorry ass behind if I didn't know you'd get Porter to drive you out here anyway. And then I'd have two pricks to deal with."

I gripped the door handle as he took a curve with more speed than even I'd try. "Don't kill us before we get there."

"Scared?" He stared at me when his eyes needed to be on the road.

"Douche." I wanted to hit him again.

He returned his gaze to the blacktop and sped down the highway toward Millie Lagner's place. Her son had been the man we'd met at Judge Ingles' house, and from the looks of things, he was the one who set fire to the firm. I had to assume it was on the judge's orders. Why else would he do it?

"You need to leave Arabella alone." The swagger had left Logan's voice, but iron replaced it.

"Mind your own business."

"That's what you're missing here, college boy. Arabella *is* my business."

"You two aren't together."

"That's not the point." He passed a logging truck, bits of bark bouncing off the windshield.

"I get it. You think you need to do some big brother routine and protect her. But what you're missing is that I don't give a shit what you think." I tried to peer through the trees ahead to catch sight of Arabella's cruiser, but she'd had too much of a head start.

"Big brother?" He white-knuckled the steering wheel. "I don't think so."

"Please." I shook my head. "You plow every single chick under fifty in this town—and some who aren't single—on a regular basis. I know, because Porter plows the same ones. So don't give me that shit. Arabella is too good for you, and she definitely doesn't want a ride on the same merry-go-round that everyone else has already worn out."

"Oh, and you live like a saint, right?"

"I never said that. But I definitely have finer tastes when it comes to my bed partners."

He shot me a glare. "And now you've got a taste for Arabella?"

"Like I said, that's none of your business."

"She's not going to fall for your bullshit. You think you're better than everyone. She knows that. She can see right through your poor little rich boy routine."

"If I didn't know better, I'd think you were worried."

"Worried about a shit stain like you?"

I smiled, the same smile I used on difficult witnesses. "Calling me names doesn't change the fact that you have a flame burning for Arabella, but she isn't interested in you at all. And now that I've come along, you finally realized that you never had a shot with her to begin with. You don't have what it takes to make a woman like her happy. Not short term. Not long term." I wanted to add "isn't that right?" but we weren't in front of a jury, and I'd made my point.

"You don't know what you're talking about."

"Okay." I did my best at Porter's shit-eating grin.

It worked, because Logan kept his eyes ahead, but said, "When this is over, I'm going to knock that fucking smile right off your face."

"We'll see." I gave as good as I got, so I looked forward to another chance at him.

Silence fell like a lead weight between us. I wouldn't be the one to break it. It didn't matter to me that Logan had a hard-on for Arabella. He'd had years with her, but never made a move. Or maybe he'd made one, but she'd shut him down. Either way, it was his mistake.

We turned onto the lane leading to the Lagner home. Arabella was just getting out of her cruiser, one hand on her gun, the other holding a flashlight. The house seemed dark despite the rising sun. No lights were on, the curtains drawn. Maybe Mrs. Lagner hadn't woken yet. Unease crept through me, coloring all my thoughts with alarm.

Logan pulled up next to Arabella's car as she climbed the stairs to the porch and knocked on the door.

"I'd tell you to stay here, but you're too dumb to follow ord—"

I was out of the car before Logan even finished speaking. Arabella ignored both of us as we walked up behind her.

"She home?" Logan asked.

Arabella pointed to the Buick in the driveway. "I think so, but the house is quiet."

Logan flipped the button closure on his holster, leaving his pistol at the ready. For the first time since all this started, I wished I had a gun.

She knocked again and hung on the doorbell, which sounded over and over again inside. No movement. Trying the door handle, she shook her head. Locked.

"You've got probable cause that a crime has been or is being committed." I stepped back. "I can kick it in."

"We know we have probable cause. Jesus. This is our fucking job." Logan backed up to stand next to me.

Arabella finally turned and looked at us, her gaze straying to my sore eye and then Logan's darkening jaw. A disappointed shake of her head was all she gave us before moving to the side.

Logan reared back and kicked before I even got set. The door creaked, but didn't budge. "Fuck!" He stepped away and rubbed his knee. "She got a burglar bar back there or something?"

I aimed for the spot right next to the handle and drew my leg back, then shot out, nailing it with all my might. The wood at the latch splintered, and the door raced inward, slamming against the wall and sticking, the handle likely embedded in the drywall.

"Lucky shot." Logan stopped nursing his knee and walked past, drawing his gun as he entered.

Arabella put a palm to my chest. "Stay out here until we clear it."

I didn't like the idea, but I wasn't armed. "Can I get the shotgun from your cruiser?"

She glanced down the hall as Logan disappeared into the sitting room, her teeth worrying away at her bottom lip. "Garvey's going to kill me." She pulled her keys from her pocket, then handed them to me and drew her weapon as she entered the house.

I ran down the steps and opened the car. It took me a couple tries to figure out which key went to the locking mechanism between the seats, but once I got the shotgun free, I hurried back up the stairs.

"Mrs. Lagner?" Arabella's voice was faint. She must have been at the back of the house.

I bypassed the rooms along the hall and walked into the kitchen as Arabella grunted.

"Shit." I set the shotgun on the table and knelt beside her as she struggled to roll over what had to be Mrs. Lagner's body.

"It's clear back here." Logan walked in as we both pushed her over.

"God." Arabella fell back, knocking into the kitchen counter, as I struggled to process what I saw.

Dark red marks circled Mrs. Lagner's neck, her vacant eyes bulging and red. Someone had strangled her with a cord, the dark wire embedded in her throat, the skin puffy around it.

Logan walked around to her other side and took her wrist, then let go. "She's stiff, cold. Been here a while."

Arabella scrambled back to her knees. I grabbed her elbow and helped her up, silently inviting her to lean on me.

"You okay?" I squeezed her arm.

"I'm fine." She let out a deep breath. "Text Chief Garvey and Porter. Let them know what we got out here."

Logan holstered his pistol and pulled out his phone.

"There's a garage out back. Behind that is Leonard's house." She kept her pistol in her palm, and her voice was eerily calm. "We need to clear both of them."

"You think Leonard did it?" Logan finished his message, pocketed his phone, and retrieved his weapon.

"I don't know. But it doesn't matter. We need to find him and take him into custody. We can ask questions later. Benton, I need you to stay here."

"No way." I lifted the shotgun. "I can help."

"I can't risk a civilian getting hurt." She swallowed hard and her gaze returned to Mrs. Lagner's face. "Another civilian."

"I'm in this, okay?" I moved in front of her so she had to look at me and away from the horror on the floor. "Let me help."

"He's going to follow anyway. Like a mangy fucking puppy." Logan gripped the door handle. "Might as well use him."

"He's right." I flicked the safety off. "Except for the mangy part."

Logan edged the door open and peeked into the yard. "Seems clear. Nothing's moving. Can we send college boy out first?"

"Logan, get your head in the game." Authority rang in her tone. "And Benton...just stay behind us. Anything happens, you run."

"Sure." *No way.*

This was the part where I should have kissed her for luck, but she may have shot me for trying. With a calculated grace, she motioned for Logan to open the door.

Frigid wind rushed inside as Logan took point, his pistol up, and hurried across the grass toward the barn. Arabella followed, and I kept to her heels despite her admonition to stay back. I wasn't going to let anything happen to her.

She let out a curt whistle, and motioned for Logan to bypass the barn. We all crept up the side nearest the tree line, gluing ourselves to the clapboard sides. When we got to the corner, Logan bobbed his head out to check the area.

"Nothing," he whispered. "But there's a truck next to the shack back here."

"Wasn't here before." Her breath fogged. "Leonard must be inside."

"We rushing him or you want me to call out?"

She glanced at me. "Stay here and cover us. If anyone comes out of the garage or comes up from the house that you don't know, give a warning shot, unless you see a weapon. If you see gunmetal, shoot to kill."

"He'll piss his pants before he'll pull that trigger."

Logan's quiet snort had me gripping the stock a little too hard.

"Because that's what you would do?" I smirked at him over Arabella's head.

His laughter turned into a snarl. "You don't even—"

"Boys!" Arabella hissed. "Shut up, and let's get this done."

"I'll go." Logan flipped me off, then darted around the side of the garage. He stayed low and eased up to one of the shack's front windows. Arabella followed, her steps silent as she edged around the stairs and molded herself beneath the other window. She was too short to see in, but she had her pistol trained on the front door.

I kept my head on a swivel, looking behind us at the house and garden, then glancing to the garage's back door every few seconds. Adrenaline made everything move in triple time, even though nothing seemed to be happening. I held the shotgun against my shoulder, my left hand steadying the barrel and my right on the stock near the trigger.

Logan slowly rose, his eyes just north of the windowsill, then sank down again. He held up one finger and pointed to the window above Arabella, then pointed at the ground. She moved to join him as he eased up the stairs, both of them standing on the small front porch on either side of the door. My heartbeat pounded in my ears, and I had the urge to run up there, grab her, and pull her away from whatever danger lay inside. But I couldn't. That wasn't who she was.

She reached for the door handle. It turned. They shared some silent signal between them, then Logan pushed through the door. Arabella followed, disappearing into the dimness beyond.

A shot pierced the air, the muzzle flash lighting up the interior of the shack, and I broke into a run toward Arabella.

## 24

## ARABELLA

*I* dropped to my knees and returned fire as Logan fell in front of me.

"Fuck!" Logan yelled. "Stop! He's down!"

I was breathing hard, my hands shaking as I pointed my gun at the dim corner of the shack. A thin sliver of light slashed across the floor from the window and illuminated a limp hand with a pistol in it. Lunging forward, I snatched it away, yanking it toward me as I scrambled back and aimed my pistol at the figure again.

A gurgling noise barely cut through the ringing in my ears, but the pale fingers in the shaft of light shivered. When a shadow fell across the door, I swung my gun up. Benton stood there, his shotgun trained on the man in the corner. I dropped my pistol to my side and took a gulp of air. The realization that I could've shot him out of pure fear was like a bucket of ice water on my already frozen psyche.

"Are you all right?" He eased to one knee beside me.

"I'm fine. He didn't get me. Logan?" I reached toward him.

"Fucker tagged me in the leg."

"Bad?" I gripped his arm.

"No. I mean, it hurts like a bitch, but it's not the artery."

Relief washed over me. Benton turned and slapped his hand along the wall until an overhead light flickered to life.

The same man we'd seen at Judge Ingles' house lay in the corner, a hand towel pressed to a wound in his abdomen. The towel was a crimson red, but as I moved closer, I realized it had been white, but was soaked with blood.

I glanced at Benton. "Watch the door. Someone shot him before we even got here."

His eyes were closed, his breath coming out in labored gasps.

"Leonard?" I checked his other hand to make sure he didn't have another weapon handy. Not that he was in any shape to use it.

"Mom?" He coughed, flecks of blood spraying onto his pale lips.

I grabbed his wrist and felt for his pulse. It was slow and barely noticeable. He didn't have long.

"What happened?"

"Mom?"

"Leonard, I need you to tell me who did this to you. Who hurt you and your mom?" I put my palm to his face, his skin cold and clammy.

"Eyes." He shuddered, the movement sending him into

a weak, bloody cough.

"Eyes?" I leaned closer. "Do you mean the man with the light eyes?"

A distant siren warred with his rattling breath.

"Leonard." I shook him gently.

His hand dropped from the wound in his abdomen, the gurgle in his chest falling silent.

"Leonard!"

He didn't move. I sat back on my ass, my gaze glued to him. His unearthly stillness created a wrongness that could never be righted.

"Arabella." Benton knelt next to me as the siren blared close by. "He's gone."

"I shot him."

"No." He pointed to pockmarks in the wall to Leonard's left. "You missed. And it doesn't matter. He was a goner before we ever showed up." He cradled my face in his warm hands. "Come on. Come away from him."

I blinked a few times. So much death, and I wasn't able to stop any of it.

"I'm bleeding too, you know," Logan grated.

"Logan." I turned to him. He was lying on his back, his right pants leg red with blood just below his knee. "Let me see."

Benton walked to his other side and bent down. "At least everyone in the room was a terrible shot."

"Fuck off." Logan winced as he tried to sit up.

"Stay down." I grabbed the hem of his pants leg and pushed it up until I found the wound. It was a clean entry, blood oozing from around a hole in his calf. I couldn't see the back of his leg to check for an exit.

Shucking off my jacket, I wadded it up and pressed it to his calf.

Logan gritted his teeth as I applied steady pressure.

"Benton!" Porter's voice.

"I'm in the building behind the garage! We need an ambulance. Logan's been shot."

"I'll call it in." Porter's heavy boots hit the porch and he stopped in the doorway. "What the hell happened in here?"

"The fuck does it look like, *Sheriff?*"

"You still got a smart mouth even after you got popped in the leg like an amateur?" Porter shook his head, then put his phone to his ear. "Yeah, gonna need an ambulance out at the Lagner residence, and step on it. Logan Dearborn's going to bleed out if you don't hurry, and what a terrible, terrible loss that would be."

"Where's my gun?" Logan reached for it, but I smacked his hand.

"You need to stay still." I kept the pressure on his leg. "Porter, Mrs. Lagner's in the house, deceased. This is her son, Leonard. He was already shot when we got here. I need you to put out a BOLO on the shooter. About six feet, slim build, light blue eyes, blond hair, Jersey accent. Armed and extremely dangerous."

"I'll get the rest of my guys running the roads to see if we can find the creep. Do you have any more officers to spare?" He texted, his thumbs flying over his phone.

"No, we don't have enough for what's already happened. Chief Garvey may need to call the state for rein—"

"Like hell I will." Chief Garvey stomped up the steps

behind Porter. "We don't need those state assholes ruining this investigation. Unless you're saying you can't handle it, Arabella?" He peered at Logan and gave him a disgusted look.

"I'm not saying I can't handle it, but Chief—"

"Good. I'm glad we're on the same page. Logan gonna make it?"

"Thanks for the concern, Chief." Logan groaned. "Really appreciate it."

"I've been shot three times, son. And I'm none the worse for wear. You'll get over it." He pointed at Leonard's body. "He tell you anything?"

"I think he identified his killer. The man with the light eyes."

Chief Garvey's mustache twitched. Nothing huge, just a slight jump. No one would have noticed, but I was looking up at him. I didn't miss it. A sick feeling swirled in my gut.

"You put out a BOLO on any man in the county with light eyes?" He hitched one thumb into the waistband of his pants. "That's a lot of people, Arabella."

My tongue felt glued to the roof of my mouth. He knew something about the man with light eyes. He *knew* and hadn't said anything. I dropped my gaze to Leonard. If the Chief had been straight with me, could I have saved him? What did the Chief know, and how long had he been watching me try to solve this case while withholding crucial information from me?

"Arabella?" Chief's voice filtered through my thoughts.

I met his gaze again. "Yes?"

"I asked if you'd checked the garage?"

"No. Not this time."

Logan reached down and clutched my jacket, pressing it to his leg. "You go." He gritted out, "But take one of those idiot Kings with you. I'll be fine here."

"I'll stay with the crybaby." Chief shuffled inside and leaned against the wall. "I doubt anyone's in there, but better safe than sorry."

I tried to search his face for any hint of lies, or maybe some sort of plot. Was the killer lying in wait for me in the garage?

"I'll go." Benton grabbed his shotgun. "I'll get Porter to search with m—"

"I'm coming." I pushed to my feet. No way I'd let Benton take a bullet for me.

"Check it, but if you find someone in there, shoot first and ask questions later. Don't risk yourself." Chief covered his concern for me with his usual gruffness, but it rang true all the same. He knew something he wasn't telling me, but he wouldn't send me toward danger. Would he?

I walked out of the shack as mistrust warred with my knowledge of Chief's character, of our history together.

"It wasn't your fault." Benton kept his voice low as we walked through the fading grass toward the back of the garage. He'd mistaken my worry for distress over Leonard.

"I know."

"Okay. You just seem shaken is all."

"I've never fired my weapon at someone." The scary part was that it had been easy. And I knew I could do it again if I had to.

"That's a good thing, and I hope that's the last time." He cut in front of me and cautiously opened the door.

I wanted to pull him back so I could go first, but he eased inside, his gun up. My pistol was warm in my palm, and I had nine rounds left. Plenty to put someone down if need be.

"Hang on." I pulled the heavy flashlight from my belt and clicked it on. The strong beam cut through the gloom, revealing the same array of rusting parts and unused tools as before. We stuck close to the husk of a car and swept the place. Nothing. Then I turned around and caught the rickety ladder in the beam of the flashlight. "There."

Benton maneuvered toward it, the hollow sound of metal clanking through the dusty space as he knocked over an ancient gas can. "Shit."

"Do me a favor and keep your finger off the trigger." I moved up behind him, the path to the ladder even narrower, dusty tarps covering mystery junk, lawn mowers, and an array of wire spools pressing close on either side.

At the base of the ladder, he stopped and turned to face me. We were close, my chest almost touching his as dust motes swirled through the flashlight's ray.

"You okay?"

"I'm fine." I stared at the open collar of his shirt, unsure if I could meet his eyes. Too many dark thoughts were passing through my mind, all the what-ifs around what had just happened. What if it hadn't just been Logan's leg?

His palms warmed my upper arms, the same gentle grip from his house this morning—from when I wore only a towel. "You're freezing." He pulled me against him and opened his coat, wrapping it around me.

"I'm fine." Despite my insistence, I melted into his cocoon of warmth. It was what I needed, even though I couldn't admit it, and certainly couldn't ask for it. No one could see. It was just the two of us, hidden in the dark, pretending all of this was normal, pretending that maybe there was a connection between us.

I clicked off the flashlight.

"You're safe." He tucked my head under his chin. "When I heard the gunshot, I thought..." His voice faded, but his arms tightened around me.

I closed my eyes and breathed him in, the clean scent of his soap and the underlying hint of something else—maybe of him. It was foolish, and I knew I was kidding myself, but I needed what he was offering. A simple touch to get my feet on the ground again, to push away the terror and the worry and the uncertainty that seemed to whirl around us like a tornado.

My eyes began to sting, and I had to bite back tears. I didn't even know they were there, lurking beneath my armor. Why did kindness bring them to the surface faster than anything else, even pain?

"You're safe," he repeated, as if he was reassuring the both of us.

We stood for a while, until the threat of tears receded, and my skin warmed under his embrace.

I turned my head to the side and rested my ear against his chest. "If you tell anyone about this, I'll deny it."

He shook with quiet laughter and nuzzled into my hair. "I wouldn't say a word. Frankly, I was relieved you didn't knee me or stomp my foot when I took the liberty of holding you."

"I should have." I sighed.

"Oh, come on. It's not so bad, is it?"

I smiled, and it was real. "I guess it could've been worse." Stepping back, I missed his warmth.

"Here, take this." He started to peel off his jacket, but hit his elbow on the ladder. "Shit."

"Keep it. I've got a coat in the cruiser. Besides, I don't need anything else weighing me down when I go up the ladder." I clicked my light back on.

"I'll go." He put a hand on a rung, his low voice like an invisible caress.

"No. I'm lighter." I focused the beam on the wood. "It might not even hold me, but I need to see what's up there." I holstered my gun and scooted past him.

He moved around until he was behind me, his arms on either side of the ladder, caging me in. "I'll hold onto it. Be careful."

I tested the first rung with a kick. It didn't break, so I put my weight on it and pulled myself up. He pressed his chest to my back, his hands locked on the side rails. *Focus.* I took another step, then another, my flashlight thunking against the rungs as I climbed. I could almost see over the edge of the landing when the rung I was on splintered.

"Shit!" I fell, but not far.

"Gotcha." Benton cupped my ass in his palms, then gave me a push. I pulled myself over the edge of the landing, the wood sturdy beneath my knees.

"You good?" he asked.

"Yeah. Thanks."

"Anytime." I didn't miss the amused inflection.

I trained the light ahead of me and moved forward into the cramped loft. The roof beams were right overhead, and I had to hunch to make progress. Compared to below, the loft was nearly empty, only a few odds and ends tossed on the floor. I inspected the wooden two-by-fours beneath my feet. They were old and splintering just like the ladder, but there was a clear path where the dust had been disturbed. I followed it a few paces until I reached a large steamer trunk, the kind that those antiques shows would say was worth a small fortune. It was unlocked, so I lifted the top, the joints creaking. When it was open, I blinked to make sure I wasn't hallucinating.

"See anything?"

Focusing the beam on the trunk, I stared. "I should say so."

"What?"

"From the looks of it? About ten thousand dollars."

25

BENTON

*P*orter counted out the last stack of bills and set them on Millie Lagner's dining room table.

"How much?" Chief Garvey stood in the doorway, casting glances down the hall at the crime scene tech.

"Twelve thousand and change." Arabella finished the tally in her notebook.

Chief Garvey whistled. "What was Leonard doing with that kind of money?"

She flipped a few sheets back in her notes, then set the pad down. "I think that Leonard was working for Judge Ingles on multiple fronts. And it all comes back to the judge's money. If I can figure out where it came from, maybe I can figure out why the murders are happening. It has something to do with the man with light eyes." She glanced at Chief Garvey, then continued. "I think he or Leonard killed Randall King and Letty Cline, probably on the judge's orders. Maybe the judge sent the man with light eyes out here to clean up his loose ends by killing Leonard."

Chief Garvey furrowed his eyebrows. "I'm hearing a lot about what you 'think' happened. What do you know?"

"We know the judge ran. We know someone in his house took a shot at me. Maybe Leonard, maybe Light Eyes. We know the judge is the one with a money trail that doesn't add up." She rose. "The next step is to search his place on the edge of the county."

I nodded my agreement, and the chief shot me a glare.

"I just need to find the judge, and I need him to talk." She seemed certain she could manage it. "He's the thread that runs through all of this."

Chief Garvey seemed to chew on her words, his mustache twitching before he finally stilled. "All right. Let's get out there. I've been wanting to see it ever since you told me he had a secret mansion."

"I'll come, too." Porter eyed the cash, the green bills stacked up neatly inside a black garbage bag. "It's out of the county, but I know Ted, the Coffee County Sheriff. He still owes me a favor for that time I helped his mistress out of a DUI when she and her smoking hot sorority sister—"

Chief Garvey held up a hand. "We can use all the help we can get, especially now that Logan's going to be spending his evening at the hospital. Arabella, head out. I'll follow you."

"On it." Arabella strode down the hall and said a few words to Pauline, then hurried to the front door. "How many deputies can you—"

Chief Garvey grabbed the bag and hefted it over his

shoulder as his phone rang. He pulled it from his belt and grimaced at the number. "Hang on." He stepped onto the porch.

"I'm coming with you." I followed Arabella into the hall.

"I've got Garvey and Porter, plus Porter's deputies." She seemed so confident, the moment in the garage gone. "You should hang back, check on Charlotte."

"Like hell I will. I'll ride with Porter. I'm not letting you out of my sight."

"I don't need you to save me, Benton. I'm not that kind of woman. Never have been."

"I know that." I stepped closer to her, forcing her to meet my gaze. "It's one of the things I like about you. But that doesn't mean you don't need me at all." I'd work as hard as I could just to hear those words from her lips— *"I need you."*

Porter edged past us and out the front door, but not without giving me a knowing glance.

"You could get hurt." She shook her head as I stepped closer.

"I could." I pressed my index finger under her chin and tilted her face up to mine. "So could you."

She didn't smack my hand away. Instead, her lips parted on a soft sigh. "This is my job. I agreed to take this risk the second I signed on."

What I wouldn't give just to taste her. I leaned closer. "I'm a deputy these days. All about some danger."

She smirked, the corner of her mouth tempting me. "I'm pretty sure you're a starched shirt attorney. At least you were when I met you a few days ago."

"A lot has happened since then." Closer still, our lips were only a breath away from touching.

Her eyelids lowered as I ran my fingertips down her neck, her pulse fluttering under my touch.

The door opened, jarring us out of the stolen moment.

She stepped back and cleared her throat.

"Chief Garvey just took off," Porter announced.

"What?" Arabella pushed past me and stared out the door at his disappearing cruiser. "Why?"

"He said the hospital called. Lina woke up." Porter pushed his hat back on his head. "I guess that means he's out, at least for this part of the investigation."

"Lina's awake?" Arabella seemed stunned, but then the ghost of a smile crossed her face. "Thank god. That's the first good news we've had in I don't know how long."

Porter scuffed his boot on the concrete porch. "Since, um, the chief's out, would you mind letting Benton ride with you? I've got some stuff to do."

"While you're driving?" She cocked her head at him.

He put one hand on his hip. "I'm a very important sheriff, Arabella. I have to multitask, even when I'm driving."

I knew he was full of shit. Arabella did, too, but she simply walked past him and down the stairs.

Porter gave me a grin and waggled his eyebrows. "Now you owe me one."

"You're an idiot."

He followed me out into the driveway. "You still owe me one."

Arabella cranked her cruiser, and I dropped in next to her, closing the door as Porter walked by with a wink.

"He's not obvious or anything." She put the car in reverse as I returned the shotgun to its spot between the seats.

"Subtlety has never been his strong suit."

"Oh, I remember."

I didn't like the way she'd said it, but I tried to keep my tone even. "Were you two close in high school?"

She shot me a sideways glance. "What are you really asking?" She turned onto the highway leading out toward Coffee County.

"Were you two, you know…" *Please say no.*

"Were we together? No. Did we hang out sometimes, drinking beer we were too young for and smoking cigarettes that made us cough? Yeah."

Sounded like Porter. "I wish I'd known you back then."

"Yeah?" She shook her head. "I'm pretty sure you wouldn't have looked at me twice. After all, I wasn't quite up to the King standard."

"I was a prick in high school." I settled lower in my seat. "Loved rules, especially playing by them. Porter was my nemesis. I couldn't stand how he'd fly by the seat of his pants, but somehow still manage to come out on top."

"Like the way he became sheriff?"

"Exactly like that." I still couldn't believe he'd won the county election. "I was always trying too hard. All of it just so I could impress my dad, make him think I was worthy to carry on the family business. It was all I thought about, really. Porter was out chasing skirts, and I was at home studying for exams." A wry chuckle escaped me. "The truth was—and I'd never tell him this—was that I wished I could be like him. He didn't care about what

Dad thought, not like I did. And it seemed to make Dad think even more of him. But if I stepped out of line..." I clenched my jaw shut, thinking of some of the harsh words my father had thrown at me over the years. He'd always reminded me I was the elder, the one who was responsible for the other two.

"Doesn't seem like he treated you equally." Arabella's voice was soft even as she tore up the asphalt toward the judge's house.

"He didn't." And I hadn't realized how much resentment I still bore from it.

"There are so many perks to being an only child." She smiled, lightening the mood. "All the Christmas gifts, mine. No pesky siblings to fight with. Nobody vying for the attention that was mine, all mine."

"Sounds heavenly."

She shrugged. "Lonely."

I peered through the small window into her past. "So you were a wild child in high school?"

She smiled, a memory tickling some spot in her mind. "I did some stupid things—many of which your brother was witness to and has been sworn to secrecy about—but I managed to get good enough grades to go to community college. Mom instilled in me from a ridiculously young age that I needed to be able to support myself. Didn't need to rely on a man, only myself. Not that she needed to tell me that, since she raised me on her own."

"How did you meet Vivi's father?"

She stayed silent and chewed her bottom lip as we rocketed around an 18-wheeler, red and blue lights flashing.

"Sorry, I didn't mean to push—"

"No, it's fine. I met him while I was working at the Skate N' Shake close to school."

"You wore roller skates and served up fried food?" I tried to imagine her in the shorty-shorts and tank top the restaurant required. *Hell.*

"Yep. It paid for my books. He came in one day, then the next, and on and on for weeks on end. Every time he asked me out, I said no. I didn't have any plans to be someone's girlfriend, and definitely not a wife."

"What made you change your mind?"

"He was persistent." The wistfulness in her voice made me jealous of a man I'd already decided to despise. "I eventually gave in, and he was charming...at first." She slowed and peered at the left side of the highway where dirt roads meandered off into the trees at intervals. "They always are at first. Abusers and drunks and any sort of bad news, really. They start off great. Thoughtful, caring, just what you're looking for. And you're the frog in the pot, the water getting hotter and hotter until you're boiling."

"He hurt you." My hands balled into fists. It wasn't a question. I knew.

"Yeah." She said it as if the scar didn't hurt, as if she'd covered over any lingering ache. "He did. I was young and dumb. Thought I could change him. We went on like that for years. Fighting and separating, but we just couldn't stay away from each other. Even though I knew he'd eventually kill me if I stayed with him."

I wasn't prone to violence. Didn't make the first move in the few fights I'd been in. And definitely didn't break the law. But I was ready to pummel this man until my fists cracked.

"When I got pregnant with Vivi, things changed a little at first. But then he went back to his old ways. Drank more, slept around more. To be honest, the week after Vivi was born when he didn't come home, I was relieved. Having her made me realize that he'd have to go one way or another. I think it was better that he left like he did—a coward. It ensured that I'd never take him back, not that he ever tried."

"He was a fool." How could a father leave his child? Not to mention any man who hurt a woman wasn't fit to lick Arabella's boot. I'd had it so easy. Never worried about money. The only thing that made me lose sleep at night was letting my father down. And in the light of all his secrets and lies, I'd come to realize that *he* was the one who let *me* down.

"I'm glad to be rid of Dale. If he showed up now, I probably wouldn't even recognize him. It's more likely he's dead. Either from a bottle or a needle." She slowed as we passed an "Entering Coffee County" sign peppered with buckshot. "It's somewhere along here."

We passed a few more dirt roads, then slowed when we saw a paved one, the black asphalt soaking up the midday sun.

"This has to be it." She turned onto the winding lane that took us through a new-growth stand of pines, up and over a rise, and then down the other side where the trees thinned out and a pasture fence rose on either side of the lane.

"He cleared all this land." My gaze roamed over the

rolling landscape, the grass growing high as cattle grazed off to the right near a man-made pond, the perfect circle reflecting the blue above.

"All I can see is money." She pointed to a barn with deep crimson siding and what looked like a brand-new metal roof gleaming in the sunlight. We kept going until the road curved up another slope, the steepest yet. On the other side, a valley lay sprawled below. A huge house sat in the center, the front like a French chateau, with a separate garage, a tennis court, and a large pool sparkling behind it.

"Holy shit." I leaned forward, gawking.

She slowed to a stop. "And I thought the King place was a mansion."

I couldn't tell if I wanted to defend my homestead or simply agree. The grandeur of this place was unmatched. How he'd managed to get all of this built without some sort of paper trail or even a whisper of gossip in Azalea was beyond me.

We eased down the hill and came to a stop near the bottom where a sheriff's cruiser sat parked.

A deputy rolled down his window. "Howdy."

"Seen anyone?" Arabella asked.

"Nope. Hasn't been a peep." He had to have been a deputy long before Porter arrived on the scene. His droopy eyes and gray beard gave him the appearance of a slightly sloshed Santa.

"We're going in."

"Got a warrant?"

"Don't need one. We've got enough dead bodies and probable cause that the judge is behind it."

He whistled, the whiskers around his mouth bristling. "The judge you say? Damn."

"It's a mess." She glanced at her rearview mirror. "Porter should be here in a minute. He'll let you know what he needs. We're going to go ahead and find a way in."

"Ten-four." He tipped his hat as we drove by.

Arabella rolled the rest of the way down the smooth lane. "Did he remind you of—"

"Santa Claus."

She smiled. "Yep. I should have gotten his number so he could come to the house and play Santa for Vivi."

"When we were little, my dad always…" The gut punch from the memory was unexpected, knocking the wind out of me. Dad dressed as Santa, even when Porter and I were old enough to know it was him. He'd do it for Charlotte, and even my stoic teenage self got some joy out of seeing her eyes light up when "Santa" walked in.

"We're close." She took my hand. "We're going to find who did this."

"I know." There wasn't much I was sure of anymore, but Arabella had fast become my touchstone. Her word was golden.

We'd find the killer. And more than that, I'd solve the mystery of who my father truly was.

## 26

ARABELLA

The front door had two panels of wrought iron with sheets of glass behind each. There was no way to get in without welding equipment, so we skirted around the landscaping at the edge of the two-story home until we came to a side door. It was wrought iron as well, though not quite as ornate.

"Let's keep going." I warily glanced at the wide pasture at our back. We were completely exposed and in broad daylight. The day had warmed a bit, but the chill lingered as we turned the corner to the back of the house, the pool glinting to our left.

"There." Benton pointed to a set of wood and glass doors that led into the house from the pool area.

Placing my hands on the glass to shield from the sun, I peered inside. A well-appointed living area, the white furniture sleek and modern, lay beyond. "Don't see anyone, but I'm pretty sure his furniture is worth more than my house."

Benton yanked on the door handles, but they were

locked up tight. "Want to keep looking, or will this work for you?"

I scanned the back of the house, but didn't see any more obvious entrances. "Let's do this one."

He handed me the shotgun. "They open outward, so kicking won't work, but this looks like tempered glass." He backed away and gripped the edges of a marble planter, fading pink blooms spilling over the sides. With an easy motion, he picked it up and walked it over to the door, though it had to weigh at least fifty pounds. He shot me one more look, his eyebrows up in question. I nodded.

With a hard shove, he pushed the planter through one of the plate glass doors. It shattered into several smaller pieces, and the planter landed with a thud on the tile floor beyond.

"Nice one."

I jumped as Porter walked around the side of the house and inspected the damage. "You need a bell."

"Not even a bell could save you from my ninja skills." He put his hands up in what I supposed was a karate move.

"Where's your backup?"

"The guys—" he shot me a look, "—and ladies. I hire ladies, too, you know." He coughed into his palm. "They'll be here soon. I left one on Letty Cline's place and another is watching the courthouse. Santa's going to stay put out front, let us know if we got company."

"What's his actual name?" Benton kicked the remaining glass from the door frame.

"Santa's?" Porter tilted his head back, as if looking at the sky could give him the answer.

"You don't even know his *name*?" Benton retrieved his shotgun and stepped through the door.

"He answers to Santa. What do you want from me?"

Benton held out his hand for me.

Porter smirked. "After you."

"Shut up." I took Benton's hand and stepped through the busted door.

Despite the cavernous space—the living area was two stories with wide windows at the top—the air was stale, as if no one had been here in a while.

"No alarm system at the *Chateau de Ingles*?" Porter asked, using a horrid French accent.

"Suppose not." I turned right into a spotless kitchen. "It's like nothing here has been touched." I opened the first drawer I came to. Empty. I walked down the row of custom cabinetry, each one as barren as the last.

Porter opened the fridge. "Not even ketchup. What kind of psycho doesn't have ketchup?"

"He didn't live here." I peered into a wide pantry, the shelves bare. "He just built it, furnished it, and let it sit. That's why no one in Azalea ever gossiped about it. He was never here."

Benton walked into the dining room, an ornate table and chairs matched with a sideboard and china cabinet dominated the room.

"Fancy schmancy." Porter opened the sideboard. "But no booze."

A thin film of dust coated the table.

"Why build a house and never live in it?" Benton continued his examination, Porter and I following behind. We moved through a formal sitting room with a fireplace big enough for me to stand in, a library full of leather-bound volumes that looked brand new, two bedrooms that were sumptuously appointed, and two bathrooms that had never seen the flush of a toilet.

"There's nothing here." I peered out the front door and caught a glimpse of Santa in his SUV.

"Let's try upstairs." Porter took the steps two at a time.

"What do you make of this?" Benton leaned on the bannister and stared up at the crystal chandelier. "Why would the judge spend all this money for no reason?"

"There was a reason." I followed the silver inlay that ran through the marble foyer. "There's a pattern here. We're still too close to it to see the whole thing. But the judge didn't make the money for this." I waved my hand at the thick moldings and sleek décor.

"He didn't inherit it either. I've heard the story of how he came from nothing about two hundred times, starting from when I was barely old enough to walk. Judge Ingles would even tell it in the courtroom to put jurors at ease. He was an everyman, grew up poor here in Azalea and became one of the most respected members of the community."

"The money came from elsewhere. From outside Azalea."

"Where?"

"I don't know yet. But I suspect the man with the light eyes is—"

"God, I'd kill to take a bath in this master tub. It's got all these jets. I could fit three women in there with me." Porter reappeared on the landing.

Benton scoffed. "Did you find anything of use?"

"Nope." He thumped down the stairs.

"Let's check the garage." I headed back through the broken glass, past the pool, and to a simple white door at the back of the garage. Locked, of course.

Porter walked over. "Allow me—"

I reared back and kicked the door near the handle. It rocketed inward.

"Damn, girl." Porter whistled as Benton gave me an appreciative look.

"What?" I shrugged, the picture of nonchalance despite being secretly pleased with myself.

We walked into the gloomy garage, and I felt around until I came to a row of switches. I flicked each one of them on, and the room lit up in a sea of glints and reflections.

"Is this heaven?" Porter strode in and peered at the first car he came to—an iridescent sports model.

"The cars alone are worth a fortune." Benton walked between the bumpers, the gray concrete floor polished to a bright sheen.

"Can I impound these? That the right word?"

"I think the word you mean is 'steal.'" I looked past the glitz to see if there was anything of interest.

"No, I mean the thing where we take custody of the items that are, you know, contraband, and keep them in our—"

"She knew what you meant, Porter. Then she used sarcasm to shut you down. You're just too slow to catch up to it."

"That's just, like, your opinion, man." Porter moved on to the next car, this one shiny black.

Benton muttered under his breath.

I peeked into the pristine car to my right. "This was a total bust."

"You have got to be kidding." Porter shook his head. "This is the coolest shit in Mississippi. Maybe even in the south."

"But we're no closer to finding what we're looking for." I walked past the chrome and glass until I came to an outer door on the other side of the garage. Flipping the deadbolt, I swung it inward.

"Look." Benton pointed to a low structure with a set of doors about twenty feet to the side of the garage. "What's that?"

The doors had been painted a deep green, which would have camouflaged them pretty well in the summer. But they stuck out in the browning grass, the metal almost technicolor in the sun.

"Maybe it's a storm shelter?" I hurried to it, the door shutting behind us as Porter continued his tour of each car in the garage.

"Yeah, that's probably it."

I stopped short and stared at the chain around the handles. "Who padlocks a storm shelter?"

Benton knelt and pulled on the thick chain. "No way we're getting into this without a key to the padlock or—"

"Bolt cutters." Porter appeared behind me, free from the garage's spell. He clicked on the radio at his shoulder. "Santa, come in."

"Yes, boss."

"I can't believe he answers to Santa." Benton rose and stared at the doors.

"Drive on down here. You got some bolt cutters or a crowbar?"

"Got both. Heading down there now." An engine cranked in the distance.

"We're out back next to the garage. You can drive right up to it."

"Be there in a few seconds. Santa out."

I pulled out my phone and snapped a photo of the storm shelter doors.

"What do you think he's got down there?" Porter toed the edge of the rectangular entrance.

Images from movies flashed through my mind. Women in chains. Torture implements. Organs in jars. I made myself shiver. "I guess we'll find out."

Santa walked around the corner of the garage, bolt cutters and a crowbar in his hands as promised. "Boss."

"I think the bolt cutter should do it." Porter took the handles and bent down.

"You need to cut the link where the lock is." Benton pointed.

Porter moved the cutting mechanism to the appropriate link. "I knew that."

Benton pulled the chain taut.

They made quick work of the chain, the links rattling against the metal doors as they pulled them free.

"Santa, stay here and keep watch."

"You got it." He patted the gun positioned at the edge of his portly stomach.

"Let's do it." I pulled my pistol, aiming it at the doors as Benton and Porter pulled them open.

The interior was pitch black, but fluorescent lights

kicked on to reveal a rough set of wooden stairs leading down, the walls on either side compacted dirt.

"I can go first." Benton moved closer.

"I got it." Placing my foot on the first step, I eased down. The slope was harsh, almost like a ladder, and the earth above my head made me break out in a cold sweat. Tight spaces weren't my favorite.

A few more steps, and the floor evened out. Thick support beams lined the sides of a small room, no bigger than Vivi's room at home. A bench sat against one wall, so perhaps the space had truly been designed as a storm shelter. However, a small desk sat to the side, a laptop and some banker's boxes stacked on it.

I stowed my pistol and snapped a photo.

"That's the file." Benton slipped past me and examined the top box. "The one that was missing from the file room."

"What's the other one?" I tapped the bottom box.

"Not sure. It could be from the firm, but it isn't labeled. The one from the firm has to do with—" he ran his finger along the words printed in a neat hand on the side of the box, "—looks like my subdivision." He picked up that box and set it on the ground.

I opened the bottom box. It was full of manila folders, none of them labeled. "What's this?"

Benton pulled out one of the thicker folders and paged through the documents inside. "Renovation costs." His brow furrowed. "For the law firm."

"No offense, but the firm looked like it hadn't been updated for quite some time."

"It hadn't." He pulled out one sheet of paper and read

from it. "Replaced flooring in all offices, 5000 square feet of Brazilian mahogany, labor, extra materials." He flipped to another page. "This one says they gutted the bathrooms and installed Italian marble. Has a receipt. My father paid in cash."

"I used the bathroom at the firm. That was definitely not Italian marble."

"None of this is true." He flipped through a few more pages. "But Dad's signature is on half of these documents. He signed for work that was never done, and he paid for it. I've never heard of any of these businesses."

The picture was finally becoming clear. "He was washing cash. Had to be. He and the judge both. This house? I'd be willing to bet that Judge Ingles paid for this construction with mostly cash. And he didn't use locals, either. Whoever he paid was part of the scam."

He plucked another piece of paper from the file. "This receipt is from a business in New Jersey."

"The man with the light eyes. He had a Jersey accent. The money is coming from there. Straight to Judge Ingles and your father. They were washing it for someone else— maybe drug money or something equally illegal—and taking a cut."

Benton dropped the folder back into the box as if it were a scorpion. "I want to say my dad would never do that." His eyes hardened, but I knew heartbreak lived just beneath the surface. "But the truth is, I didn't know my dad. Not like I thought I did."

"I'm sorry." I didn't know what else to do. I wrapped my arms around him. "I'm sorry you found out like this, and I'm sorry he hurt you."

"Me too." He accepted my embrace and pulled me close.

We stood in silence for a while, him in mourning and me in thought. Something had to have gone wrong for the New Jersey side of the equation to turn on Randall King and Judge Ingles. But what? The open safe seemed like a pretty big clue. Did someone get a little too handsy with the cash?

"Thank you." He squeezed me gently. "For everything."

I shook my head against his chest. "Seems like things have been pretty shitty in your life ever since I walked into it."

"I don't think so. I think things were already shitty, but I just didn't realize it. You showing up was the best thing that could've happened."

Something warm and tingly danced inside me.

A sharp crack filtered down the stairs. *Gunshot.* My gut knew it before my head did.

"Porter?" Benton called.

I turned and ran to the stairs right as the door slammed shut, throwing everything into darkness.

## BENTON

*A*nother sharp crack shattered the air as I tried to climb the steps in the dark.

"Stay inside!" Panic blazed through Porter's yell. "Santa is down. There's a shooter in the woods."

"Where are the rest of your men?" Arabella blindly gripped my hand as she climbed onto the stair behind me.

"Yeah. That." A beat, then, "Randy, Chester, Harris—where the hell are you? Someone's out here shooting at me. Santa took a bullet in his side. I need an ambulance and for you to get your asses out here!"

"We're almost there." A voice crackled back.

"A couple of you peel off to the left, and go into the woods. The shooter is on the garage side. He's at least 100 yards away from the house, got a high-powered rifle. See if you can sneak up on him from the back. The rest of you get out here and help me with Santa."

"Ten-four." The crackling fell silent.

"We can't let him get away. It has to be the man with the light eyes. Has to be." Arabella tried to push past me.

"Whoa." I put my hands on her shoulders and pushed her against the dirt wall, no space between us in the narrow stairwell. "If you go out there, he'll pick you off."

She tried to shove me off. "If I don't go out there, he'll get away."

"Porter put his people on it. Have faith."

"In Porter?" I didn't need to see her face to sense the sarcasm.

"You can't go out there and get shot. Vivi would never forgive you. Or me, for that matter."

"I could use one of the doors as a shield, and then maybe get back into the garage. There were some four wheelers in there—"

"No." The thought of her taking a bullet scared me more than I could comprehend.

She gripped my wrists. "Hey, I don't need you babysitting me. I'm the lead detective on this case. People are depending on me. If we don't get this guy and he kills someone else, that's on me."

"You can't control what other people do." I didn't remove my hands from her shoulders. "This whole mess was in motion long before you got involved. You don't deserve to get shot because of it, because of what my father did, or what Judge Ingles did."

"I'm going out there." She put metal in her voice. "And you're going to let me go. So take your hands off—"

I kissed her. I couldn't let her go, but I couldn't think of any other way to convince her to stay. It was dumb and rash, but also perfect. She stiffened, her grip squeezing my wrists as I ran my tongue along the seam of her lips, finally tasting what I'd been fantasizing about. It was even better in real life.

Her hold loosened as I pressed her against the wall, her body molding to mine, her soft curves delicious and warm. She let her hands drop to my waist, and I ran my fingers through her hair, gripping lightly. The fact that she hadn't pushed me away left me in a euphoria all its own. I wanted to tell her how good she felt, but that would require me to stop kissing her. Not happening.

I darted my tongue across her lips once more, urging her to open for me. There could've been a full-on firefight outside, but I could only focus on the woman in my arms. Keeping her safe, keeping her with me. With a soft sigh, her lips parted. I took the chance I'd been given and caressed her tongue with mine. The sweet moan that lofted from her lungs was a sound that I would never be able to forget. I delved deeper, tasting her, making some small part of her mine, and giving her a piece of me in return.

She let go and wrapped her arms around my neck, giving herself to this moment, sharing it only with me. I placed my free hand at her throat, her soft skin heaven on my fingertips. Would the rest of her be even softer? Everything inside me was already keyed up, but that thought was like kerosene on an unrelenting blaze. I wanted more, so much more from her, and the way she clung to me told me that she wanted it, too.

A creak, followed by blinding light, and then Porter's voice, "What the hell, you two?"

Arabella broke our kiss, her pouty lips luscious even in the low light. "Is it clear?"

I didn't let her out of my hold. Porter be damned.

"My guys are chasing someone through the woods right now. It has to be the shooter. But stay low just in case." He held the door open, using it as a shield the same way Arabella had suggested earlier.

"Benton?" Arabella gave me an expectant look.

"You have to let her go, you dope." Porter grinned.

I released her, and she hurried up the stairs.

"I think you're going to need a minute." Porter made a show of glancing at my crotch. "Wouldn't want to take a bullet in the boner."

"Fuck off." I adjusted my pants and followed Arabella around the side of the storm shelter.

Santa leaned against the structure, one hand at his side where blood soaked a small area of his khaki Sheriff's deputy uniform.

"How bad is it?" Arabella knelt next to him.

"Just grazed me."

"Right in the old bowl full of jelly." Porter cocked his head to the side as a now-familiar siren pierced the chilly air. "You'll be fixed up in no time."

Santa, though pale, still managed a smile. "I'm the first Morrison County deputy to be shot in the line of duty since the 70s."

"You're right, Santa." Porter patted him on the shoulder. "You're a big fucking deal."

Arabella scanned the tree line. "Any idea where the shot came from?"

"Nope." Porter pointed in a wide, useless arc. "Somewhere over there."

"We lost him." A voice crackled through Porter's radio. "He may have already hit the highway by now."

"Damnit!" Arabella rose, any hint of her earlier softness gone. "Let's get those boxes and get back to town. Whatever is in them is the key to this mess." She kept her eyes on the trees. "We have to figure it out before the next body drops."

* * *

CHARLOTTE STARED as Porter and I carried the banker's boxes into the police station. I'd called her down to the station. We couldn't risk leaving her unprotected at my place, not to mention she wanted in on the investigation.

The officer at the front desk breathed a sigh of relief as Arabella strode in. "Ms. King here tried to argue her way into your office. Garvey's too."

"It's all right, Helen. The Kings are helping me with the investigation."

"Logan shot, a deputy shot, the Chief busy with Lina— it's like the whole place is coming down around us." Helen, an older woman with a flustered air blanched. "Has there been someone else? Another murder."

"No, I think we have plenty, don't you?" Arabella hurried past and pulled open a set of double doors to an office area.

"What are those?" Charlotte tapped my box as we followed Arabella past the reception desk.

"Files from the judge's place. One of them is from the firm." I hefted the box a little higher as Arabella led us to a conference room to the right.

"Maybe we should have gone to my office." Porter frowned at the peeling dry erase board and the pock-marked table. "Why do I have such better stuff?"

"Because you get way more funding from the county and the state." Arabella pulled a chair across the dull tile floor and sat down. "We get whatever the town gives us, which isn't much."

"Right." Porter examined one of the plastic chairs and sat.

"Why did Judge Ingles have stuff from the firm?" Charlotte opened her laptop and searched the wall for an outlet.

"Either Dad gave it to him or he took it." I sank into another one of the chairs, this one with a worn cushion.

Arabella propped the door open with a brick that seemed to be sitting outside the room for just that purpose. "Helen! Can you brew us some coffee?"

"Sure thing," Helen yelled back.

No one else was in the office. "When do you think Chief Garvey will be back?" I pulled a chunk of folders from the firm box, while Charlotte took the other half and set them in front of her.

"With Lina awake? I don't know. He may not come back today." Arabella glanced at a clock above the white board. It was ten minutes slow. "I've got a few hours to work with before bedtime. Let's—"

"You're going to *bed*?" Porter gawked at her. "There's a killer on the loose and you're—"

I kicked his chair. "Bedtime for her daughter, you idiot. She's got to go put Vivi to bed."

"Oh." He grinned sheepishly. "My bad, Arabella. I forgot you had that little one."

"It's fine." She grabbed a dry erase marker and began writing names on the board. My father's name materialized at the top of a circle. Light Eyes and Judge Ingles shared a spot in the center.

"Let's see what we have here." Charlotte set down her laptop bag and flipped open the first folder.

I grabbed one and did the same as Porter drummed his index fingers on the table. The noise quickly became maddening.

"Try the laptop." I pulled it from the box and slid it to Porter.

He opened it as I started combing through the file. Documents concerning my subdivision—specifically receipts—lay inside. I flipped through them. Plenty of them were from businesses in and around Azalea. But they were all paid in cash. Invoices from construction firms had been paid in cash, as well. It wasn't normal practice, not when it came to such large expenditures. But the invoices had been broken up over weeks, so each payment didn't seem so damning.

"These are from a New Jersey business. Ray's Roofing." Charlotte pulled out her phone, her thumbs flying. After a few moments, she said, "It's not a thing. At least not in the town listed on the receipt for work done."

I flipped back a few pages. "For roofing, right?"

"Yeah."

"What lot is that receipt for?"

"This is lots four and five—the ones around the corner from your place with that big oak tree between them."

Pulling out a document, I slid it over to her. "Same here."

She picked up the paper. "This is for Gary's Roofing. Lots four and five."

"They double billed for costs." I thumbed through some more records. "It's like they built the subdivision twice over. One set of bills getting paid with cash. The other set entirely make believe."

Arabella stopped writing. "They did the fake ones to defray tax costs, right?"

"Yeah, that has to be it." I grabbed another manila folder. "The real work would get paid for in cash, which is a smart way to wash dirty money."

"How does money get dirty, exactly?" Porter stared at the laptop screen.

"It's not physically dirty, it's—"

"I *know* that."

I continued, "It's money that doesn't have an explanation. Like money made selling drugs or prostitutes or underground gambling operations. Illegal money that doesn't get reported to the IRS. Because it isn't reported—and it's all cash—it's dirty. And because it's dirty, it can't be used."

"Why not?" Porter cocked his head to the side, likely imagining a Scrooge McDuck pool of cash and wondering why he couldn't spend it.

Arabella jumped in. "Because if you went and bought, let's say, a house for half a million bucks or even a hundred thousand dollars, you can't show up to the closing with all that in cash. The seller wouldn't accept it because the IRS would be all over them and you, wanting to know where that money came from. That kind of money can't just appear out of thin air without raising questions."

"Right." I nodded. "The only way to use it is to go to businesses that only take cash. But you can't live like that, not anymore. You need credit cards and bank accounts and an entire electronic trail to purchase houses or real estate or fancy cars or that yacht you've had your eye on. If you tried to buy those things with unaccounted-for cash, the IRS would swoop in and bust you in no time. If you went to your bank and tried to deposit half a million in unaccounted-for cash, the IRS would get you there, too. Dirty money. To make it clean, you've got to give it a history, get it into the banking system steadily. Then it's laundered."

"So, Dad and Judge Ingles were washing the money by getting it into banks without raising suspicion?" Porter's eyebrows drew together as he followed along.

"Looks like it. The New Jersey people would send the money, all dirty cash, to Judge Ingles and Dad. Then they'd take that money and pay for what they could in cash. Like the subdivision improvements or—"

"The shitty burger joint's renovation." Charlotte held up a thick file. "Same thing. Two sets of receipts. There's the florist here as well as the antique shop and a few more businesses."

Porter cocked his head to the side. "But if they paid the dirty money for stuff, how did they get clean money back?"

Arabella leaned over my shoulder and studied the documents. "When Benton and his neighbors bought their houses. They paid clean money for them. That entire subdivision is a giant cash-washing machine. When Letty made money on flower sales. When the burger place got customers. Those last two are heavy cash businesses. But their actual operations likely served more as a tax harbor than anything else. No way they made more than they spent."

"Oh." Porter nodded as if he grasped it all, but I wasn't so sure.

"Even with all that, there must be more somewhere. Something we're missing. Those things were somewhat finite. The subdivision was built. The businesses aren't churning much money. There's something else." Arabella returned to the board, writing out clues, names, and bits of information.

I settled in to review every piece of paper I could get my hands on. "We're going to need more coffee."

ARABELLA

"Bennon?" Vivi looked up at me with her big eyes.

"He's working on something." I stroked my hand down her hair and placed the fourth story of the evening on her bedside table. Mom guilt.

"He want to come see me?"

"Of course." I couldn't help but smile. "He did, but we're trying to fix something, and it's taking a lot of extra work."

"That why you not home?" She hugged her unicorn stuffie tight.

"Right."

She dropped her voice. "Sarah Ellen said people got dead. She said you were supposed to find who made them get dead." Her eyes widened. "Are you going to get dead?"

I took a breath as the gut punch resonated through me. "No, sweetheart. I won't get dead." I kissed her hair.

"Don't get dead, Mommy." She threw her arms around me and squeezed. "Please."

I hugged her and swayed back and forth, rocking her slowly the way I used to do when I could cradle her in my arms. "Nothing's going to happen." I kissed her crown again, then pulled the sheet over her as she lay down.

"Promise?" She still had round cheeks, the baby not completely faded from her. I could still kiss her cheeks and hug her until she protested and informed me she was a big girl. Sassy and full of heart. I hoped she'd never change.

"I promise." I dropped another kiss on her nose and stood. "Now get to sleep. School in the morning."

"Will you take me?"

"I'll try to, baby."

"Bring Bennon?" A sly smile twisted her cherub lips.

"I don't think so."

"Bring Bennon." The question was gone, replaced with a command.

"I'll think about it. Now go on and get some sleep." I flipped the light off and met Mom in the hall.

"You can't go back out there." She put a hand on her hip, her fragile frame even smaller in the dimly lit living room.

"I have to." I swept my hair back and grabbed a pony-tail holder from the odds and ends drawer just inside the kitchen.

"No, you don't. What you have to do is be here to raise that baby. Vivi needs you. *Alive*." Her scolding felt just as rough as it had when I was an unruly teenager. She could somehow manage to put four buckets of guilt into a thimbleful of words.

"Mom, this is my job. I'm the one—"

She grabbed my chin and tilted my face down to hers, her lips pressed in a thin line and her eyes searching my forehead.

"What are you doing?" I finished tying my hair back.

"Looking for a lightning scar, since you clearly think you're the chosen one."

"Oh my god, Mom!" I gently pushed her hand away, then skirted the edge of the couch to escape her. "You've been watching Harry Potter too much with Vivi. This is what I do, okay? I'm going to solve this case and make the city safe for us."

"We *are* safe. It's the rich bastards around here that keep winding up dead."

"What, Mom, what?" My fatigue began to boil over into anger. "You just want me to let them get picked off one by one and do nothing to stop it?"

"They aren't us."

"I promised to protect and serve everyone in Azalea, not just us!"

"They don't give a damn about you! They don't need you. Vivi does. I do. Those people were happy to lord their money over us—over you—the whole time you were growing up, and even after. Why are you so desperate to sacrifice yourself for them?"

"It's not about us versus them!" I slammed my hand on the back of the couch. "It's about doing what's right. It's about—"

"Mommy?" Vivi's voice stopped me cold.

"It's all right, baby. Go to sleep. Love you." I kept my voice light as I glared at Mom.

"She's what matters. Not the Kings, not any of them."

She shook her head, a rusty sigh escaping her scarred lungs, the fight leaving her like rain falling from a leaf.

"Don't you think I know that? I would do anything for her. Anything. But I have to take care of this case. I can't let a killer slip through my fingers. I thought you'd—"

She coughed, tried to play it off, then went into a full-on coughing fit. I leaned down and pushed the small cart with her oxygen tank over to the sofa. "Sit."

Still coughing—deep, gut-wrenching sounds that reminded me the cancer was one bad scan away—she sank to the cushion. I helped her wrap the tubing around her ears and turned on the air. The coughing fit subsided, and she took several deep breaths through her nose.

Her eyes watered, but I couldn't tell if it was from coughing or fighting. She took my hand, and I sat next to her.

"I'm just so afraid." Her voice softened. "Losing you. I couldn't bear—" Her voice broke, and a piece of me broke with it.

"You aren't going to lose me." I squeezed her hand. "I promise."

"You can't promise that, Belly."

"I can. I'm not going to put myself in danger. But I am going to solve this case. I'm close, Mom. So close. I need a little more time, a lot more coffee, and just one break."

"You need rest."

I gave her hand another squeeze and rose. "Not tonight. I'm almost there."

She leaned back, her breathing calming. "You always were a stubborn little devil."

"Some things don't change."

"They sure don't, since Vivi's just like you. Maybe even worse. Though you're a hard one to top."

I walked to the door and shrugged on my coat. "I love you too, Mom."

* * *

I RUBBED my eyes as the time ticked over into the a.m. Papers were spread all over the conference table, and the whiteboard was covered with data on properties, transactions, business fronts, and a host of other dirty dealings.

Instead of Judge Ingles at the center of the web, I'd changed it to BRLC, LLC. That was the most recent shell corporation that had been used to purchase several large tracts of land in the county.

"Here's another." Charlotte held up a document. "The two hundred acres near the Tillman farm. Sold by CLRB to BRLC just six months ago for a high sum, along with another phony cashier's check drawn on a bank that doesn't exist. But it was all cash. Just like all the rest. Judge Ingles signed off on the sale as judge of probate and recorded it in the county records to hide it in plain sight."

"How many times has it changed hands?"

"This is the…" She counted up tally marks on her legal pad. "Fifteenth time in the past three years."

Porter snored lightly at the table, his forehead resting on his arms. His job had been to crack the password on the laptop we'd found. He gave up after about ten minutes, played on his phone, then promptly fell asleep while pretending he was studying some papers.

Over the past hours, the rest of us had discovered a

vast scheme to launder money by buying and selling county properties over and over again, from one shell corporation to the next. Randall King prepared the paperwork, Judge Ingles signed off on the transfers, and the money changed hands without anyone raising an eyebrow. Millions of dollars had been funneled through these transactions, all unbeknownst to anyone except the few who were in on it. But we couldn't pinpoint the organization behind it. Only that whoever, or whatever, it was, started with a 'C.' Charlotte's cursory research on her laptop turned up a Colletti syndicate that ran game up and down the New Jersey coast. An outfit of career criminals, drug dealers, and illegal gambling rings—they were our prime suspect.

The Colletti Family was on the board with a big question mark. I finished writing the code from Benton's business card—the one I'd found in Letty's hand—on the board beside it. Another snippet whose relevance floated just out of reach. Strain ached along my shoulders and down my back. I needed a break. We all did.

I capped the marker. "I'm going for some air. Let's all take a break."

Charlotte grunted and continued poring over a sheaf of documents.

Benton rose and stretched. "I could use a reprieve, if only for a minute."

"Don't go far. Killer on the loose and all that." Charlotte waved a document at us as we left her to it.

I reached over my head, trying to ease the tension in my shoulders.

"I'd offer you a massage, but that would be pervy and

all." Benton shot me a smile, though his eyes wore the same tired look mine did.

It didn't sound pervy at all. Heavenly? Yes. But I couldn't go there with him. I'd already gone too far with that kiss. My heart kicked up a notch at the memory, tiny electrical currents firing along my skin. Where had he learned to kiss like that?

"What are you thinking?" He pinned me with his gaze.

The heat in my face jumped to four-alarm fire status. "About the case."

"Mmmhmm." He pushed open the door ahead of us. It led into a small courtyard—the only smoking area at the police station—that was sheltered from view.

The brisk air should have been refreshing. Instead, I sank onto the nearest concrete bench, too many worries eating away at me.

Benton sat next to me, and when he put his arm around my shoulders, I didn't shrug him off. He was warm, smelled good despite our long day, and had a habit of giving me what I needed right when I needed it. Like that moment.

"Did Vivi miss me, at least?"

I snorted. "She gave me hell. Wants to see you in the morning, in her office, bright and early."

He laughed. "She's a real hard-ass, that one."

"I know." I leaned against him and rested my head on his shoulder. Whatever propriety I had was gone, collapsed under the load of needing human comfort—and needing it from one person in particular.

He kissed my hair. I closed my eyes.

"We're going to solve this." His warm breath tickled along my scalp. "I promise."

I wanted to believe him. But I was a small-town cop with no resources. Porter's men were spread out across the county, but there was too much area to cover. The man with the light eyes had slipped through my fingers, just like Judge Ingles.

"We know what's going on now. We know who was involved."

"It had to be a chunk of money. That's what your father had in the safe." I chewed my lip. "Well, what he was *supposed* to have in the safe."

"Agree." He wrapped his other arm around me, pulling me against his chest.

God, he smelled good. The only man I got this close to was Logan, and he always reeked of tobacco, whiskey, and a late night at the bar.

"We'll find the money."

"Then what?" I'd been asking myself that question ever since I formed the theory on the money laundering. Would the man with the light eyes stop if I found it before he did? Or would he come after it, no matter what?

"Hookers and blow?"

I laughed, the sound rising from deep in my belly. Pulling back, I looked up at him.

His smile was gorgeous, lighting up his eyes. His gaze flicked to my lips. "I didn't ask last time, but would you mind if I—"

"Kiss me."

His lips were sudden, firm but not rough. I let myself have this little piece of delight in the midst of darkness.

Opening my mouth, I relished his tongue as it swept inside. Each caress, each touch between us had me clutching him tighter. Then I ran one hand through his hair, mussing it and sifting through the soft strands.

He groaned, the sound tickling against my lips as he slanted his mouth over mine. I was hungry for him, wrapping my arms around his neck as he pulled me into his lap. One large palm on my hip, he ran the other through my hair, his fingertips teasing the base of my neck. Warm, attentive, and spine-tingling—all words I wouldn't have associated with him when we met. But now, he was all those things to me and more.

Goosebumps raced across my skin as his fingers edged beneath my shirt, the soft pads of his fingers grazing along my waist. Such a simple touch, it wound the coil of delicious tension inside me even tighter. I wanted to feel all of him, run my hands along his perfect jaw and find out what he looked like shirtless…and pants-less. Wicked thoughts, too many to count, filled my headspace.

He broke the kiss, and I took a gulp of cold air as he trailed his lips down my neck. I gripped his shoulders, holding on while he moved his hand fully under my shirt, his fingers spread along my side. The heat from his hand warmed me everywhere until I wriggled on his lap, his lips pressed to the skin at my open collar.

"If you keep doing that…" His voice was polished marble.

I wriggled again, his hard length apparent beneath my thigh. "Inside, first room on the right."

He bolted up, me in his arms and dashed to the door.

"Fuck!" He opened it, then accidentally kicked it shut, then opened it again.

I laughed as he barreled into the evidence room, a couple of desks in the front, and all the evidence locked in a separate area behind them.

"Here?" He glanced around.

"It's all I have, but if you'd rather wait—"

He claimed my lips again as he set me on the closest desk, a log book falling flat on the floor and a few pens rolling away. His hands were at my chest, the buttons of my top undone in record time. I yanked his shirt free from his pants and didn't bother with buttons. Running my hands beneath his shirt, I explored his stomach, his chest, the hard planes of his body.

"Fuck." He bit my neck, then lowered his mouth to my breast. With a quick pull, he displaced the cup, my hard nipple popping free.

I moaned as his warm mouth encircled it, his hands going to my waist and unbuttoning my pants. Running my hands through his hair, I threw my head back as he feasted on me, each touch another shot of jet fuel on the fire. Pulling my bra the rest of the way down, he cupped my other breast, giving it the same attention and heightening my desire.

With undeniable haste, I scrabbled at his fly. I popped the button, then unzipped his pants. When my hand brushed against his hard length, he groaned against my breast. Reaching inside his boxers, my fingers couldn't close around him.

He straightened, pressing me to him with one hand while using the other to shuck my jeans. I kicked them off, my shoes dropping to the floor, until I wore only my bra and panties. With a steady grip, he pulled my panties down my thighs, his eyes on mine as he knelt and eased them all the way off.

Standing again, he looked at me with an intensity that sent my heart into a frenzied pace. Like a rabbit being chased, I couldn't slow this down. There was no time-out, nothing that could stop us.

"Benton." I spread my legs wide.

He gripped my ass and yanked me to the edge of the desk, his cock pressing against my slick core. "Damn, Arabella. Just damn." He rubbed his cock against me, his lips finding mine again as my clit began to buzz with each stroke from him.

I bit his lower lip, then pulled back, my hand on his cheek. "I-I haven't done this in a long time." God, it was embarrassing to hear it out loud.

"Neither have I." He pressed his forehead to mine. "Years, honestly."

His confession soothed the rough edges of my heart. "You think we remember how?" I smiled and brushed my lips against his.

"I stick it in your belly button, right?"

I laughed, the worry rolling away from me like ocean waves. "Just when I think I have you figured out, you hit me with something new."

He pressed his thumb beneath my chin gently, tilting my face up to his. "I hope you like what you find."

The vulnerability in his eyes matched my own. I moved my hips, rubbing my slick folds against him. "So far, so good."

"Shit," he hissed, one hand going to my hair, the other gripping my hip. "Let's see if I can't surprise you a little more."

I arched my back and spread my legs wide, every part of me desperate to feel him moving inside me. "Give it your best shot."

He reached down and positioned himself at my entrance. With a push, his head eased inside.

I gasped as a ripple of delicious sensation coursed through me. "More."

He pushed again, his thick cock hitting me in all the right places, but our bodies still weren't flush. God, there was more. "I need to see you." I yanked at his shirt.

He reached behind his head, grabbed the shirt, and pulled it over. The broad expanse of his chest, the center dusted with dark hair, was made for my mouth. I leaned up and nipped at him above his nipple.

"Christ!" He surged the rest of the way inside me. "Are you all right?" He stilled.

It pinched, but that quickly subsided. I reached behind me and unclasped my bra. He pressed me to him, one strong arm around my back, the other at my hip. With a smooth movement, he pulled out, then moved back in.

I gasped and clung to him. "More."

Another thrust, then another, and then more. Skin on skin the wet sounds from between my thighs were loud in the small room. I wrapped my legs around his waist as he filled me again and again, our bodies working in unison. He couldn't keep his lips off me, his kiss saturating me with warmth as his body propelled me into a frenzy of need.

My hips worked with him, grinding my clit against him with each stroke. His fingers dug into my hips, likely leaving bruises. I didn't care, just as long as he didn't stop. I chased my release, my tongue tangled with his, my hard nipples brushing against his chest. Each slap of skin heightened my arousal until I was near the precipice.

"I'm close," I breathed. Spreading wider, I increased the friction between us.

He thrust harder. "I want to feel you coming around my cock."

I think my eyes rolled back in my head as he sucked the skin along my throat. "I'm—" The orgasm rushed through me, toppling anything I'd ever felt before. I couldn't think, could barely breathe, as everything inside me constricted and then burst outward. Each wave of pleasure rolled into the next. I must have been loud, because Benton pressed his palm over my mouth, his cock still working me relentlessly as I squeezed him.

"It's too good." He pulled out. Hot spurts of come coated my stomach as his cock jerked against me. The illicit sight added to my pleasure, my orgasm rolling a few more times before subsiding into pleasant aftershocks.

He rested his palms on the desk next to me, sweat sticking dark hair to his forehead. I ran my hand through it, pushing it back.

"Sorry I couldn't hold it." He looked at me from under his eyebrows.

"You were perfect."

"No, you." He dipped his head down and nuzzled my breasts. "So beautiful when you come. Beautiful all the time, really."

He'd already melted my body into a puddle, and he seemed to be going for my heart.

He straightened and glanced at my stomach. "Let me, um—" He turned and gave me a view of his toned ass. "Find you some tissues."

"Look in the bottom left drawer." I pointed to the other desk as he pulled up his pants and obscured my view.

"Got it." He came back with a box of cheap tissues, but they'd do the job.

Once I was cleaned up, we both got dressed. Unspoken words piled up between us like layers of snow as we pulled on our clothes and righted ourselves.

I reached for the door handle, but he pulled me back.

"Hey." He brushed my hair behind my ears. "I don't know what that meant to you. And I don't want to pressure you." He brushed his thumb along my cheek. "But I want more. Do with that what you will." He placed a soft kiss on my lips, then opened the door for me.

I had to get away from him before my heart turned to goo, and made a mistake like telling him that I wanted more, too. Stepping into the hall, I stumbled into someone's back.

Logan turned around, an orthopedic boot on his leg. "There you are. I've been looking—"

I knew the exact moment he looked behind me and saw Benton, because that's when everything went to hell.

29

BENTON

*F*or a guy with a gunshot wound, Logan could move damn fast. He careened toward me, one fist shooting out blindly toward my face.

I ducked back. "Whoa!"

"Logan!" Arabella grabbed the back of his shirt. "What the hell are you doing?"

"I'm going to rip this motherfucker apart. That's what I'm doing." He powered forward, rage twisting his haggard face.

Easily feinting to his left, I avoided his swings. I could have knocked him flat with a simple sweep of his bad leg, but I wasn't that guy.

"Let go, Arabella." He stopped, breathing heavily.

"Not until you stop acting like a lunatic."

"You let this asshole touch you." He turned toward her with a wobble. "This asshole who thinks you aren't good enough to lick his shoe."

"What I do is none of your business, Logan." Her tone sliced through the air like a knife.

283

"He doesn't give a shit about you. He's just another rich douche bag who thinks—"

"I'm done talking about this." Arabella crossed her arms over her stomach. "And if you're done with this macho pissing contest, we have work to do." She turned on her heel and strode down the hall.

Logan pinned me with a glare. I returned it, though I didn't make a move toward him. It would have been gratifying to beat him senseless, but it would piss Arabella off, and I figured it was best that I left that up to Logan.

He jabbed his finger at me. "You aren't fooling me, college boy."

"I haven't been in college for a decade. You need new material." I brushed past him, giving him a little more shoulder than necessary.

He stayed upright, and his clunky steps echoed behind me as I followed Arabella to the conference room.

She was already back at the board, the marker in her hand. I yanked my chair out and sat, the movement waking Porter from his nap.

"What'd I miss?" He stretched and yawned.

I didn't respond. I was too busy unpacking what had just happened between Arabella and me. Just the memory of her on that desk had blood rushing to parts south. I shifted in my seat and tried to get a handle on the tangle of emotions inside me. Logic tried to have its say, reminding me that I was in the midst of a stressful and traumatic situation, which could be the reason for my unexpected feelings for Arabella. But that reasoning was hollow. There was something far deeper that resonated between us.

Logan limped in and collapsed in a chair next to Porter. He tried to cover his huffing and puffing with a cough, but he was clearly winded. Good. Maybe he would hold off on any more attacks.

"What's that number?" Porter stared at the digits from the card in Letty's hand.

"We don't know." Arabella backed up a step. "Could be the digits for an electronic safe, maybe some sort of code. Too many digits for coordinates, too many digits for an analog safe—it doesn't fit anything we can find on the Internet."

I had the urge to pull her into my lap.

She pointed at it. "It was written on the card Letty had in her hand when she was killed."

"It's familiar." Porter leaned back and rubbed the stubble along his jaw.

Everyone in the room seemed to stop breathing and stare at him.

"Familiar how?" Arabella urged.

Porter stared for a few more moments. "It'll come to me. Give me a minute."

Charlotte shook her head and returned to her papers. "Typical."

"Let me think." Porter let his head loll on his shoulders, his eyes clenched shut in concentration.

Arabella hadn't moved, her attention on Porter. I grabbed another file. More likely than not, Porter had no idea what the number was. I had faith in my brother, but not on subjects involving numbers, math, or clues in a murder investigation.

"Logan, how's your leg?" Charlotte asked from her seat on the floor.

"Apparently well enough to start a stupid fight," Arabella snapped.

"Huh?" Charlotte looked up from her papers.

"Nothing." Arabella returned to the board.

Logan glowered and swung his leg up on the chair next to him. "It's fine. I'll heal up in no time. Thanks for asking. At least someone around here cares."

Arabella whirled on him. "You're being a baby. A jealous, stupid baby!"

"Yeah?" He leaned forward. "I can't say what you're being in mixed company."

"That's enough." I stayed in my seat, my hands clasped in front of me. "You say another word to her like that and I will toss your sorry ass out of here."

"You and what army, prick? I don't care if my leg is fucked up, I can still kick your ass six ways from Sunday."

"Try me." I pushed my chair back and rose. His jealousy routine was going to come to a halt, and I couldn't wait to be the one to end it.

"Knock it off, both of you." Arabella stepped between us.

"If you're going to fight, do it outside." Charlotte motioned to various stacks of papers. "If you mess up my property research, I might just shoot the both of you."

Logan struggled to his feet. "I'd be happy to take this piece of shit outside. Come—"

"Property research." Porter rocketed to his feet, ignored the simmering tension, and walked to the board. He tapped the numbers from Letty Cline. "Property research!" His triumphant tone momentarily stunned the rest of us.

"The fuck is wrong with your brother?" Logan leaned back in his chair.

"Don't you see?" Porter snatched the marker from Arabella and drew dashes between a few of the numbers. "I think that one goes there. I don't remember all the way. Anyway, you get the idea, right?" He snapped the lid back on the marker.

"Porter, if you don't explain what you're on about, I may strangle you." Charlotte rubbed her eyes.

"It's a place." He tossed the marker in the air and caught it.

"No, I told you, too many digits to be coordinates." Arabella frowned.

"Not coordinates." Porter walked to the table and pulled Charlotte's laptop over to him. "When I was working as a process server, I had to find people on properties all over the state. There's a county database with addresses and stuff for property taxes, crap like that, but those are county-specific."

"So?" I scooted over to see what he was typing.

"So, when you have the correct credentials." He grinned. "Sheriff and all. There's another database that the state maintains on properties. It's for taxes, too. But you can only get into it if you are a certain sort of state employee."

"Like you?"

"Actually, no." He pulled up a login screen and typed in his personal email address. "It has a listing of every property in Mississippi, and it uses its own number identification thing. Something to do with how the revenue department evaluates this or that or something or other. Not sure. But it's an internal state system. The number on Letty's card is from there."

"If the system's only available to a handful of state employees, how did you get into it?"

His grin grew even wider. "When I was a process server, there was this hot clerk in Jackson at the Secretary of State's office—that's who keeps the records. And let's just say I took her out for a nice dinner, let her get some special treatment from the prince, and then—"

"The prince?" Arabella cocked her head to the side.

I winced as she fell right into his trap. He'd concocted this line when we were teens, and he'd used it on every unsuspecting female since then.

"The prince, Arabella. I'm the King, so the big bastard down below, he's the prince."

Arabella rolled her eyes.

"You're an idiot." I drummed my fingers on the table. "What's the password?"

"Not sure." He tried something.

Error.

Tried something else.

Error. And a little message popped up that he only had two more tries before he was locked out.

"Slow down." Arabella's voice kicked up an octave.

"Concentrate." I clasped my fingers together.

"Let me try—" He typed deliberately, then hit enter.

Error.

"Think, Porter!" Nothing in the history of humankind

could stress a person out more than a screen saying a lockout was imminent.

"I am! I tried all my usual ones. Prince69. BigPrince. MegaPrince."

"I've never been happier that I wasn't born with a dick than I am at this very second." Charlotte stood and crowded behind Arabella and me.

"Shh." Porter's brow furrowed. "I'm trying to think."

He typed a few letters, then erased them.

"Nothing comes to mind?" I wiped my sweat mustache.

"I've got one more I use sometimes, yeah. But I don't know if I capitalize it or not on this one."

"What happens if it locks us out?" Arabella peered around Porter.

"I don't know. It just says contact tech support, but they won't be open until the morning."

"Fuck." Logan winced as he shifted in his chair.

"You can do this, Porter." I tried for a supportive tone.

"Right. I got this." He took a deep breath and typed slowly. His finger hovered over the Enter button as we held our breath.

Hesitating for a moment, he swallowed audibly, then clicked the key. The screen began to redirect.

"I'm in!" Porter clenched his fist. "Yes!"

I clapped him on the back right when the words "Error! Contact technical support to reset your password" appeared onscreen.

## 30

ARABELLA

"Come on, baby. I need you."

I stared at Porter as he sweet talked the clerk from the Secretary of State's office.

"I know it's late. I know, but I need your help." His voice was low and smooth. It was likely the same voice he'd used to trick the clerk into helping him the first time. "I haven't been in Jackson. That's the only reason why—" He leaned back in his chair, balancing on the rear legs. "No, baby. I swear. If I had been in Jackson, I would have called you up first thing."

Logan grunted as he tried to reposition his leg.

"Does it hurt bad?" I threw him a bone, even though I was still pissed at him for butting into whatever was going on between Benton and me.

"It's been better. But at least I'll have a story to tell about being shot in the line of duty." A ghost of Logan's cocky smile crossed his lips.

"Maybe you should go home. Get some rest."

"No way. Not when we're this close."

Porter gripped the edge of the table as he held the phone away from his ear. "*She'll do it,*" he mouthed with a wink.

"Doesn't sound like it." I eyed his phone, a voice still squawking from it.

He put it back to his ear. "You remember that thing I did? That thing with my tongue that had you making squirrel noises?" He paused for a reply. "That's what you're gonna get the next time I'm in Jackson."

Charlotte rose. "If I have to hear any more of this, I will definitely barf." She walked out and pushed through the doors to the lobby.

Benton sat quietly, his ears attuned to Porter's conversation as his eyes followed me while I paced in front of the whiteboard.

Porter tapped a few keys. "Yeah. I'm there. Okay, I can wait." He fell silent, and I pulled a chair over and sat beside him.

Ringing echoed through the squad room. Chief Garvey's phone had been going off every hour or so. I finally asked dispatch who kept calling. It was the mayor and the DA, and I had zero interest in talking to either of them. I'd save that for Chief Garvey when he returned.

Porter tapped a few more keys. "That's it. Thank you so much, baby. I'll be seeing you soon. Keep it warm for me."

Benton held up his hand and circled his finger in a "hurry up" motion. Porter said his goodbyes, then got down to business on the laptop, his thick fingers moving carefully.

"It was Prince69 all along. I should have known that

one." He clicked on a link to the property database, then clicked to search by unique identifier. "Okay, what's the number?"

I read off the code from the board for him. When he hit enter, I held my breath.

"We got one hit." He pointed to the sole search result.

"What is it?" Benton leaned closer.

Porter clicked on the tab. "It's a piece of property here in the county. A big plot of land, mostly timber."

Charlotte hurried back in. "Did you get it?"

"Yeah." I scoured the property information until I came to a number that matched the local county plat designations. "Charlotte, see which property matches 658-342-33."

She plopped on the floor and began searching through her records.

"It looks like this one stayed in the name of the original LLC." Benton pulled the laptop closer to him. "Why didn't they buy and sell this one like the others?"

I stood and began pacing in front of the board again. "Maybe to fly under the radar with this one? Maybe there's something there that they didn't want looked at."

"I've got it." Charlotte pulled a stapled packet of documents from one of her piles. "It looks like Dad bought it at a tax foreclosure sale a few years ago."

My hackles rose as more puzzle pieces snapped into place. "Did it originally belong to Theodore Brand?"

She flipped the page. "That's right. He was the previous owner. How did you know?"

I snapped off the top of the marker and wrote the property information beneath the state identifier. "I interviewed Mr. Brand as a possible suspect in the murders. I didn't think he was our guy."

"You should have let me play bad cop with him." Logan shook his head.

"No. I still don't think he's our guy." I tossed down the marker. "But I overlooked the importance of his property. He lost it in a tax foreclosure, and Randall King bought it out from under him. When I went out to speak to Brand about it, he said that he'd attempted to go out to the property once he'd gotten out of prison, but there was a new gate along the front road. That tipped him off to the change in ownership. When he found out about the tax sale, he went to Randall, who then got a restraining order against him from Judge Ingles. After that, Brand let it drop. He told me he couldn't afford to go back to prison, especially when, at the time, he had a daughter on the way. So, Judge Ingles and Randall King got the property free and clear for a pittance and managed to shut Brand up while they were at it." I walked into the main squad room and grabbed my jacket and gun from my desk.

"Hold up." Benton followed at my heels. "We need some sort of plan."

"The plan is to get out to that property, find the man with the light eyes and Judge Ingles, arrest them, and make sure no one else dies." I shrugged on my jacket.

"I'm coming." Logan limped from the conference room.

"No. You need to stay here. I want you to call all the guys we got—pull Brody and everyone else—and send them out to the property. Tell them to give me a half-hour head start to keep it quiet, then hang at the entrance and around the edges. Stop anyone they see leaving. I don't want anyone getting away."

"I'm your partner. I should be the one who—"

"You'll just slow me down." I pointed to his leg.

He winced, and I knew I was being an asshole, but it didn't change the fact that I couldn't take him with me.

"We got this." Porter pressed his hat onto his head. "Looks like this is a county matter anyway."

"Arabella, come on." Logan's tone turned pleading.

"Stay here with Charlotte and wait for the chief to come back. When he gets here, let him know what's going on. I expect to be bringing someone in tonight, maybe light eyes, maybe the judge, hopefully both. Get this place ready."

Charlotte leaned on the conference room door frame. "I'm cool with staying here. Guns and danger aren't exactly my strong suit." Her eyes narrowed as she looked at Benton. "But make sure the man who killed our father gets what he deserves."

"I will." He nodded.

I would have given a speech about how we weren't going to engage in vigilante justice, but they wouldn't listen, and I didn't have the time. I'd deal with any issues as they arose. "Let's roll." I strode into the lobby, feeling Logan's fiery gaze on my back the entire way.

The frigid night air hit me like a wall as I walked outside. A cloudless sky overhead was pricked with stars and a low moon.

"I'll ride with you." Benton strode to my cruiser as Porter climbed into his SUV.

I cranked up the car, the engine grumbling to life as I

palmed the cold steering wheel. "This tract is out on route seven. About half an hour away. See if you can pull up some satellite images from Google as we go. The more information we have, the better."

He got to work on his phone as I pulled out of the station parking lot. The streets were deserted, everyone warm in bed on this brisk night. My thoughts wandered to Vivi—the way she always slept with her arms above her head, her sweet breaths steady as she dreamed. She didn't know what sort of night existed beyond the comforting confines of her fluffy blankets. I wanted to keep it that way, to keep her safe and warm and unafraid. Because once you see what lives in the darkness, sleep will never come as easily again.

"Arabella." Benton reached over and took my hand in his. "Are you all right?"

"What do you mean?" I focused on the pavement ahead of us.

"I don't know, you just looked so…lost, there for a second. What were you thinking about?"

His fingers were warm, his gaze even warmer. I'd opened up more to him in a few short days that I had to anyone else in years. But I still couldn't give him what he was asking for—unfettered access to my thoughts, my feelings, my trust. And it wasn't just because of what had happened with Dale. It was more that I didn't have only myself to worry about. Vivi would always be the number one concern in my life.

"Just about the case." Despite my reasoning and my justifications, the lie still tasted sour on my tongue.

"Okay." He didn't sound convinced, but he didn't push.

"The land is mostly pulpwoods with a few marshy acres along the back. Main road is off Route 9. Looks like there's another way over towards Jones Ferry where it hits Route 9 close to the old sawmill."

I let go of his hand and reached for the radio. "Porter, you there?"

"Right behind you." His headlights had followed me steadily out of town.

"Can you go up Jones Ferry Road to get to Route 9? It'll take you a little longer, but you can get onto the property without using the main road."

"Sure thing. I'll creep up and meet y'all in the middle."

"Sounds like a plan." I hung up the mic and gripped the wheel. If I took Benton's hand again, another layer would melt inside me, and I couldn't let that happen. He was already too close.

"Hey." When he said it like that—softly, like he was speaking to me as we lay in a warm bed on a cold night like this—I had to take a breath.

"Yep?" I responded, a little too loudly.

He smiled—even though he was worn out, had a hell of a week, and was on the way to confront his father's killer, he still managed a smile for me. "Everything's going to be fine."

"You can't kill the guy, you know." I let him take my hand again.

He brought it to his lips and blew warm arm between our palms.

"Did you hear me?"

"I did." His lips brushed the back of my hand.

"I mean it. I'd have to arrest you for murder."

"I know." He dropped our hands to his lap and pressed mine between both of his. "I don't intend to kill him. I just want to know the truth."

"So do I."

"And maybe hurt him some."

"Benton—"

"He'll probably try to escape or something. I don't know. If he gets his ass kicked during the attempt, there's nothing wrong with that."

I sighed and turned onto Route 7. "There's plenty wrong with that. I intend to bring him in. Alive. Question him at the station."

"You think he'll talk?"

"Light eyes probably won't. But Judge Ingles, maybe."

"If he's still alive." Benton stared out at the road as we ate up the miles. "I don't see the Colletti family leaving any loose ends down here now that they're winding up their business. Once they get what they came for, the judge is as good as dead."

"I don't understand what started all this. What was the catalyst? Why did your father suddenly decide to play fast and loose with a crime family?"

"No idea." He shook his head. "It doesn't make sense. Dad was always careful." He frowned. "Even more careful than I'd ever suspected. He hid the Lina thing and this entire money laundering charade from me."

"I guess the reason why doesn't matter anymore. It won't bring any of these victims back. Neither the guilty or the innocent." Poor Mrs. Lagner's bulging eyes flashed through my mind. "But I still intend to find out."

"You know what I keep thinking about?"

"What?"

He squeezed my fingers. "Did Dad know that he'd start this domino effect when he did whatever he did? Did he know his actions would lead to all this senseless killing? I keep trying to square the man who'd put all these lives on the line with the man who raised me." His heavy sigh weighed him down. "I still can't."

"He did some bad things, but I can't imagine he wanted Letty to die, or anyone else. Maybe he thought he was going to get away with it. Honestly, that's probably it." I slowed as we passed mile marker 18. "Criminals never think they're going to get caught. They don't consider that chance. That's why they do it."

"It's so odd."

"What?"

"To hear Dad referred to as a criminal."

"Sorry." I glanced at him and wished I could do something to ease the hurt in his eyes. "I really am."

"It's not your fault. It's his." He peered through the darkness, a steep hollow falling away from the road to our right. "We should be almost there."

"Yeah, I think the next curve is the edge—"

"Look out!"

I didn't see the truck until it was crashing into us, pushing us off the road and into the deep, cold woods.

## 31

## BENTON

*a*rabella's scream embedded itself in my head like a bullet. I reached for her as we careened down the wooded embankment, the car glancing off trees, glass shattering, and metal screeching. The car bumped over a fallen log, tilted to the right, then slammed into a tree along the side of a deep ravine. We came to a stop, the car rocking with steam pouring from under the hood.

"Arabella." I grabbed her hand, though it was hard to see her in the dark.

"What the…" She stirred and coughed.

"A truck. It came from behind us, lights off. Are you okay?"

She pulled on her seatbelt, the strap still tight against her chest. "I think so, but I probably have a stripe going across me from this."

"Better a stripe than something worse." I pushed her hair from her face. "You're bleeding."

She turned to me. "Benton." Reaching up, she pressed her palm against my forehead. "You've got a bad cut."

"Damn." I blinked and realized blood had been clouding my vision. "Doesn't matter. We have to go."

She shot a look over her shoulder. "Whoever did that will be coming for us."

An engine idled on the road above us. We needed to get moving.

Arabella unstrapped her seatbelt and felt her pocket. "My phone." She leaned forward and reached beneath her. "I can't find it."

I pulled the shotgun free and leaned down to help her search.

The crack of a shot followed the thunk of a bullet into the trunk of the car.

"Shit!" I grabbed her arm. "Forget the phone. I've got mine."

"Okay." She grabbed the door handle. "Let's go."

I threw my door open and scrambled out.

"Benton! My door's jammed."

Another shot and a chunk of pine tree exploded just a few feet ahead of me. I leaned into the car and grabbed Arabella's upper arms. With a yank, I pulled her across to me. We both tumbled into the dirt, the pine needles not giving enough cushion as I got the wind knocked out of me.

"Come on." She crawled around to the front of the car.

I followed as another shot shattered the night.

"We have to get to the bottom of this ravine. That'll give us enough cover to cut across toward the property." Arabella wiped her sleeve across my forehead. "I have a first aid kit, but it's in the trunk."

"It's not worth it. I can barely feel it." I gingerly felt around the cut at my hairline. "It's just bleeding a lot because of where it is. Hang on, I need to tell Porter." I pulled out my phone.

Another shot thudded into metal.

"Hurry. The longer we sit here, the easier it will be for him to pick us off."

With only one bar, I speed dialed Porter.

"Yeah?" Country music blared in the background, then quieted.

"There's a shooter out here on Highway 9 near the main entrance to the property. He ran us off the road, and we're on the run through the woods. Send whatever deputies you have available."

"All I heard—shooter—woods…"

"Porter." I spoke hard into the phone, as if that would help with connectivity.

"Can't hear…"

"Goddammit Porter, we need help!"

"Can't hear—damn—saying. Fuck it, I'm going to send deputies over that way." The one moment of clarity ended as my service died.

Arabella nodded. "Let's go." She pulled her pistol. "I'm going to lay down some covering fire. Hopefully, he'll hide and we can get far enough away. Ready?"

"As I'll ever be." I hefted the shotgun as my heartbeat surged on pure adrenaline.

"On three." She maneuvered to the edge of the car and pointed her pistol up the slope. "One, two, three."

We darted away from the car as she fired three shots.

The undergrowth yanked at my calves as I rushed into the dark with Arabella keeping up at my side. She fired two more rounds just as a slug kicked up the pine straw in front of me. He was a good shot. Fuck.

"Left!" I hurdled a fallen tree, then turned and caught Arabella as she came over.

We hit the bottom of the hollow and raced away from the wrecked car. A shallow stream ran between fern-covered banks. We slogged through it, keeping a hellish pace until the sides of the ravine grew sharper, rock outcroppings giving us impenetrable cover.

"Jesus, my feet are frozen." Arabella stopped, her hand resting against a mossy stone.

I hustled her around to the side of the rock, then pulled her into my arms. We both shivered, the icy water seeping into our shoes and up our pants.

"The cold may kill us before the shooter does." Her teeth chattered.

"We just have to keep moving. It'll keep us warm."

"Right." She stomped her feet a little, as if to shake some heat back into them.

"I don't think he followed." I wasn't sure, but I thought I'd heard the sound of an engine growing louder, then disappearing.

"If he's smart, he'll loop around onto the property and wait for us to come out of the woods."

"I think it's safe to say he's pretty smart. We just need to be smarter." I gave her one more squeeze then let her go.

"Let's keep going." She pulled her coat together and buttoned it.

I took her hand, and we picked our way along the side of the stream, moonlight glinting off the surface as a frosty wind rattled the dead leaves still left on the trees.

"We're close." She jumped across the water as the landscape flattened out to our right, the stone embankment growing impassable on our left.

"Yeah, satellite showed the trees thinning out at the edge of the property. It looked like they clear cut the center of the pulpwoods a long time ago and kept it clear. Maybe for cattle?"

"Could be." She cast a glance over her shoulder. "Probably some old homestead out here or something. No doubt creepy."

"Let's hope not."

Our footsteps seemed too loud, our puffs of breath too obvious. Sound carried in icy air, the rumble of a log truck from the highway making it all the way to us. But we were still hidden in the woods. No need to get stealthy just yet. We tramped along for fifteen more minutes, our steps growing quieter as tall grass began to fill in the open spaces between the trees.

We passed what was left of a decrepit fence, the timbers long since rotted, a feast for the termites and ants.

"I think we've been on the property for a while, but this is the clearing I saw on the satellite images." I slowed and peered through the dark.

"Let's just stand and listen for a minute." She pulled me behind a thick pine tree, and we moved so we were back to back. The brief respite of warmth was welcome—for her, too, since she leaned against me.

A small rise blocked my view of what was ahead, but I

was scouring the trees back toward the road. If the shooter had come around to cut us off, that's where he'd be. A few minutes passed, my cheeks going numb as my body heat dropped.

"I don't see anything." The words came out on a shiver.

"Me neither." I turned and pulled her into my arms, trying to give her what little bit of warmth I had. "If he was out there, he would've taken a shot by now. I think we're in the clear, at least for the moment."

"Jesus, I should have planned this better." She pressed her nose against my throat; it was even colder than I was.

"We're all running on adrenaline at this point. And you couldn't have planned for some asshole to run us off the road."

"Maybe not, but I should have known he was there. He must have been following us ever since we left Azalea. I was too keyed up to notice." She shook her head as much as she could. "Rookie mistake."

"Stop beating yourself up. I'm pretty sure Chief Garvey is going to do it for you later. Give him a fresh target, why don't you?"

A tired laugh shook her. "You know, when I met you, you were the biggest asshole on the planet. Now, we're huddled up together and you're telling me jokes to cheer me up. How did that even happen?"

"Just lucky I guess."

She snorted. "Come on. Let's keep going."

I kept my head on a swivel as we strode to the top of the rise. After narrowly avoiding an anthill that was bigger than a toddler, I turned my gaze forward.

We topped the rise.

Arabella gasped.

I hefted my shotgun and pulled the trigger.

## 3 2

### ARABELLA

The shotgun blast set off a ringing in my ears as I drew my pistol and fired three rounds at the man with the light eyes. He rolled away from his rifle and scurried behind a beat-up pickup truck parked in front of a large barn. He'd been lying in wait for us, but the rifle must have jammed. Or maybe he'd taken a shot right as Benton fired. It didn't matter. I had to take him down either way.

"Come out with your hands up!" My voice sounded strong, though my heart seemed to shiver in my chest.

There was no cover, so I cut a semi-circle around to the right, my pistol trained on the truck. Benton pumped the shotgun once, a spent shell landing in the grass as a fresh one took its place.

"I said come out!" We kept moving, each step slow, until we got even with the back side of the truck. No one was there.

Benton dropped and peered under it. "He's gone."

When he rose, he held up a finger with a red streak across it. "But one of us winged him."

"He could be in the barn." I checked the bed of the truck, then opened the door. Nothing amiss, other than the fact that it had been wrecked when it ran us off the road.

He peered at the ground and walked past the barn door.

"Benton!" I pressed my back to the sturdy wood as he peeked around the corner.

"He went toward the far tree line. There's more blood over here." He returned to my side and pulled out his phone.

Porter's voice grumbled through the speaker. "Where the fuck are you two?"

"There's a barn. Wasn't in the satellite images. It's pretty new, from the look of it. If you follow the back road—"

"The back road is for shit. Someone put up a concrete barrier. Can't even get around it in the four-wheel drive because it's marshy as fuck. I'm stuck in the fucking mud from trying."

A frustrated roar constrained itself to Benton's throat. It died down, and then he spoke again, "The man with the light eyes is here. He shot at us. Ran us off the road."

"I'll radio the deputies to watch for him."

"He's on foot and injured. On the south side of the property near the main entrance. Send whoever you can onto the property. There's a barn just off the main entrance. And hurry up and get your ass over here!" Benton ended the call and shoved the phone in his pocket.

"We need to check it out." I jerked my chin at the barn. Light shone through a crack in the door.

"I know, but I was hoping Porter would be here to back us up. I mean, it's not like he's the sheriff or anything. This is *just* like him." He sighed.

"We got this, but there's no sense taking stupid risks." I swallowed, my mouth suddenly dry. "If anything goes down, we get the hell out and hunker down until the cavalry gets here."

"I think the cavalry will be dealing with the biggest threat. Light Eyes isn't fucking around. Whoever might be in the barn won't hold a candle to that creep."

"Let's find out." I eased along the side and gripped the door handle closest to me. I yanked it, but it didn't move, and the clang of a metal chain rang from inside.

"Someone's in there." Benton blew out a white puff of breath.

"We can't get in, not without a battering ram." I shot a glance to the mangled truck. "Which we may just have."

Benton already took my meaning as he ran around and checked the driver's side. "Key's here. Back up." He gunned the engine, then turned the rickety truck in a wide circle, ending with the broken headlights pointed squarely at the barn entrance.

I reversed course and stationed myself several feet from the doors, far enough to avoid any backlash.

"Ready?" he called.

"Hit it." I held my ground as he floored it, the truck bounding forward over the terrain until it made contact with the doors. Wood splintered, glass shattered, and the truck busted into the barn with a ruckus that probably carried for a mile.

I ran over as Benton climbed from the driver's side, the truck's engine sputtering and dying.

"You okay?"

"I'm fine." He pulled his shotgun from the seat as I surveyed the barn.

A naked bulb hung in the center, and all the stalls were empty. No hay graced the floor, and it was clear that no animal had ever set foot in there. Ahead, a desk sat beneath the bulb, a laptop perched on top and stacks of banker's boxes strewn around.

"More files?" Benton walked over as I peered into the dark corners, my gun up. Nothing moved, but the doors had been bolted from the inside. Someone was here.

He flipped the lid off the closest box. "Holy shit."

"What?"

He pulled out a stack of bills. "Cash."

I turned in a circle and peered up into the loft.

Another box top hit the floor. "Cash. All of it is cash."

"That must be—"

"Seven hundred and fifty thousand dollars." Judge Ingles walked from the shadows, his eyes glinting under the harsh light.

Benton brought up his shotgun, but I already had my gun trained on the judge's head.

"I'm unarmed." He held up his hands and leaned against one of the barn's support beams. "I can't run anymore. Not now that he's here."

"Who? Benton?"

He shook his head with a tired sigh. "Colletti's guy. The one who killed Randall and Letty."

"You knew all along, didn't you?" I didn't drop my gun. Not until I knew for sure he wasn't dangerous.

"Yes."

"I could have protected you. If you'd have just *said* something, I could have saved Letty. No one else would have had to get hurt. To die."

"There was no sense in that." He adopted a reasonable tone, one he probably used while wearing his robes and sitting in judgment on others. "Besides, Letty had it coming. She started all this. After what she did to Lina over—"

"Letty hurt Lina?" Benton walked to my side, his shotgun at his hip, though still pointed at Judge Ingles.

"Lured her out to that ravine and pushed her in." He nodded.

"What do you mean 'she started all this'?" I took a step closer, trying to gauge if he was telling the truth.

"She hurt Lina, which got Randall to thinking about leaving and turning his back on our arrangement."

"The money laundering scheme."

He smiled, his teeth crooked like old tombstones. "Good work, little detective. He wanted to take a chunk of the unwashed money—" he tilted his head toward the boxes of cash, "—take Lina, and disappear."

The pieces fell into place in my mind—one at a time. "But the Collettis found out somehow."

"He didn't make a payment on one of the properties. It only took the Collettis a few days to notice the missing payment. Randall was dumb enough to think he'd have plenty of time before they came looking. He was wrong."

"So what's your plan?" Benton cocked his head to the side. "I take it being trapped in a barn with the shooter outside wasn't on your agenda?"

"No." The placid façade fell away, the judge's face wrinkling into a glare. "You led him right to me. How'd you find this place, anyway?"

Unease trickled down my spine like ice water when I realized that we should have had some deputies out here by now. Where were they? I tightened my grip on the gun. "Letty left us a clue."

"That bitch gummed up the works from day one." He snarled, putting more force into his words than I thought he had. Perhaps he wasn't as frail as he'd been leading everyone to believe.

"It's over. There's nowhere for you to run. Put your hands on your head and get on your knees."

"I'm afraid I can't." He shook his head.

"Get on your knees!" I took another step toward him.

"Going to jail for murder isn't high on my bucket list."

"Murder?" Benton moved to my right, his shotgun up.

The judge laughed. My hackles rose.

"The Lagners. You didn't figure that one out? Didn't think decrepit old Brad Ingles had it in him?"

"Show me your hands. Now!"

"All right." He raised his left hand, his right hand obscured by the thick support beam he'd been leaning against.

"Both of them!" My finger danced along the edge of the trigger.

He raised the other, and the thump of blood in my ears lessened a bit.

"Now get on the ground."

"It'll take me a minute." He leaned to the side and bent one knee, half of him hidden behind the post.

"Don't!" I aimed for his head.

He shot me a sly look. "I'm doing what you said."

I gave him one more chance. "Stop!"

He didn't take it.

A shot cracked through the barn, and Judge Ingles fell forward, a pistol clattering from his hand and onto the concrete.

"What the—" Benton tackled me before I could finish my thought as two more shots boomed nearby.

We crawled to the desk and pressed our backs against it as slow footsteps echoed around the barn.

"You two don't have to die," the man with the light eyes called. "I'm here for the cash. Nothing else. Just let me take what's ours, and you'll never see me again."

Benton started to swing the shotgun around the desk. I grabbed the barrel and held him still. The shooter would pick us off the second we showed ourselves.

"How can I be sure you won't come back?"

Benton's eyes widened as he gave me an incredulous look.

"I got no reason. Our business here is concluded." He was circling to our left.

"So if we give you the cash, you'll let us go?" I sent up a silent prayer.

Benton shook his head vehemently.

"Sure thing." He'd almost cleared the desk.

With a shove, I threw myself away from the desk and rolled, firing all the while.

The shooter dove while firing back at me. White heat seared through my upper arm. I couldn't stop my scream as I emptied my magazine.

Benton cut from the other side of the desk, the boom of his shotgun filling the enclosed space.

I crawled into the nearest stall as blood seeped through my coat. Dropping my gun, I clutched the wound, applying pressure as scorching agony ripped through me.

Three more booms and pumps from the shotgun, then a click. Benton was out of shells. Scuffling footsteps, and then he dropped down next to me, his hands going to my arm.

"Did we get him?"

"I don't know." His eyes grew grave as he stared at my arm. "It's bad. I need to stop the bleeding. Where the fuck is Porter?" He shucked his jacket off, then yanked at the hem of his button-down, ripping off a strip of fabric.

"Make sure he's down." Spots swam in my vision. Shock. "Make sure we got him."

"Let me tie this first." He wrapped the fabric around my arm just below my shoulder and tied it off.

"That's sweet." The man with the light eyes walked around the end of the stall, bloody spots marring his shirt and pants. Benton had pegged him with buckshot, but not enough to stop him. A bigger wound bled from his shoulder, and he had a limp. "Taking care of your girl. Real sweet."

"Let her go." Benton held up his bloodied hands. "She has a kid at home, okay? A little girl. Her name is—"

"Shut the fuck up." He pointed the pistol at my head. "You know that's not the way this is going to end. But I have one little question first." He dropped to his haunches, the gun still pointed between my eyes. "Who else knows?"

"Knows what?" Benton asked.

The man tsked. "You want me to make her hurt? I can." He aimed at my leg.

"Wait!" Benton put his hand over my knee, as if it could stop a bullet.

"Ready to talk?"

"Yes."

"Who knows?"

"Ah, well—"

"Don't tell him shit." I stared up into the cold eyes that had seen more death and violence than I could even imagine. "Do your worst, asshole."

He seemed taken aback, then nodded appreciatively. "Damn. You've got a set of brass balls, lady. I'll give you that."

"Just do it." I didn't drop my gaze. I refused to be cowed by this murderous piece of shit.

"Spare her—"

"I'll send your kid your regards." He returned his aim to my face, his finger on the trigger.

Benton took my hand in his.

A single shot. An end. A fall into darkness.

33

BENTON

*I* draped myself over Arabella as the man with the light eyes staggered and fell face down. He landed just inches from us. I reached over and yanked his gun from his hand so hard that I may have broken one of his fingers. Not that he minded—a mushy pulp on his temple oozed blood.

"Arabella?" A deep voice came from the front of the barn.

"Chief?"

"You okay?" He hurried up, his pistol still in his hand.

"Yeah."

"No." I pointed to her arm. "She's been shot."

His bushy eyebrows lowered as he knelt and peered at the wound. "Damn."

"I'll be okay."

His mustache twitched as he surveyed the dead man. "He had that coming and then some."

"Where's Porter and the rest of them?" I needed to get Arabella to a hospital, and fast.

319

"On the way." He stood and huffed a grunt. "Why didn't you shoot this guy before I got here?"

"I'm out." Arabella frowned. "And shot."

"I emptied the shotgun. That guy was like the Terminator."

"Terminated all right." Chief Garvey toed his body. "He have a gun on him?"

"Yeah." I held it up.

"Go ahead and hand it over. Evidence."

I reached up, but Arabella rested her hand on my forearm. "Chief?" The question in her voice seemed more loaded than the pistol in my hand.

His mustache twitched again. "Don't make this hard."

"What?" I tightened my grip on the pistol.

Chief Garvey pointed his gun at Arabella.

"The fuck are you doing?" My voice rose.

"What I have to. Now hand over the gun."

I glanced at Arabella.

"Just do it." She stared straight ahead, ignoring the barrel pointed at her.

"Listen to her, son." Chief Garvey held out his meaty palm.

"Give it to him." She turned to me, her skin pale.

I swallowed hard, then handed the gun to Chief Garvey.

"Smart choice." He stuffed it in the back of his pants, and moved his aim to me. "Now your phones."

Benton handed his over.

"Arabella?" The Chief held out his hand.

"Mine is still in the car wreck."

He dropped my phone to the floor and smashed it with his boot, then pulled his cell from his pocket and hit a speed dial button. It rang as he stared at Arabella, an almost remorseful look in his weary eyes. No answering ring sounded from her pockets. He stowed his phone.

"Told you." She shrugged, then groaned.

"Don't move, Arabella. You'll just make it hurt more." He pointed at me. "You are going to load those boxes into my cruiser. Don't try anything, or I'll have to shoot you. I don't want to, but I will."

"You knew all along, didn't you?" The pain in Arabella's voice was like a gut punch.

Even Chief Garvey's eyes softened a little. "I didn't know the particulars, no. But I knew there was a lot of money changing hands in the county. Seemed best for me to put my head down and ignore it. Which is what I did. Until Lina." His mouth tightened. "Until they hurt her. And then I began to figure things out. I suspected Letty all along, but I didn't have proof. Not until Lina woke up. It's a shame Letty got off so easy." He motioned the pistol at me. "Come on. Get to work."

I stood and walked toward the boxes.

"Cruiser's just outside the door behind the truck. Try anything, and I'll shoot Arabella."

"You lied to me." Her voice broke. "This whole time, you've been lying."

I hefted a couple of boxes and walked them to the cruiser, setting them in the backseat. I quietly tried to open the front door to get to the radio, but he'd locked it. *Shit.*

"—had to." He coughed. "All these things were already in motion. If I'd told you the truth, you would have gone after the Collettis' man. He would have shot you dead the second he found out you'd made him. Don't you see? I did this to protect you."

"Protect me?" She spat. "You taking off with all this cash was to protect me?"

"I'm taking Lina far away from here. Somewhere she can recover, and we can live in peace. An early retirement."

"You left a trail of bodies in your wake just so you could retire?"

I kept listening as I loaded boxes and wished for Porter to show up with a line of deputies behind him.

"It's not like that, and you know it! I've worked my ass off for this town. I gave my years. And what did these assholes go and do? They invited a goddamn crime syndicate to turn this place into a money laundromat!" His voice shook. "They got what they deserved. All of them!"

"And the Lagners?"

His voice quieted. "Collateral damage."

I loaded the last of the boxes in the cruiser and returned to Arabella.

"You'll get caught." I sank by her side and took her hand in mine. Her skin was too cold and covered in a clammy sweat. Grabbing my coat, I wrapped it around her.

"By the time I get Lina and hit the highway, that idiot brother of yours won't even have his thumb out of his ass."

"What are you going to do with Benton and me?" Acid coated her words. "Kill us too?"

"No." He shook his head. "You know I couldn't." He dropped his aim. "I love you and Vivi." He gestured toward me. "But I'd kill him, so don't try to be a hero."

"Please don't do this." A tear leaked from her eye as she stared up at him.

"I have to." He backed away. "Stay put. They'll get out here eventually."

Anger crested inside me. "She could bleed out—"

"She won't. She's tougher than you think." He backed away, his gun still pointed at us. A few moments later, his engine roared to life, and he took off, leaving us behind in the cold barn.

"Porter will be here soon." I scooted Arabella between my legs and wrapped my arms around her, clasping my fingers together against her ribs. "I'll keep you warm till then."

"He was like a father." She snorted a rueful laugh. "So no wonder he took off."

"He loved you."

"He just pointed a gun at my head." She sniffed.

"There's no way he would have pulled that trigger."

"Then why did you help him?"

"Because he would have shot me as soon as look at me." I kissed her forehead. God, she was cold. Too cold.

"True." She snuggled closer, but groaned when she moved her arm.

"It's going to be okay." I tucked her head under my chin.

"Cold."

"I know." I eyed the blood still seeping from the wound in her arm. Something icy slithered around in my heart, and I pushed the dark feeling away. "You're going to be fine."

The sound of the Chief's engine had long since faded when another low hum met my ears. "Do you hear that?"

"Mmm."

"Arabella." I gently pulled her away from me. Her head lolled forward. The icy slither intensified, wrapping my heart in frigid barbed wire. "Hey!"

Her head popped up and her eyes fluttered open, but they were unfocused. "Yeah?"

"Stay awake." I brought her back against my chest, and let out a relieved breath.

"I thought I *was* awake."

"Someone's coming."

"Someone else who wants to kill us?"

"Surely someone in this damn county wants to see us make it another day, right?"

"Doesn't seem like it." Her breathing turned shallow.

"Shh."

The engine grew louder, and someone skidded to a stop outside the barn. Boots crunched on splintered wood. I tensed, probably gripping Arabella too tightly, but she didn't protest.

"Benton?"

"Porter!" I'd never been more relieved to hear his voice.

"Where are you?"

"Back here, first stall. Arabella's been shot. We have to get her to the hospital!"

"Shot?" He hurried into view, then peered at first Judge Ingle's body then the man with the light eyes. "Holy shit."

"Porter, focus! Help me get her up."

He dashed over and held onto Arabella as I scooted her out of my embrace, then stood. When he moved to pick her up, I leaned over. "I got her."

"I'll drive." He rushed out the door.

When I got outside, the back door was already open and he was in the front seat talking into his radio.

I slid in, gingerly holding Arabella on my lap, then closed the door.

"What the hell happened? Chief Garvey rode up, said he didn't see the shooter, everything was fine, and that you two were going to walk out to the road."

"Then why did you come?"

He glanced in the rearview mirror as he drove away from the barn. "You know I've never been too good at following instructions."

"Thank god." I pulled Arabella tight against me, but she still groaned when Porter went too fast over the bumpy terrain.

"Sorry, Arabella."

"Just go." I hated for her to hurt more, but the faster we got to the hospital the better. "Blast the heat."

"I am." He jabbed his finger into the up arrow a few more times, just to be sure. "Now tell me what the hell happened."

I recounted the story as his deputies blew past us

toward the barn, their lights flashing. When we hit Route 9, he floored it, siren blaring. He radioed for a paramedic intercept outside Azalea and sent Logan over to the hospital to guard Lina. Chief Garvey had quickly become the most wanted man in the county.

"That's—wouldn't let—call in the state police." Arabella mumbled against my chest.

"What?" I stroked her hair.

"He wouldn't let me call the state police in to help. That's why. He knew. He'd been planning to take the money." Her voice was thinner than a piano wire, and her lips had faded to the same pale shade as her skin.

Panic gripped my heart and squeezed. "Porter, faster!"

"I'm going as fast as I can without killing us all!"

"Benton?"

"Yes? I'm here."

"I can't feel you."

"I'm holding you in my—" My voice caught on the last word, and I couldn't continue.

"Take care of Vivi."

"We both will, okay?" My eyes burned.

"Please. Mom is too sick." Her labored breath slowed her words.

"I'll love her like my own. But I'll do it with you at my side." A lump formed in my throat, and my vision hazed as I stared down at her.

A faint smile twisted the corner of her lips. "Sounds like...you love a girl ... from Razor Row."

"I do." I kissed her clammy forehead. "Please stay. I'll even move to Razor Row if my comeuppance will make you happy."

"It would." She opened her eyes for only a moment, her green irises still striking even in the shadowy car. "Promise me. Viv." Her eyelids fluttered closed, shutting me off from her.

"I promise." I clutched her to me, my heart breaking as hers slowed.

## 34

### BENTON

*T*he doors remained closed as I paced back and forth in front of them. There'd been no word ever since we'd arrived at the emergency room. The triage nurse had taken one look at Arabella and rushed her away toward surgery and a waiting doctor.

Porter had left to chase the chief. After grabbing the cash, Garvey had stolen an ambulance and his daughter, hitting the road out of town before we'd made it to the hospital. Every law enforcement officer in Mississippi was on the lookout for him.

Logan pushed through the doors at the other end of the hall and hurried toward me with a pronounced limp. "I knew you'd get her hurt or killed!" His hands curled into fists.

He was right. I leaned against the wall, waiting for his onslaught, not even bothering to defend myself. She could die because of me. Because I wasn't strong enough to keep her safe.

Logan stopped right in front of me, his face drawn, ire

oozing from every pore. When he met my gaze, it seemed like some of the steam left him, as if something in my eyes gave him pause.

"They're working on her. That's the last I heard, and that was half an hour ago," I offered. "She'd lost so much blood..." My voice faltered as I remembered how pale she was, how faint her breaths had become.

"Fuck!" He punched the wall across from me.

"All we can do is wait." I couldn't shake the useless feeling.

"This is bullshit." He limped to the door. "The chief, that asshole judge, your father—they all did this to her." Turning, he glared at me. "You did this. You fucking Kings, lording over this town. If it weren't for you—"

"Simmer down, Logan." May Bell shuffled toward us, trailing her oxygen tank behind her. "He didn't do anything. If you want to blame somebody, blame that good for nothing Garvey." She coughed, the sound shallow and wheezing.

I took her elbow. "You all right?"

"As much as I can be."

"Who's watching Vivi?"

She arched a brow at me. "What do you take me for? My friend Vilma is helping out."

"Sorry." I helped her to the row of seats in the waiting area off to the right, a TV humming quietly as a man snored in the corner chair.

She let out a labored breath as she settled, her house shoes peeking out from beneath her flowery mumu. "How's my Belly?"

"This asshole got her shot. She's still in surgery." Logan sat across from us and crossed his arms over his chest.

"That's not helpful." Her cross tone was enough to chill the room.

"Sorry, May Bell."

"Tell me what happened." She patted my knee with a calmness that would have been believable if I hadn't noticed her shaking hand. "I could use a good story."

"Yeah, I'd like to hear it, too." Logan chewed his words as if they were an overdone sirloin.

I took a breath and turned to May Bell, then began to tell her about the properties changing hands, the money running through the county, and what happened in the barn. By the time I was done, Logan was leaning forward, elbows on his knees, and May Bell had paled a shade.

"She's going to make it." May Bell took my hand in hers. "She will."

I could only nod and hope that the conviction in her words stuck. "I promised her I'd take care of Vivi." I bit back tears. "And I will. You and Vivi."

"It won't come to that." She squeezed my fingers.

The hall doors swung open. I jumped to my feet and rushed toward them, Logan right behind me.

Doctor Evans, his hair under a surgical cap, strode out.

"Doc?" May Bell stood in the doorway to the waiting room.

"Let's sit down." The doctor gestured toward the chairs.

"No." The steel in May Bell's voice reminded me so much of Arabella that my chest ached. "Tell me right now. How's my baby girl?"

"She lost a lot of blood. The bullet clipped her brachial artery and did some more damage on the way out. But she's a fighter. She's going to make it."

I could finally breathe again, my lungs filling all the way as relief coursed through me. May Bell took a step, and almost faltered, but I grabbed her arm and steadied her.

"Thanks, Doc." She gave him a thin smile. "Can I see her?"

"She's in recovery. The anesthesia will wear off over the next half hour, and then we'll work on pain management."

Her hard stare cracked his clinical exterior. He nodded. "Yes, you can see her. But only one at a time."

I helped May Bell through the doors. She continued down the hall, the doctor at her side, until they turned along a corridor on the left.

I sagged against the wall, going out of my skin with the need to see Arabella. But I'd have to wait. I glanced at Logan, who glowered right back at me. Great.

He opened his mouth to speak—

"Save it." I held up a hand. "I've heard all you've got to say."

He dug in his pocket and pulled out a tin of snuff. Tapping the top, he smiled faintly. "She hates this, you know?" The tin settled in his palm. "Hates all my bad habits." He opened the lid, took a pinch of tobacco, and settled it between his lip and gum. When he snapped the lid closed, his gaze returned to mine. "But I keep doing them. All of them. This—" he tapped the can, "—drinking, women, you name it."

I wasn't sure where he was going, but I was too beat to stop him. At least we weren't fighting.

"She thinks I can be a better man." He shook his head. "She's wrong. Always has been." His deep sigh matched my own exhaustion. "I'm not going to change my ways. I can't, or maybe I won't."

"You're saying you aren't good enough for her." Realization hit me in the gut.

"Of course I'm not." He leaned over and spat into the trash can just inside the waiting room. "Doesn't mean you are, though."

"That's true. But I'm willing to try and be better for her."

"You ever going to tell her your alibi for the night your father was killed was pure bullshit?" He smiled, pulling the skin under his lip taut along the lump of snuff.

I kept my poker face. "What do you mean?"

"You and Porter—both of you lied about where you were that night. He said he was with Vorayna Clearwater. A lie. You said you were at home or some bullshit. Also a lie."

"How do you know?"

"There's plenty I know." He shrugged. "Porter, I can understand. When your alibi is a married woman—and the mayor's daughter at that—you don't want to spread that around. But you don't make sense at all. Why lie?"

"Some things are personal." I hadn't thought about the lie since I'd told it. Now, I dreaded explaining myself to Arabella.

"There's no shame in going to dance class." He grinned.

333

I hid my wince with a cough. "My father arranged classes. He wanted the firm to have two entries in that stupid Dancing with the Stars thing next year. I was humoring him. So, yes, I was at Jacquelin Alabaster's studio that night. Not that it did much good."

"You saying you didn't learn to dance?"

I shook my head. "Jacqueline said I was by far the worst student she'd ever had in her thirty years of teaching."

"She told me the same thing about you." He spit again. "Shoot straight with me, college boy." He gave me an up and down look. "I'm not even going to tell anyone we had this conversation. None of this ever passed between us. But answer one thing for me. Did you know what dear old Daddy was up to?"

"Absolutely not." I stood straight, looking him right in the eye. "I never knew."

He nodded slowly, then relaxed against the wall again. After a while, he said, "I'm a damn good dancer, myself."

Somehow, a truce had just been struck between us, one built on my utter lack of rhythm. After a few more minutes of blessed silence, the doors opened again.

"She's asking for Benton." The doctor turned to me. "May Bell says that's you."

"Yes." I followed him as Logan grumbled behind me.

The doctor walked without urgency, to the point where I wanted to jump ahead of him, but I didn't know which way to go.

Finally, he slowed and turned into a room near a nurse's station. "In here."

May Bell sat next to Arabella, both of them speaking softly.

My mind stopped buzzing, everything inside of me calming as I saw her, her eyes open. When she looked at me, I couldn't get to her fast enough. Pushing past the doctor, I rushed to her side.

"Hi." She smiled up at me.

"I'm going to go console Logan." May Bell stood and shuffled toward the door.

Arabella intertwined her fingers with mine.

"Are you all right?" I peered at the bandages around her right arm, all of them clean and white.

"I'm flying. Thanks, anesthesia." She turned her head toward me, her dark hair making a halo behind her.

"I was so worried." I eased onto the bed, careful not to disturb her.

"I know. You even told me you loved me. Must have been out of your mind."

I stroked her cheek, happy to find her warm, the life flowing inside her where before she'd been pale. "I meant every word."

She blinked, her eyes growing misty. "You can't love me. You don't know me."

"I know all I need to. And I meant every word about Vivi, too."

"This is crazy."

"Probably." I squeezed her fingers.

"You're crazy." She smiled despite her words.

"Definitely."

"I'm sleepy."

"Get some rest. I'll be here." I wasn't going to leave her. Not ever.

Her eyes closed, her hand still in mine. I kissed the back of her knuckles.

"I love that." Her breathy sigh warmed every bit of me.

"Then I'll keep doing it." I kissed her hand again. "For as long as you let me."

"In that case, you're in for a lot of kissing."

"Promise?" I leaned forward and pressed my lips to hers gently.

EPILOGUE

"If your mom could see you right now, she'd probably cry all over you." I leaned down and tweaked Vivi's nose.

"Hey!" She swatted at my hand and grinned, one of her front teeth missing, her bubble gum tongue showing through.

"Who is this stunning lady standing before me?" Porter dropped to his knees and opened his arms.

Vivi ran to him, and he caught her, then picked her up and stood.

"Where'd you get this pretty dress?"

"Bennon." She adopted a shy tone, though there wasn't a timid bone in her body.

"Well, you look like a little angel in it."

She blushed and squirmed.

"Run along now." He set her down. "I think you've got a job to do here in a minute."

She disappeared through a door at the side of the vestibule.

"Such a cute kid, man." Porter ran his hands down the front of his black tux and light blue tie. "And damn, I look hella fine in this getup. I might adopt the tuxedo as the new uniform for the sheriff's department. That way I can show everybody up even more than I already do."

I took a deep breath and let it out, only half listening to Porter's nonsense.

"Nervous, huh?" He smiled and clapped me on the back.

"No. I'm just…" *Nervous.*

"Look, I know this will come as a shock to you, but on the wedding night, you'll be expected to perform what we experts like to call 'the sex.' This will necessarily include the insertion of the—"

"Shut up." I couldn't stop my smile. My brother was such an idiot.

"There it is." He grinned. "There's the smile. The uptight douchebag is dead and gone. Ever since you met Arabella, you've been the type of guy I'll actually admit I'm related to."

The sanctuary doors opened, and one of the ushers told me it was time to take my place up front.

"I wish…" Porter's grin faded a bit. "Nothing."

"I wish he was here, too." I couldn't help it. He was my father. Even though I didn't know him like I thought I did, even though he'd kept things from all of us, he was still my dad. His sins—though many—couldn't erase the profound effect he'd had on the King family. On me.

Porter cleared his throat. "Got a report from a Texas border town that maybe the chief was hanging around."

"Any truth to it?" I raised a brow. We hadn't seen or heard from Chief Garvey ever since he stole the money, an ambulance, and his daughter from the hospital. But there were sightings every now and then.

"No. But maybe one of these days we'll recover the—"

Charlotte burst through a side door, one hand in the pocket of her pink dress. "Here."

"What?" Porter turned as she thrust a box at him.

"The rings."

"Oh, shit." Porter flipped open the box. "That does seem kinda important."

Charlotte rolled her eyes. "It's about to start. Benton, what are you doing back here?"

"I was just—"

She shooed me into the sanctuary. "Go!"

I hurried down the aisle, the people seated on either side passing by in a blur. The church was full to the brim. I was the eldest King, the one who inherited what little cachet my father still had in Azalea. But the filled seats told me the name still meant something. Maybe it was because I'd invested in the town by rebuilding the law firm on a new site, dedicating the old location as a city park, and doing what I could to repair the mess my father and his associates had made. But I couldn't have done it without Arabella at my side. As the new chief, she closed the murder cases and did the best she could on damage control.

I took my spot at the front and nodded to the pastor. Clasping my sweaty palms together, I stared straight ahead. Minutes passed, each second ticking away as I replayed all the moments I'd had with Arabella and Vivi since I first met them. How did I manage to survive so long without them in my life?

The elderly organist began playing, though she seemed to miss every third note.

"Ready, son?" The minister patted my arm.

"Yes, sir." Despite my nerves, I had no doubts whatsoever. Arabella was the one.

The vestibule doors opened and Vivi skipped down the center aisle, forgetting to throw the rose petals, but looking too cute for anyone to stop her. She grinned and ran up to me.

I picked her up as the bridesmaids and groomsmen began to file in. "You did that perfectly."

"I know." She shrugged. "We getting married?"

"Your mom and I are getting married, yes."

"I can't wait." She kissed me on the cheek, then wriggled to get down. She ran over to May Bell and sat on her lap, then kicked her feet up on Logan's knee as the rest of the wedding party filed in.

"Rings are A-okay." Porter patted his pocket.

"I should hope so. You've only had them for fifteen minutes."

He elbowed me. "Calm down. You don't want to faint."

"I won't faint." I scoffed, but took a deep breath.

The organist changed songs, the notes unmistakable, and everyone in the room rose.

I peered at the vestibule doors. When the ushers opened them, and Arabella appeared, my mouth went dry. She was a vision in a white gown, a thin veil covering her face as she walked slowly toward me. My heart banged against my ribs, and I felt like someone had punched me right in the gut. But instead of winded, I felt like I was flying.

I could see her smile through the veil, and I returned it. When she reached me, and I took her hand, I wanted to pull her in for a kiss right then and there.

"Patience, Mr. King." The minister's eyes twinkled as he began to speak about love and commitment.

But I couldn't concentrate on him, not when Arabella was standing next to me.

"You look amazing." I squeezed her hand.

"You do, too."

"I can't wait to get that dress off you."

Her smile grew wider. "Stop."

"It's gorgeous, but I think it'll be even nicer on the floor."

Even through the veil, I could see her cheeks growing pink. God, I loved her.

"Are you ready for the vows?" The minister motioned for us to begin.

We promised ourselves to each other, and I can't recall anytime happier than the moment I slid the ring on her finger, lifted her veil, and kissed her in front of the whole town. She clutched my shoulders as I dipped her, our embrace verging into inappropriate as Porter laughed and Vivi squealed from the front row.

Setting her back on her feet, I kissed her hand. "Thank you."

The organist began to play as the crowd applauded.

"Thank you?" Her green eyes shimmered. "For what?"

"For saving me. For saying yes. For Vivi." For so much more that I couldn't even name. She'd brought me back to life when I hadn't even known I was dead. "I love you so much." I smoothed my hands around her waist, the lace tickling the tips of my fingers.

She wrapped her arms around my neck and moved in closer, her crimson lips tantalizing. "I love you, too. Now kiss me again, and let's really give Azalea something to talk about."

* * *

Enjoy this read? Try The Maiden, a dark, mysterious romance that will make you question everything.

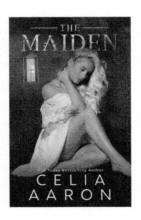

SHEER WHITE FABRIC covers me from neck to toe. I keep my eyes on the dirt path ahead of me as I move through the dark, my thin shift a beacon in the night calling every sort of predator to me. I try not to shiver. Keeping my steps even becomes my world, my only focus. One step, then the next.

I can't think about the crackling branches, the footfalls through the crisp leaves, the low chant floating through the chilly air, or the women ahead or behind me. No. Only my own steps. Right, then left. The frozen earth beneath my bare feet. The momentum that carries me deeper and deeper into the woods.

Firelight casts a faint glow as we continue moving forward, each of us rushing toward the cage, desire in our hearts, and fervor in our souls. We want to be shackled, owned, moved only by the spirit of our God. And our God has anointed one on earth to embody His good will. The Prophet Leon Monroe.

The deep chant thrums through my veins as I approach the firelight, the orange glimmer flickering over my dirty feet and up to play against the soft fabric of my nightgown. Though clothed, I am bare. I enter the circle of men, each one of them dressed in white pants and shirts—holy men, handpicked by the Prophet himself.

I follow the girl ahead of me until all of us form an inner circle, pressed between the fire and the men along the outside. It's a new circle of hell, promising an agonizing burn no matter which way I move.

A woman in all black walks along the line of women, handing each of us a small pitcher of water. My head bowed, I don't look her in the eye as she approaches. But I already know who she is—Rachel—first wife of the Prophet. Her limp gives her away. I take my pitcher, the weight of the cold water steadying the shake in my hands.

A strong voice silences the chanting. "We thank God for this bounty."

"Amen," the men chorus.

"We remember His commandment to 'Be fruitful and increase in number.' As a sign of our obedience to His will, we take these girls under our care, our protection. We also take them into our hearts, to cherish as if they were of our own blood."

"Amen."

His voice grows louder as he walks around the circle. "Just as Rebekah was called by the Lord to marry a son of Abraham, so have these girls been called to serve the godly men gathered here tonight."

A pair of heavy boots stops in front of me. A light touch under my chin pulls my gaze upward until I'm met by a pair of dark eyes. The Prophet peers into my soul.

"Do you remember the tale of Rebekah, Sister?"

"Yes, Prophet."

"I'm sure a child of God like you knows all the stories in the Bible." He smiles, his white teeth bleached like a skeleton's.

"Yes, Prophet."

"'The woman was very beautiful, a virgin; no man had ever slept with her. She went down to the spring, filled her jar and came up again.' And then what happened to Rebekah?"

"She was taken by Abraham's servant."

"That's correct." He leans closer, his gaze boring into mine.

A shiver courses through me. He glances down at my

chest, a smirk twisting the side of his lips as he sees my hard nipples through the gauzy fabric.

He releases my chin and steps back, continuing his circuit as he speaks of Rebekah's destiny. I steal a look at the man standing opposite me. Blond hair, blue eyes, a placid expression—the Prophet's youngest son. Something akin to relief washes over me. Being Cloister Maiden to Noah Monroe wouldn't be so bad. He was rumored to be kind, gentle even. I let my gaze slide to the man standing at his left. Dark hair, even darker eyes, and a smirk like his father's on his lips as he stares at me—Adam Monroe. I drop my gaze and silently pity the Maiden to my right.

"We will keep you safe. Away from the monsters of this world who would seek to use you, to destroy the innocent perfection that each one of you possess. Remember the story of Dinah: 'When Shechem, son of Hamor the Hivite, the ruler of that area, saw her, he took her and raped her.' And so it is with any man who is not within this circle. They would take you, hurt you, and cast you aside once they've spoiled your body and heart. Only in the Cloister can you lead peaceful lives without fear."

I wonder if Georgia heard the same speech. She must have. How long did they let her live after this ritual? The thought churns inside me, surprisingly strong, and hate begins to override my meek persona. Breaking character for a split second, I glance back up at Adam Monroe. Had he been the one to slit her throat? Had his large hands done untold violence to Georgia while she was still alive?

He scowls at the shivering Maiden standing in front of him, then snaps his gaze to meet mine. His eyes round the

345

slightest bit, and I drop my focus back to the dirt, then close my eyes. I shouldn't have done that. I silently berate myself as Leon—*no, he's the Prophet*—as *the Prophet* continues his lesson on the safety of the Cloister. I let my disguise fall back into place. I am a devout follower of the Prophet and eager Cloister Maiden. The hum of my thoughts grows louder, and I realize the Prophet has stopped talking.

I open my eyes and peek at the Maiden to my left. She's lifted her pitcher, her eyes still downcast. I do the same.

"The water signifies an offering from Maiden to her Protector. A righteous man—one who will teach her and lead her in the light of the Lord our God. The Protector is sanctified by God, and his decisions will always be made in the best interest of the Maiden under his protection. Just as God instructed in Genesis, the man is leader, the woman his helpmate. And so it will be here. The Protector—with God in his heart—shall lead his Maiden and show her the ways of true believers."

"Amen." The men's voices seem to have grown louder, hungrier.

"Now, Maidens, offer yourselves as vessels made to carry the knowledge and light of our Lord, to your Protector."

With shaking arms, I hold out my pitcher. A brief brush of fingers against mine, and the weight lifts. After a few moments, the drained pitchers fly over our heads and crash into the fire at our backs. A primal roar rips from the men—wolves with appetites whetted for blood.

"Protectors, lead your gentle lambs back to the Cloister where we will welcome them into the fold."

A hand appears, the wide palm up. I take a deep breath and remind myself that Noah is a good draw. Slipping my hand into his, I lift my eyes to find the entirely wrong man attached. Noah leads a different woman away from the bonfire.

Adam's smirk darkens as he grips my hand too tight. "Shall we, little lamb?"

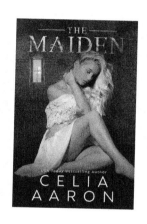

## ACKNOWLEDGEMENTS

hanks to Mr. Aaron, mainly for listening to me jabber on and on about keeping up with snakes I've let out of the can. . . Also for reading the beginning of this story multiple times as I kept tinkering.

Thanks to Viv for reading the first few chapters and assuring me it wasn't a pile of poo. (For some reason, most authors always find their work to be a pile of poo until someone magical comes along and tells them otherwise. Mr. Aaron and Viv are my magic.)

Thanks to Jeff, my editor, for always pondering my odd word choices and suggesting less-odd ones. Stacey, you're the best at catching typos. Thank God.

Pear, thanks for letting me send you pics of one pear molesting another pear and never ever reporting me for it. Also, I couldn't have lovely covers without you.

Thanks PopKitty for always being there to help me out with teasers. Despite me being last minute. And vague. And scattered. And, ya know, me.

To my Rabid Readers—y'all rock. Thanks for being

there for me when I need you. Acquisitions, y'all are the most supportive and positive group on Facebook. I can't thank you enough for all the love you give me.

JT, your Filthy video gives me life. Never stop, baby. Haters gonna say it's fake. So real.

*cough* Okay, I'm done embarrassing myself for now.

To my readers. Thank you. I can't do this without you. You are the reason for what I've got going here. Never change, loves.

What's next? Well, I hope y'all are ready to go darker. Darker. Darkerrrrrrrr. Visit www.jointhecloister.com to know when my next fucked up series goes live.

Xx,

Celia

## Dark Romance

### The Bad Guy

My name is Sebastian Lindstrom, and I'm the villain of this story.

I've decided to lay myself bare. To tell the truth for once in my hollow life, no matter how dark it gets. And I can assure you, it will get so dark that you'll find yourself feeling around the blackened corners of my mind, seeking a door handle that isn't there.

Don't mistake this for a confession. I neither seek forgiveness nor would I accept it. My sins are my own. They keep me company. Instead, this is the true tale of how I found her, how I stole her, and how I lost her.

She was a damsel, one who already had her white knight. But every fairy tale has a villain, someone waiting in the wings to rip it all down. A scoundrel who will set the

world on fire if that means he gets what he wants.
That's me.
I'm the bad guy.

## The Cloister Series

I joined the Cloister to find the truth. But I've discovered so much more, and the darkness here is seducing me, pulling me down until all I can think of is him. Adam Monroe, the Prophet's son, a dark prince to an empire that grows by the day. He is tasked with keeping me safe from the wolves of the outside world. But the longer I stay at the Cloister, the more I realize the wolves are already inside and under the Prophet's control. If Adam discovers the real reason I'm here, he'll bay for my blood with the rest of them. Until then, I will be Delilah, an obedient servant of the Prophet during the day and Adam's Maiden at night.

## Counsellor, Magnate, & Sovereign

Darkness lurks in the heart of the Louisiana elite, and only one will be able to rule them as Sovereign. Sinclair Vinemont will compete for the title, and has acquired Stella Rousseau for that very purpose. Breaking her is part of the game. Loving her is the most dangerous play of all.

## Blackwood

I dig. It's what I do. I'll literally use a shovel to answer a question. Some answers, though, have been buried too deep for too long. But I'll find those, too. And I know where to dig—the Blackwood Estate on the edge of the Mississippi Delta. Garrett Blackwood is the only thing standing between me and the truth. A broken man—one with desires that dance in the darkest part of my soul—he's either my savior or my enemy. I'll dig until I find all his secrets. Then I'll run so he never finds mine. The only problem? He likes it when I run.

**Dark Protector**

From the moment I saw her through the window of her flower shop, something other than darkness took root inside me. Charlie shone like a beacon in a world that had long since lost any light. But she was never meant for me, a man that killed without remorse and collected bounties drenched in blood.

I thought staying away would keep her safe, would shield her from me. I was wrong. Danger followed in my wake like death at a slaughter house. I protected her from the threats that circled like black buzzards, kept her safe with kill after kill.

But everything comes with a price, especially second chances for a man like me.

Killing for her was easy. It was living for her that turned out to be the hard part.

**Nate**

I rescued Sabrina from a mafia bloodbath when she was 13. As the new head of the Philly syndicate, I sent her to the best schools to keep her as far away from the life--and me--as possible. It worked perfectly. Until she turned 18. Until she came home. Until I realized that the timid girl was gone and in her place lived a smart mouth and a body that demanded my attention. I promised myself I'd resist her, for her own good.

I lied.

* * *

<u>Contemporary Romance</u>

**You've Got Fail**

She's driving me crazy. Or am I the one driving myself crazy? I can't tell anymore. Ever since Scarlet Rocket showed up in the flesh, she's turned my structured world upside down. My neatly ordered life, my hand-painted Aliens versus Vampires figurines, my expertly curated comics collection--none of these things provide any shelter from her sexy, sassy onslaught. It's a disaster of my own making. She didn't exist until I created her. Now, I can't get her out of my mind, and all I want to do is get her into my bed. Never mind that she's a thief, a liar, a con-woman. Every step she takes leaves chaos in her wake. And damn if I don't want more of it.

**Kicked**

Trent Carrington.

Trent Mr. Perfect-Has-Everyone-Fooled Carrington. He's the star quarterback, university scholar, and happens to be the sexiest man I've ever seen. He shines at any angle, and especially under the Saturday night stadium lights where I watch him from the sidelines. But I know the real him, the one who broke my heart and pretended I didn't exist for the past two years.

I'm the third-string kicker, the only woman on the team and nothing better than a mascot. Until I'm not. Until I get my chance to earn a full scholarship and join the team as first-string. The only way I'll make the cut is to accept help from the one man I swore never to trust again. The problem is, with each stolen glance and lingering touch, I begin to realize that trusting Trent isn't the problem. It's that I can't trust myself when I'm around him.

**Tempting Eden**

A modern re-telling of Jane Eyre that will leave you breathless...

**Jack England**

Eden Rochester is a force. A whirlwind of intensity and thinly-veiled passion. Over the past few years, I've worked hard to avoid my passions, to lock them up so they can't harm me—or anyone else—again. But Eden Rochester ignites every emotion I have. Every glance from her sharp eyes and each teasing word from her indulgent lips adds more fuel to the fire. Resisting her? Impossible. From the moment I held her in my arms, I had to have her. But tempting her into opening up could cost me my job and much, much more.

**Eden Rochester**

When Jack England crosses my path and knocks me off my high horse, something begins to shift. Imperceptible at first, the change grows each time he looks into my eyes or brushes against my skin. He's my assistant, but everything about him calls to me, tempts me. And once I give in, he shows me who he really is—dominant, passionate, and with a dark past. After long days of work and several hot nights, I realize the two of us are bound together. But my secrets won't stay buried, and they cut like a knife.

**Bad Bitch**

 ad Bitch Series, Book 1

They call me the Bad Bitch. A lesser woman might get her panties in a twist over it, but me? I'm the one who does the twisting. Whether it's in the courtroom or in the bedroom, I've never let anyone - much less a man - get the upper hand.

Except for that jerk attorney Lincoln Granade. He's dark, mysterious, smoking hot and sexy as hell. He's nothing but a bad, bad boy playing the part of an up and coming premiere attorney. I'm not worried about losing in a head to head battle with this guy. But he gets me all hot and bothered in a way no man has ever done before. I don't like a person being under my skin this much. It makes me want to let go of all control, makes me want to give in.

This dangerous man makes me want to submit to him completely, again, and again, and again...

**Hardass**

**Bad Bitch Series, Book 2**

I cave in to no one. My hardass exterior is what makes me one of the hottest defense lawyers around. It's why I'm the perfect guy to defend the notorious Bayou Butcher serial killer - and why I'll come out on top.

Except this new associate I've hired is unnaturally skilled at putting chinks in my well-constructed armor. Her brazen talk and fiery attitude make me want to take control of her and silence her - in ways that will keep both of us busy till dawn. She drives me absolutely 100% crazy, but I need her for this case. I need her in my bed. I need her to let loose the man within me who fights with rage and loves with scorching desire...

**Total Dick**

**Bad Bitch Series, Book 3**

I'm your classic skirt chaser. A womanizer. A total d*ck. My reputation is dirtier than a New Orleans street after a Mardi Gras parade. I take unwinnable cases and win them. Where people see defeat, I see a big fat paycheck. And when most men see rejection, it's because the sexiest woman at the bar has already promised to go home with me.

But Scarlett Carmichael is the one person I can't seem to conquer. This too-cool former debutante has it all—class, attitude, and a body that begs to be worshiped. I've never worked with a person like her before—hell, I've never played nice with anyone before in my life, and I'm not about to start with her. This woman wasn't meant to be played nicely with. It's going to be dirty. It's going to be hot. She's about to spend a lot of time with the biggest d*ck in town. And she's going to love every minute of it...

## Fantasy Romance

**Incubus**

An incubus who feeds off the sexual desires of others, Roth de Lis has never been denied the pleasure of a woman's body...until now. Lilah, once a warrior maiden in the service of a goddess, languishes on earth after being cast out from the slopes of Mount Olympus.
Lilah will do anything to return home, including betraying Roth. As she spins her web of lies, Roth begins a slow, wicked seduction that eventually threatens to consume them both. But when Lilah's deceit comes to light, will their torrid love affair be able to overcome a pact with the darkest of gods?

**Blood Prince**

He's searched for her across centuries. But he's not the only one . . .

Paris, heir to a vampire kingdom he has never claimed, is adrift on earth and in the Underworld. The bounty on his head keeps him on the run. When he realizes the woman whose death haunts his dreams could be alive, he will risk everything just to touch Helen again. But her past can't be erased, and neither can her old enemy--a demon who will destroy worlds just to possess her.

# ABOUT THE AUTHOR

Celia Aaron is a recovering attorney and USA Today best-selling author who loves romance and erotic fiction. Dark to light, angsty to funny, real to fantasy—if it's hot and strikes her fancy, she writes it. Thanks for reading.

Sign up for my newsletter at celiaaaron.com to get information on new releases. (I would never spam you or sell your info, just send you book news and goodies sometimes). ;)

*Stalk me:*
www.celiaaaron.com